A F CHA    **AUG 17 2018**
Saint errant
Charteris, Leslie, 1907-
1993, author.

WITHDRAWN

# SAINT ERRANT

## FOREWORD BY DICK LOCHTE

D1252952

# THE ADVENTURES OF THE SAINT

# SAINT ERRANT

LESLIE CHARTERIS

SERIES EDITOR: IAN DICKERSON

The characters and events portrayed in this book are fictitious. Any similarity to real persons, living or dead, is coincidental and not intended by the author.

Text copyright © 2014 Interfund (London) Ltd.
Foreword © 2014 Dick Lochte
Introductions to "Jeannine," "Teresa," "Judith," and "Dawn" originally published in *The Second Saint Omnibus* (1951)
Publication History and Author Biography © 2014 Ian Dickerson

All rights reserved.
No part of this book may be reproduced, or stored in a retrieval system, or transmitted in any form or by any means, electronic, mechanical, photocopying, recording, or otherwise, without express written permission of the publisher.

Published by Thomas & Mercer, Seattle

ISBN-13: 9781477842874
ISBN-10: 147784287X

Cover design by David Drummond, www.salamanderhill.com

Printed in the United States of America.

*To Bunny*

# PUBLISHER'S NOTE

The text of this book has been preserved from the original edition and includes vocabulary, grammar, style, and punctuation that might differ from modern publishing practices. Every care has been taken to preserve the author's tone and meaning, allowing only minimal changes to punctuation and wording to ensure a fluent experience for modern readers.

# FOREWORD TO THE NEW EDITION

More than half a century ago I discovered a copy of the first American hardcover edition of this book, which seemed to be waiting for me, tucked away in a back room of the Basement Bookstore in my home town of New Orleans, Louisiana. It was, I felt at the time, a fabulous find, rarer than pearls.

Why? Well, what could be more irresistible to a teenage boy, a diehard fan of Leslie Charteris's famous swashbuckling character, than a book filled with nine unread Saintly adventures, each featuring a beautiful female? And that's not including Patricia Holm, who graces several of the stories. I should explain also that, in the Crescent City at least, this was not the best of times for Saint addicts. The radio show had gone west. The TV series was still a few years away (and would not actually appear in New Orleans until its color seasons). The local newspaper, *The Item*, had discontinued the comic strip (causing some of us to spend entirely too much time in the only library in town that carried the *New York Herald-Tribune*). And even Charteris had admitted, in his afterword to *The Second Saint Omnibus*, that he could no longer state with assurance that the Saint would be back.

For about a year, my friend Jacques and I had been scouring the newsstands and bookstores for Charteris titles and had scored a nice pile of not-quite-ancient Avon paperbacks, along with one or two tattered hardcovers. But, the copy I found at the Basement Bookstore was (and still is) encased in plastic and pristine.

And, as it turned out, the nine stories were all as exciting and entertaining as I'd supposed.

They cover a fifteen-year span of the author's writing career, beginning with the tale, first published in a 1933 issue of *American* magazine, in which Simon agrees to help the beautiful "Judith" recover plans for a gearless car that had been stolen from the inventor. At the other end of the timespan is a story that debuted in the Winter 1948 issue of *Mystery Book* magazine, in which Simon is framed for attempting to blackmail the Chicago gangster husband of would-be actress "Iris."

"Judith" was, according to Charteris's introduction in *The Second Saint Omnibus*, "a sentimental piece" for three reasons. It was the first short he ever sold to a slick paper (as opposed to pulp) magazine in the US. He was paid considerably more for it than he'd ever been paid for a short, and it was the first sale he made after arriving in America with "about fifty dollars in my pocket and nothing but an unshakable faith in my own destiny to support me beyond that."

It was shortly after the sale of "Judith" that he first got the idea for a collection of stories "primarily involving dames."

And the dames are as different as they are intriguing. "Lida" is a socialite friend of Pat's who dies, possibly by her own hand, at a Miami nightclub whose host Simon sums up in a typically amusing thumbnail description as "(s)omething tall, dark, and rancid."

The Saint meets "Lucia" in what passes for a hotel on the outskirts of a tiny Texas border town where she's working for her father, the owner of the establishment. When both father and daughter are placed in jeopardy by the arrival of a gangster, Simon steps in. Moving on to Mexico, he meets "Teresa," who convinces him to assist her in locating her husband, last seen in the territory ruled by the legendary bandido El Rojo.

"Luella," the toothsome lure in a badger game setup, has the misfortune of catching the interest of Simon and Pat, who are visiting a post–WWII Los Angeles. For "Emily," the Saint continues on alone to Northern California's gold country to teach a couple of swindlers a lesson in selling worthless mines.

It's hard to pin down exactly where Simon meets "Dawn," since not even he can come to grips with the events that transpire in what is generally considered the most unusual of all of his recorded adventures. And, like the story, the lady is special. "She came warily into (Simon's) cabin, disheveled, her dress torn provocatively so that sun-browned flesh showed through, her cloud of golden hair swirled in fairy patterns, her dark eyes brooding, her mouth a parted dream . . . She was glamorous beyond belief." Wow!

And yet, for me, personally, it was "Jeannine" who proved to be the most fascinating of all the females. I could be wrong, but I think she may be the only woman, besides Pat, to ever make a second appearance in a Saint story. Even better, the story is beautifully crafted, with a particularly satisfying close. And, adding a cherry to the top of this Saintly sundae, the events take place in my hometown.

Starting to read "Jeannine," I blinked when I arrived at the sentence identifying the location where Simon and Detective Wendel were dining. "They sat in a booth in Arnaud's, which Simon had chosen over the claims of such other temples of New Orleans cuisine as Antoine's or Galatoire's because the oak beams and subdued lights seemed to offer a more propitious atmosphere for a meal which he wanted to keep peaceful."

Because my father's company insured Arnaud's, we'd dined there often. I'd probably sat in that same booth. Certainly I'd experienced, as presumably had Charteris, the ambiance the beams and lighting produced. To a fourteen-year-old fan, this connection to both writer and character seemed monumental. Now, having spent the last several decades as a journalist, screenwriter, and novelist, I've met face-to-face with a fair share of my favorite authors and other celebrities. I've corresponded with Leslie Charteris and even spent a pleasant afternoon with the best of all the interpreters of Simon Templar, Sir Roger Moore. One might presume that at this point in life, I might be just a little less affected by the Saint's visit to a place where I have not lived for many, many years. Instead, rereading "Jeannine" for this introduction, I was transported back to that time and place and experienced that same sense of teenage wonder at the idea that the Saint and I had shared not only the same city, but the same restaurant.

I guess the lesson to be learned is: once a Saint fan, always a Saint fan.

*—Dick Lochte*

# SAINT ERRANT

# JUDITH

# INTRODUCTION

This story is a sentimental piece to me because (1) it was the first short story I ever sold to a smooth-paper American magazine, (2) I got paid more for it, many times more, than I had ever received for a short story until then, and (3) this was the first sale I made after I landed in the United States in 1932, with about fifty dollars in my pocket and nothing but an unshakable faith in my own destiny to support me beyond that.

You may well ask why such an ancient manuscript should crop up so late in not even the *First*, but actually the *Second Saint Omnibus*.

The reason turns out to be very simple.

A writer writes short stories and sells them at intervals to magazines. Presently he has enough to make a collection suitable for publishing in volume form. And if he wants to milk his work for the last golden drop, he does just that.

I went a little further. Long ago I had the idea for the title *Saint Errant*, which would be a book of short stories primarily involving dames. This story, "Judith," would be the first.

Now it is only a matter of record that fifteen years went by before that imagined collection was complete.

I wrote other stories in between, and even whole books. But *Saint Errant* did not complete itself until 1947. And in the *Omnibus* we are dipping into the books in the order in which they were published, without regard to the order of first publication, or even conception, of their ingredients.

I hope this explanation will satisfy the most fanatical of my self-appointed bibliographers, who have picked the hell of a subject to give themselves ulcers about.

And while we are at it, one more amplification seems to be called for. I said in the foreword to this monument that I had not tried to revise any of the stories, or bring them up to date. And a glance at this story makes me realize that that was only a half-truth.

I have not changed anything between the source volumes and this one. But the story originally began in Paris, and ended with the Saint on his way to Stuttgart. When *Saint Errant* was finally being readied for the printers, that kind of movement would have invalidated a plot point for contemporary-minded readers. So I simply switched the geography across a few thousand miles of ocean.

There was nothing to it, really. Any other writer could have done the same, with a mere wave of his magic ball-point pen.

—*Leslie Charteris (1951)*

Simon Templar had to admit that the photograph of himself which adorned the front page of the copy of the New York *Daily Gazette* on his knee left nothing to be desired.

Taken only a couple of years ago, at the studio of an ambitious photographer who had clearly seen the potentialities of future revenue from an authentic likeness of such a disreputable character, it brought out to perfection the rakish curve of his jaw, the careless backward curl of black hair, the mocking challenge of a gay filibuster's mouth. Even the eyes, by some trick of lighting in the original which had been miraculously preserved through the processes of reproduction, glinted back at him from under the bantering lines of eyebrow with all the vivid dangerous dance of humor that was in his own.

The story illustrated by the picture occupied two columns of the front page and was continued somewhere in the interior. One gathered from it that that elusive and distressingly picturesque outlaw, the Saint, had set the Law by the ears again with a new climax of audacities: his name and nom de guerre waltzed through the bald paragraphs of the narrative like a debonair will-o'-the-wisp, carrying with it a breath of buccaneering glamour, a magnificently medieval lawlessness, that shone with a strange luminance through the dull chronicles of an age of dreary news. "The Robin Hood of Modern Crime" they called him, and with that phrase the Saint himself had least fault of all to find.

At the next table on his left a fair-haired girl was struggling to explain the secret of successful Rumhattan mixing to an unsympathetic waiter. At other tables, other guests of the Windsor Hotel's Peacock Alley read their evening papers, sipped cocktails, chattered, argued, and gazed incuriously at fellow birds in that pleasantly gilded cage. Outside, but inaudible in that discreetly expensive sanctuary, flowed the common traffic of Montreal, the last outpost of Old France in the New World.

In those surroundings anyone but a Simon Templar might have been embarrassed by the knowledge that a lifelike portrait of himself, accompanied by an account of his latest misdeeds and a summary of several earlier ones, was at the disposal of any citizen who cared to buy a newspaper. The Saint was never embarrassed, except by warrants for his arrest, and in those days he was most careful to leave no legal grounds for one of those.

He folded his paper and lighted a cigarette with the comforting assurance that any casual glancer at his classic features would be far less likely to suspect him of a hideous past than to suspect the eminent politician or the debutante victim of a motor accident whose portraits, in smaller frames, had flanked his own on either side. Certainly he saw no reason to creep into a corner and hide.

At the next table the girl's gray eyes wavered in humorous despair toward him, meeting his own for an instant, which to a Simon Templar was sufficient invitation.

"*Ecoute, toi!*" The Saint's voice lanced through the air with a sudden quiet command, the edge of a blade so sweetly keen that it seemed to caress even while it cut, sapping the waiter's wandering eyes around like a magnet dropped within an inch of twin compass needles. "Mademoiselle desires that one mix three parts of Ron Rey with one part of sweet vermouth and a dash of Angostura. After that, one will squeeze into it a very thin piece of lemon peel. It is quite simple."

The waiter nodded and moved away in a slight daze. In his philosophy, foreigners were not expected to speak his own patois better than he did himself, nor to cut short his studied obtuseness with a cool self-possession that addressed him in the familiar second person singular. In the doorway he paused to explain that at length to a fellow waiter. "*Sâles Américains,*" he said, and spat. Simon Templar was not meant to hear, but the Saint's ears were abnormally sensitive.

He smiled. It would never have occurred to him to report the waiter to the management, even though he was sure they would have been grateful to be warned about such a saboteur of goodwill. To the Saint any city was an oyster for his opening, a world for conquest; anything was an adventure, even the slaying of an insolent waiter and the rescue of a damsel in distress about nothing more serious than a cocktail.

He let his cigarette smolder in absolute contentment. The Rumhattan arrived. The girl tasted it and grimaced ruefully—he decided that she had a mouth that couldn't look anything but pretty even when it tried.

"It's a good idea, but it needs co-operation," he said.

"I wish I could speak the language like you do," she said. "I'd have something to tell that waiter."

"I've spent more time in Paris than any respectable man should," said the Saint cheerfully. "I used to be the *concierge* of a home for inebriate art students in the Rue des Deux Paires de Chaussettes de M. Alexandre Dumas. We all lived on absinthe and wore velvet next the skin. It went very well until someone discovered that half the inmates were wearing false beards and reading Ellery Queen in secret."

The gray eyes laughed.

"But do you know your way about here?"

"Montreal is yours," said the Saint with a gesture. "What would you like? Respectable night clubs? Disreputable saloons? Historic monuments?"

She seemed to be thinking of something else. And then she turned towards him again in a pose very like his own. The deep friendly eyes had a queer wistfulness.

"Tell me, stranger—where do you think a girl should go on a great occasion? Suppose she had something rather desperate to do, and if it went wrong she mightn't be able to choose where she went anymore."

The Saint's very clear blue eyes rested on her thoughtfully. He had always been mad, always hoped to be.

"I think," he said, "I should take her out St Lawrence Boulevard to a quiet little restaurant I know where they make the best omelets in North America. We should absorb vitamins and talk about life. And after that we might know some more."

"I should like to go there," she said.

Simon flicked a twenty-dollar bill across his table and beckoned the waiter. The waiter counted out change laboriously from a well-filled wallet.

"Shall we?" said the Saint.

The girl gathered up her gloves and bag. Simon stood up quickly to pull the table away from in front of her. He trod heavily on the waiter's toes, overbalanced him backwards, and caught him again dexterously as he was on the point of descending, like Newton's apple, on the bald head of a customer in the next row. Somewhere in the course of the acrobatics the well-filled wallet traveled from the waiter's pocket to the Saint's own.

"*Mille pardons*," murmured the Saint, patting the anguished man soothingly on the shoulder, and sauntered after the girl.

There was a taxi crawling by, and they climbed in.

"I'm free till twelve, stranger," said the girl.

She pulled off her hat and leaned far back on the cushions, with one slim silken leg stretched out to rest a toe on the folding seat in front. The passing lights picked up her face in almost breathless perfection, and let it sink back reluctantly into shadow.

"And then do you have to hurry home before the clock strikes, and only leave a glass slipper for a souvenir?"

"No," she said, "I have to burgle a house."

There was an omelet. She had never dreamed of anything so delicate, wrapped in a gossamer skin, so richly red-gold inside, so different in every way from the dry coagulation of half-scrambled eggs which passes under the same name in so many places.

"There's a trick in it," she said with a sigh, when it was finished.

"Of course there is," said the Saint. "It's one of the higher mysteries of life, only to be revealed to the pure in heart after many ordeals and battles and much traveling."

She accepted a cigarette from his case, dipped it in the flame of his lighter. Across the table the gray eyes looked into his with the serene intimacy which must come with the sharing of any sensuous pleasure, even eating. She said, "I'm glad I met you, stranger. You take things very calmly, and you don't ask awkward questions."

In the course of his career the Saint had taken a good many things calmly enough, but he could not remember having heard it accounted unto him for righteousness before.

He perceived that he had fallen into the error of attaching himself too much to the viewpoint of his bereaved victims.

"The questions may come later," he said. "We burglars aren't easily startled."

She let a trail of smoke rise and disintegrate towards the ceiling.

"I'm going to talk to you, stranger," she said quietly. "A girl likes to talk, and nothing about this evening is real. We never met before and we shan't meet again. This is an interlude that doesn't count, except for remembrance."

"Is there a dragon in it?"

"There's a Robber Baron. Have you ever heard of Burt Northwade?"

Simon had. His knowledge of unlovable characters, in and out of prison, was very nearly unique.

He knew Northwade for one of the more unpleasant products of World War I, a man who had successfully conceived the notion of selling inferior bootlaces to the Allied armies for three times their cost, and had gained for himself much wealth by that patriotic service. The Northwade business, subsequently built up to almost monopolistic proportions, was still welding together the uppers of half the world, but Northwade himself had retired a couple of years ago to his native Canada and a mansion in Westmount, leaving the female part of his family to pursue its strenuous climb through the social gradings of New York.

"Yes, I've heard of Northwade. One of these monuments of other people's industry, isn't he?"

"He's also my uncle," said the girl. "I'm Judith Northwade." Simon Templar hadn't blushed since he was eight years old. Also he considered that his remark was very nearly a compliment compared with what he would probably have said to Burt Northwade's face, had that undesirable industrialist been present.

"You have our sympathy," he said coolly.

"My father's a professor of engineering at Toronto," said the girl. "You've probably never heard of him. You couldn't have two brothers who were more different. They've always been like that. Northwade only wanted to make money. My father never wanted it. He's just a quiet, kind, completely ordinary man—almost a child outside his work. They both started at the bottom, and they both got what they wanted. Northwade made the money; my father worked his way through school, went on to Toronto University on a scholarship, and got to where he is now. The thing that came between them was my mother. Northwade wanted her, too, but she just happened to prefer Dad." The Saint nodded.

"It wasn't Dad's fault," she said, "but Uncle Burt never forgave him. I don't think he was really jealous—maybe he wasn't really in love at all—but he'd come on something that money and success alone couldn't buy, and his vanity never got over it. Oh, he didn't say anything outright; he's always been friendly—too friendly—but Dad, who wouldn't suspect a cannibal who was weighing him, never thought anything of it. I could see. I tried to tell him, but he wouldn't believe me. He even helped Uncle Burt to make more money—he's a clever inventor, too, and during the war he designed a machine that would put tags on laces twice as quickly as the old way, or something like that. I think Uncle Burt gave him fifty dollars for it." She smiled a little. "It's beginning to sound like a detective story, isn't it?"

"It has begun," said the Saint, "but I like those stories."

She finished her glass of Château Olivier.

"It's going to sound more like that, but it's just one of those stories that are happening every day. For the last eighteen months or so Dad's been working on an infinitely variable gear for automobiles. Do you know what that means? It means that you'll just drive your car on the accelerator and brake, and whatever it's doing, up hills or down, or in traffic or anywhere, without even an automatic gear change, the engine'll always be working at its maximum efficiency—that sounds rather technical, but I'm so used to hearing Dad talk that I've got that way myself. Anyway, it's far in advance of anything that's been done in that line so far. There's a fortune in it already, but it wasn't good enough for Dad. He wanted to be sure that it was beyond any improvement. Three months ago he'd spent every penny he'd saved on his experiments. Then he went to Uncle Burt for help."

The Saint's mind moved in certain channels with the speed and precision of infinite experience. He took up his cigarette again and regarded her steadily over it.

"Northwade helped him, of course," he said.

"Uncle Burt lent him five thousand dollars. On a nominal security—purely nominal. And with a few legal documents—just as a matter of form. I expect you can guess what that means."

"I could try."

"The plans of the gear are in Uncle Burt's safe, over in Westmount— all the results of Dad's work up till now. And there's a paper with them which says that all rights in them belong to Burt Northwade—with no time limit specified. It was supposed to be until the loan was repaid, but the contract doesn't say so. Dad hasn't any mind for legal trickeries, and he signed the papers while I was away. I didn't know about it till it was too late."

"One gathers," said the Saint composedly, "that this is the house you propose to burgle."

She gazed at him without flinching, gray eyes frank and resolute, even with that strain of wistful loneliness in them.

"Listen, stranger," she said softly. "This is still the game of Let's Pretend, isn't it? Pretending that this evening is right outside the world. Because that's the only reason why I'm telling you all this. I'm going to burgle Uncle Burt's house, if I can. I'm going to try and get hold of his keys and open his safe and take those papers away, including the contract Dad signed. Dad hasn't any hope of paying back that five thousand dollars. And Uncle Burt knows it. He's practically completed arrangements to sell the gear to Ford. There's no legal way of stopping him. It's one of those cases where possession is nine points of the law. If we had that contract back, as well as the plans, Uncle Burt would never have the face to go into a court and publish the terms of it, which he'd have to do if he wanted to make any claim. Do you think I'm quite mad?"

"Only a little."

She turned the stem of her wineglass between her fingers, looking at him quietly.

"Maybe I am. But have you ever heard of the Saint?"

"The Robin Hood of Modern Crime?" murmured Simon, with only the faintest lift of an eyebrow for expression.

"I think it's the sort of thing he'd do," she said. "It's justice, even if it's against the law. I wish I could meet him. He'd understand. I think he'd say it was worth taking a chance on. You're very understanding, too, stranger. You've listened to me awfully patiently, and it's helped a lot. And now you shall talk about anything else you like, and will you please forget it all?"

Simon Templar smiled.

He poured out the last of the wine, and took up his glass. Over the rim of it his clear blue eyes raked the girl with a cavalier challenge that matched his devil-may-care smile and the mocking slant of his brows. His face was alight suddenly.

"I don't propose to forget, Judith," he said. "I am the Saint, and the safe hasn't been made that I can't open. Nor has anything else been thought of that I can't do. We'll go to Westmount together!"


"This is the place," said the girl.

Simon switched off the engine and let the car coast to a stop under the lee of the hedge. It was her car—she had been prepared for that. She had telephoned from the restaurant and it had been fueled and waiting for them at the garage.

Burt Northwade's home, an unwieldy mansion in the Napoleonic style, stood on a slight rise of ground some distance back from the road, in the center of its extensive and pleasant grounds.

Rising to sit on the door of the convertible, with one foot on the seat, Simon could see the solid rectangle of its upper part painted in dull black on a smudged gray-blue sky. He felt that he knew every corner of it as if he had lived there for years, from the descriptions she had given him and the rough plans she had drawn on the back of the menu, familiarizing him with the configurations of rooms and corridors while their coffee grew cold and neither of them cared. That had been a time of delight shared in adventure which he would always like to remember, but now it was over, and the adventure went on.

It was a night without moon or stars, and yet not utterly dark; perfect for the purpose. She saw the clean-cut lines of his face, recklessly etched in the burst of light as he kindled a cigarette.

"I still don't know why you should do this for me," she said.

"Because it's a game after my own heart," he answered. "Northwade is a bird I've had ideas of my own about for some time. And as for our present object—well, no one could have thought of a story that would have been more likely to fetch me a thousand miles to see it through."

"I feel I ought to be coming with you."

He drew smoke into his lungs, and with it the sweet smell of green leaves.

"This sort of thing is my job, and I've had more practice than you."

"But suppose Uncle Burt wakes up."

"I shall immediately hypnotize him so that he falls into a deep sleep again."

"Or suppose the servants catch you."

"I shall tie them up in bundles of three and heave them into the outer darkness."

"But suppose you are caught?"

He laughed.

"It'll be a sign that the end of the world is at hand. But don't worry. Even if that happens it'll cause a certain amount of commotion, and if you hear it I shall expect you to drive rapidly away and await the end in some other province. I shall tell them I came out here on roller skates. It's not your burglary any more—it's mine."

He swung his immaculately tailored legs over the side and dropped lightly to the road, and without another word he was gone, melting into the obscurity like a ghost.

He walked up the turf path beside the drive with the quick confidence of a cat. No lights showed in any of the front windows as he approached, but he made a careful circle of the house for complete certainty. His eyes adjusted themselves to the gloom with the ease of long habit, and he moved without rustling a blade of grass under his feet.

The ground floor was a rugged facade of raised arches and pilasters broken by tall gaunt windows, with a pair of carved oak doors in the middle that would have given way to nothing short of a battering-ram, but it is an axiom of housebreaking that those buildings whose fronts look most like fortresses are most likely to defend their postern gates with a card saying "No Admittance." In this case, there was an open pantry window six feet above the ground. Simon squeezed up through the aperture, and lowered himself gently over the shelves of viands on the inside.

He passed through into the kitchen. With the help of a tiny pocket flashlight he located the main switchboard and removed all the fuses, burying them in a sack of potatoes. If by any chance there should be an accident, the garrison of the house would be more handicapped by a lack of lights than he would. Then he made his way down the main hall and unbarred, unbolted, unchained, and unlocked the great oak portals. Simon Templar owed much of his freedom to a trained eye for emergency exits, and he carried on the good work by opening a pair of windows in the library before he gave a thought to the safe.

The girl had described its location accurately. It was built into one wall, behind a small bookcase which opened away from it like a door, and Simon held his flashlight on it for just three seconds before he decided that it was one of those situations in which neither a bent hairpin nor a can opener would be adequate.

He slid cheerfully back into the hall and stepped soundlessly up the broad staircase. A large selection of burglarious tools was not part of his usual traveling equipment, but that shortcoming had rarely troubled him. It was another axiom of his philosophy that non-combination safes have keys, that most keys are in the possession of the owners of the safes, and, therefore, that the plodding felon who finds it necessary to pack nitroglycerin and oxyacetylene blowpipes in his overnight bag is usually deficient in strategic genius. Burt Northwade was sleeping soundly enough, with his mouth open, and a reassuring drone issuing from the region of his adenoids, but even if he had been awake it is doubtful whether he would have heard the opening of his bedroom door, or sensed one movement of the sensitive hands that lifted a bunch of keys from his dressing table and detached an even more probable one from the chain around his neck.

Simon went down the stairs again like a ghost. It was the key from the chain which turned the lock, and the heavy steel door swung back at a touch with the smooth acquiescence that even Simon Templar could never feel without a thrill. He propped his flashlight over one instep so that its light filled the interior of the safe, and went to work with quick white-gloved hands. Once he heard a board crack overhead and froze into seconds of granite immobility, but he knew that he had made no noise, and presently he went on.

The plans were dissected into a thick roll of sheets tied up with tape; the specifications were packed in a long fat envelope with "Pegasus

Variable Gear" roughly scrawled on it—that, he had been told, was the name which had been provisionally given to the invention—and a short epic on legal paper was enclosed with them. There were also some letters from various automobile manufacturers.

The Saint was so busily engaged for the next ten minutes, and so absorbed in his labors, that he missed certain faint sounds which might otherwise have reached his ears. The first hint of danger came just as he had finished, in the shape of a cautious scuffle of feet on the terrace outside, and a hoarse whisper which was so unexpected that he raised his head almost incredulously.

Then his eyes dropped half instinctively to the safe which he had just closed. He saw something that he had not noticed before—a flat leaden tube which rose a bare inch from the floor and disappeared into the crack under the lowest hinge, an obvious conduit for alarm wires. The girl had told him that there were no alarms, but that was one which Northwade had probably preferred to keep secret, and it had taken the Saint off his guard.

The narrow beam of the flashlight snapped out like a silent explosion. Simon leapt through the blackness to the windows, slammed them together, and secured the catch. He was knotting a handkerchief over the lower part of his face as he crossed the room again. In the darkness his hand closed on the doorknob, turned it stealthily; at the same time his fingers stretched downwards, and could feel no key in the lock. It looked as if it might be a tight corner, a crisp and merry getaway while it lasted, but those were the moments when the Saint's brain worked at its swiftest.

He opened the door with a quick jerk and took one step into the hall. On his right, covering the retreat to the back of the house, stood an outsize butler in a nightshirt with a rolling pin clutched in one hand. On his left, barring the way to the front door, was a wiry youth in trousers and undershirt. A little way up the stairs stood Burt

Northwade himself, with a candle in one hand and a young cannon of a revolver in the other. The Saint's most reckless fighting smile touched his lips under the concealing handkerchief.

"*Bon soir, messieurs,*" he murmured politely. "It appears that you were not expecting me. I am accustomed to being received in formal dress. I regret that I cannot accept you in this attire."

He stepped back rapidly through the door, closing it after him. The butler and the wiry youth took a few seconds to recover, then they made a concerted dash for the door. They burst in together, followed by Burt Northwade with the candle. The spectacle of a completely deserted library was the last thing they were expecting, and it pulled them up short with bulging eyes.

In an abruptly contrasting silence, the night shirted butler returned to life. He tiptoed gingerly forward, and peered with a majestic air behind and under a large settee in a far corner of the room. The wiry youth, inspired by his example, made a dash to the nearest window curtains and pulled them wide apart, disclosing a large area of glass with the round goggling faces of two other servants pressed against it from the outside, like startled fish in an aquarium. Burt Northwade discreetly remained a scant yard inside the doorway with his sputtering candle held helpfully aloft.

On the top of a massive ladder of bookshelves beside the door, Simon Templar rose like a panther from his prone position and dropped downwards. He fell squarely behind Northwade, easing his fall with a hand applied to the crown of Northwade's head, which drew from the tycoon a sudden squeal of terror. The same hand pushed Northwade violently forward, and the candle which supplied the only illumination of the scene flickered and went out.

In the darkness the door banged.

"We might even get back in time to have a dance somewhere," said the Saint.

He materialized out of the gloom beside her like a wraith, and she gasped.

"Did you have to scare me?" she asked, when she had got her breath.

He chuckled. Back towards the Northwade mansion there were sounds of muffled disturbance, floating down to his ears like the music of hounds to an old fox. He slipped into the driving seat and touched the starter. The engine purred unprotestingly.

"Did something go wrong?" she asked.

"Nothing that wasn't taken care of."

The car gathered speed into the blaze of its own headlights. Simon felt for a cigarette and lighted it from the dashboard gadget.

"Did you get everything?" she asked.

"I am the miracle man who never fails, Judith," he said reproachfully. "Hadn't I explained that?"

"But that noise—"

"There seems to have been some sort of alarm that goes off when the safe is opened, which you didn't know about. Not that it mattered a lot. The ungodly were fatally slow in assembling, and if you'd seen their waist measurements you wouldn't have been surprised."

She caught his arm excitedly.

"Oh, I can't quite believe it! . . . Everything's all right now. And I've actually been on a raid with the Saint himself! Do you mind if I give way a bit?"

She reached across him to the button in the middle of the steering wheel. The horn blared a rhythmic peal of triumph and defiance into the night: "*Taaa ta-ta, taaa ta-ta, taaa ta-ta!*" Like a jubilant trumpet. Simon smiled. Nothing could have fitted better into the essential rightness of everything that had happened that evening. It was true that there had been a telephone in the library, and if there was an extension upstairs there might be gendarmes already watching the road, but they would be an interesting complication that could be dealt with in its proper turn.

Then he coaxed the car around a sharp bend and saw a row of red lights spring up across the road. He dropped his hand thoughtfully to the brake.

"This wasn't here when we came by first," he said, and realized that the girl had gone tense and still.

"What do you think it is?" she whispered.

The Saint shrugged. He brought the car to a standstill with its bumper three yards from the red lights, which appeared to be attached to a long plank rigged squarely across his path—he could not see what was beyond the plank.

Then he felt a hard cold jab of metal in the side of his head, and turned quickly. He looked down the barrel of a gun in the hand of an overcoated man who stood beside the car.

"Take it easy," advised the man with grim calmness.

The Saint heard a rustle of movement beside him, and glanced around. The girl was getting out. She closed the door after her, and stood on the running board.

"This is as far as I ride, stranger," she said.

"I see," said the Saint gently.

The man with the gun jabbed again.

"Let's have those papers," he ordered.

Simon took them from his breast pocket. The girl received them, and turned on the dashboard light to squint down the roll of plans and read the inscription on the long envelope. Her golden-yellow hair stirred like a shifting halo in the slight breeze.

"Burt Northwade hasn't got a brother who's a professor at Toronto," she explained, "and I'm no relative of the family. Apart from that, most of what I told you was true. Northwade bought this invention from a young Rumanian inventor—I don't know what sort of a price he gave for it, but he bought it. Actually there's no patent on it, so the biggest value to a manufacturer is in keeping it secret till he can come out with it ahead of the others. He was going to sell it to Ford, as I told you."

"What are you going to do with it?" inquired the Saint curiously.

"We've got an unwritten offer from Henry Kaiser."

She went forward and swung back the plank with the red lights, so that the road was clear again. Then she came back. The gray eyes were as frank and friendly as before.

"We've been planning this job for a week, and we should have done the job ourselves tonight if I hadn't seen your photograph in the paper and recognized you at the Windsor. The rest of it was an inspiration. There's nothing like having the greatest expert in the profession to work for you."

"What paper do you read?" asked the Saint.

"I saw you in *La Presse*. Why?"

"I bought an imported New York paper," said the Saint, conversationally.

She laughed quietly, a friendly ripple tinged with a trace of regret.

"I'm sorry, stranger. I liked you so much."

"I'm rather sorry too—Judith," said the Saint.

She was still for an instant. Then she leaned over and kissed him quickly on the lips.

The gun jabbed again.

"Drive on," ordered the man. "And keep driving."

"Won't you be wanting your car?" murmured the Saint.

A harsher chuckle came from the depths of the dark overcoat.

"We've got our own. I rented that one and left it at a garage for you when I had a phone call to say you were hooked. Get moving."

Simon engaged the gears, and let in the clutch. The girl jumped down from the running board. "Good-bye, stranger!" she cried, and Simon raised one hand in salute, without looking back.

He drove fast. Whoever the girl was, whatever she was, he knew that he had enjoyed meeting her far more than he could ever have enjoyed meeting the real Judith Northwade, whose unfortunate motor accident had been featured, with portrait, on the front page of the New York *Daily Gazette*, alongside his own two columns. She could never have looked anything but a hag. Whereas he still thought that her impostor was very beautiful. He hated to think what she would say when she delved deeper into the duplicate envelope and dummy roll of plans which he had so rapidly prepared for her in Burt Northwade's library. But he still drove fast, because those sad things were a part of the game and it was a longish way to Willow Run.

# IRIS

Of Simon Templar it could truly be said that to him all the world was a stage, and all the men and women merely players in an endless comedy drama designed for his especial entertainment and incidentally his cut at the box office.

To Mr Stratford Keane, all the world was also a stage, with the difference that he was the principal player and all the other men and women merely audience. This attitude persisted in spite of the fact that it was many years since the public had last shown any great desire to see him behind the footlights, and his thespian activities had been largely restricted to giving readings from Shakespeare to women's clubs and conducting classes in The Drama in the more obscure summer-theater colonies. In spite of these slings and arrows of outrageous fortune, however, he still maintained the fur-collared overcoats, the flowing ties, the long white locks, and the sweeping gestures of his departed day, and wherever he might be, the fruity resonance of his voice was still pitched to the second balcony in rounded periods from which every traditional caricature of a Shakespearean ham might have been taken.

Simon saw him advancing through the Pump Room, not in a perfectly straight line, for one of the causes of Mr Keane's eclipse was a weakness for the stuff that maketh glad the heart of man, but nevertheless with an unmistakable destination, and the attractions of Chicago fell under a slight cloud.

"Don't look now," he said to Patricia Holm, "but we are on the brink of another recital."

The main attraction of Chicago at the moment glanced up.

"Poor old Stratford," she said. "He's a good-hearted old bore. And not such a fool as you think, or why do you think he got the job of directing this new production of Macbeth?"

"Probably it was the only way they could get rid of him," Simon suggested. "So long as he's locked up in a theater in rehearsal he can't be out boring people anywhere else."

"You and your big heart," Patricia said. "It's a wonderful break for him, and he must have needed it badly."

"I'm thrilled to death at Stratford Keane getting a break," Simon assured her. "And I should be almost ecstatic if you'd never introduced him to me."

It was a little late to dream along those lines, for Mr Keane was already upon them and fully determined to make the most of their acquaintance. He held a half-filled glass over his heart and bowed deeply.

"Ah, Miss Holm! And Mr Templar," he boomed, causing people several tables away to look up and try to locate the loudspeaker. "Well met, well met!"

Patricia smiled.

"How are you this evening, Mr Keane?—Won't you sit down?" she added hastily, as Mr Keane leaned rather heavily on the table and shook a few drops out of their cocktails.

"A pleasure," Mr Keane sat down, and heaved a vast and doleful sigh. "Ah, this is indeed a haven in a world where every man must play a part—and mine a sad one . . . "

"Why, what's the matter?"

"I have just returned from the theater," stated Mr Keane tragically, as if he were announcing the end of the world. "We went through one of our final rehearsals."

"Was that bad?" Simon asked.

Stratford Keane surveyed him pityingly.

"Young man," he said, "to use the word 'bad' in that connection is to scorn all the resources of the English tongue. As a masterpiece of understatement, however, it might have some merit."

"You mean you won't be able to open on schedule?" Patricia asked sympathetically.

"On the contrary," said Mr Keane. "I'm afraid we shall."

Simon raised his eyebrows. "Afraid?"

"My dear boy," said Mr Keane heavily, "the success of Shakespeare in the emasculated theater of today is uncertain even with the most brilliant of performers, but when the lines of the Bard are assaulted by a gang of bellowing buffoons and dizzy doxies such as have been thrust upon me, the greatest play of all time would be doomed before the curtain rose."

"But isn't Iris Freeman a good actress?" Patricia asked.

"As a soubrette, yes. But as Lady Macbeth—" Mr Keane made an expressive gesture which swept an ash tray off the table. "Still, I could almost bear with her if only she would not insist on putting all her friends in the cast regardless of their incompetence—and most especially that tailor's dummy, Mark Belden, whom she picked as her leading man."

"I never heard of him," Simon admitted.

"Would that I shared your happy ignorance. Unfortunately, I have been condemned to get to know Mr Belden so well that his voice will ring in my ears until they sink into the merciful silence of the grave. A vaudeville hoofer who murders Shakespeare with every breath he takes!"

"But aren't you the director?" Patricia put in. "Don't you have anything to say about the cast?"

Stratford Keane glowered at her despondently. "My dear, your innocence is equaled by nothing but your beauty. The only voice which has anything to say about the cast is the voice of the money which is backing the production, which happens to belong to Miss Freeman."

"Shouldn't you have said that it belonged to Rick Lansing?" Simon put in shrewdly.

Patricia turned to him with a tiny wrinkle forming between her brows.

"Miss Freeman's latest husband," Simon answered. "Better known to his business associates as Rick the Barber. Only it probably wouldn't be tactful to mention that when she's around." He shifted his eyes. "Which means starting about now."

He had seen enough advance publicity pictures of Iris Freeman to recognize her as she came towards the table. It would have been impossible in any event not to notice her, for the furs and jewels which trimmed a face and figure that could have attracted quite enough attention without any artificial adornment at all were obviously worn for the secondary function of practically forcing the observer to ask who they belonged to. And the unhesitating way in which her path was headed for Stratford Keane established a connection between them that was almost enough clue by itself.

"Stratford, darling!" she cried. "I was just betting Mark that we'd find you here as usual."

"A feat of unparalleled perspicacity on your part," said Keane. He struggled halfway to his feet, rocking the table dangerously. "May I present two dear friends of mine—Miss Patricia Holm and Mr Simon Templar. This is Miss Iris Freeman, whom I was just telling you about. And—er"—he winced slightly at the exquisitely tailored male who appeared from behind Miss Freeman's patina—"Mr Belden."

Iris Freeman's beautiful dark eyes found Simon and grew wide and worshipful.

"Simon Templar?" she repeated. "You don't mean—the Saint?"

Simon nodded resignedly. It was not always convenient to be identified so readily with the paradoxical alias under which his identity had once upon a time been concealed, but those days were pretty far in the past, and few people who read newspapers were unaware of the almost legendary career of brigandage which his name stood for. He was getting more used to it all the time, and certainly there was nothing much else to do except make the best of it. Which was not always so bad, either, especially when the vague associations of his name made beautiful women look at him in that excited and expectant way.

He smiled.

"That was the name," he said, "before I saw the error of my ways."

Belden said, "This is wonderful. You know, Iris is one of your most devoted fans, Mr Templar. She's crazy about you."

Simon restrained an impulse to empty the remains of a Martini over him, and said, "I think that's a wonderful way to be crazy. But of course I'm prejudiced."

"I was just telling Mark the other day that the only person in the whole world whose autograph I'd really like to have was the Saint," Iris Freeman said.

"Isn't that sort of turning the tables on your public, Miss Freeman?" murmured Patricia sweetly.

The actress laughed gaily, with every note beautifully modulated for imaginary microphones.

"Hardly a habit of mine. But we all have our weaknesses, don't we? And the Saint's also one of mine, darling . . . Mark, do you have a piece of paper?"

Belden fumbled in his pockets and produced a folded sheet.

"Here you are."

"I suppose if I had more practice I could take these situations in my stride," said the Saint.

"You'll do all right," said Patricia. "Sign the paper and satisfy your adoring public."

Simon took out a pen and scribbled his name.

"And you must draw the Saint figure," Iris Freeman insisted. "It wouldn't be complete without that."

The Saint patiently sketched his trademark—the straight-line skeleton figure crowned with the conventional halo which had once been enough to give the most hardened citizens an uneasy qualm at the pit of their stomachs—and reflected that a lot of things had changed. Or had they?

"That's simply wonderful," Iris Freeman gushed. "You'll never believe what a thrill this is for me. I only wish I could stay and talk to you for hours, but Mark and I have to run. How would you like to come to our rehearsal tomorrow?"

"He'd love to," Patricia said firmly. "But I'm afraid he has another engagement."

"Oh . . . I see." The actress bit her lip. "Well, I'll be sure and send you some tickets for the opening, Saint. And you must come to the party afterwards, I'll manage to get you off to myself somehow—Come along, Mark."

"Yes, dear." Belden gave Simon one of those unnecessarily hearty handshakes. "It's been a pleasure to meet you, Mr. Templar. And you, Miss Holm. So long, Stratford. Don't let it get you down."

They made an exit which should have had an orchestral background, and Stratford Keane stared after them rudely.

"The only party after the opening," he said, "should be a wake, with those two as the guests of honor."

"I don't think Simon agrees with you," Patricia said. "He's discovered that there are things in Iris's favor which you never mentioned in your description."

Simon reached for her glass and finished her drink for her.

"You're very unfair to the wench," he said. "If it's a crime to be fascinated by me, what are you doing here?"

He produced folding money and handed it to a hopeful waiter.

"Buy Mr Keane another drink," he said. "And a taxi afterwards, if he needs it." He stood up. "I'm sorry we have to rush off, but I have to buy Pat some dinner. She doesn't talk back so much with her mouth full."

Mr Keane nodded broodingly.

"Good night," he said. "I shall see thee—at Philippi."

They made their escape, Simon hoped, before Mr Keane was reminded that the Pump Room was also in the business of serving food.


The encounter was typical of many similar incidents in the Saint's life—coincidental, casual, and apparently pointless, and yet destined to lead into unsuspected complications. Adventure, for him, moved in a mysterious way. Nothing ever seemed to happen to him that was completely unimportant, or that led nowhere. He had come to accept it as part of an inscrutable fate, like the people who are known to insurance companies as "accident prone": regardless of whether he took the initiative or not, something was always happening to him. He seldom thought about it much anymore, except that it may have subconsciously contributed to a pleasantly persistent euphoria, an almost imperceptible but continuous excitement which made the colors of his world just a little brighter than anyone else's.

For several hours he certainly didn't think much more about any of the three people who had just met at his table, or attach any immediate significance to the meeting—not even when he brought Patricia into his suite at the Ambassador for a nightcap, and switched on the lights and found himself looking down the barrel of a gun in the hand of an unexpected guest who had beat them to it without an invitation.

Simon Templar had looked down the barrels of guns before, and it had ceased to be a surprising experience for him. The turbulent course of his career had left enough survivors to constitute a sizable roster of characters whose principal ambition would always be to view the Saint again from behind the percentage end of a small piece of ordnance. The only remarkable thing about it was that Simon couldn't at the moment think of any particular person in the vicinity who had reason to be trying to fulfill such a whim at that time.

"Well, well, well," he murmured. "Look what people are doing now to get a hotel room."

"Shut the door, bub," said the man. "But don't put your hat down. You ain't staying long."

He had blue-black hair and a blue chin, and his suit was cut just about the way you would expect a suit behind a gun to be cut. Something about him was vaguely familiar, but Simon couldn't place it for the moment.

"That's one way to bring an invitation, anyhow," said the Saint. "Where is this party we're going to?"

"You'll find out when we get there," said the man. "Just wait till I fix the girl friend so she don't make a fuss about losing you."

He took a roll of adhesive tape from his pocket.

"I think I'm going to faint," said Patricia.

She slumped back against the wall by the door, exactly where the light switch was. As her knees buckled she caught one arm on the switch and the lights clicked out.

The gunman started to move to one side, peering blindly into the dark. He bumped into a standard lamp and set it rattling.

That was the only sound he heard before an arm slid around his neck from behind and a row of steel fingers clamped on his right hand and bent it inwards to within a millimeter of breaking his wrist. His hand opened involuntarily and the gun dropped on the carpet. Simon located it with his toe and put his foot on it.

"Okay, Pat," he said. "I've got him."

The lights went on again.

"Nice work," said the Saint. "You read all the right stories."

He released his pressure on the gunman's larynx before suffocation had seriously set in, pushed the man away, and picked up the gun.

"Now, chum," he said, "where did you say we were going?"

The man rubbed his wrists tenderly and glanced at him without answering.

The first vague impression of familiarity that Simon had felt began to come into focus.

"On second thoughts, you needn't bother," said the Saint. "I know where I've seen you before. At the Blue Paradise. You're one of Rick Lansing's boys."

"I ain't talking," said the man.

"Then we're going to find your company rather dull," said the Saint. "Why don't you beat it before you bore the hell out of us?"

The gunman seemed to have difficulty co-ordinating his ideas and his ears.

"Scram, bum," said the Saint.

The man gulped, opened the door, and departed hastily.

"Nice work yourself," said Patricia. "Why on earth did you let him go?"

"I didn't feel excited about having him live with us," Simon told her. "I might have killed him, but the management wouldn't like us to keep his body in the room, and if we threw it out of the window it might have hurt somebody."

"But aren't you a bit curious about what he was doing here?"

"I already know, darling. He was sent here to fetch me to Rick the Barber, that was obvious as soon as I placed him."

"But what does Rick Lansing want with you?"

"That," said the Saint, "is a question that Rick will have to answer himself."

Patricia picked up her wraps.

"Wait till I powder my nose," she said.

"Oh no," said the Saint. "From the type of escort Rick sent with the invitation, I'm afraid he may not be on his strictly Emily Post behavior, and even if he has hitched his wagon to a Broadway star he doesn't seem to have sworn off his old business methods. You stay here with the Old Curio and don't open the door to any strange men."

He kissed her lightly and closed the door on her argument.


The Blue Paradise was one of the gaudier cabarets in the Loop. It was not a rendezvous for the social-register set, but it did a roaring and frequently even howling trade in tourists and tired businessmen, both local and traveling. The specialty dancers specialized mainly in undressing to slow music, and the drinks were thoughtfully diluted just enough to allow the patrons to get an adequate lift without becoming unconscious before they had spent a great deal of money. Simon knew that it was one of Rick Lansing's operations, and also that there was an office in the back which was the headquarters for Lansing's other business interests, which were many and various.

Rick the Barber might have left his original vocation far behind, but he was still one of its best customers. He had dark wavy hair that glistened with oil and brushing. The skin over his tough square features was smooth and glowing from many facials. His hands were shinily manicured. He looked far more like a toughened chorus boy than what he was.

He sat behind his desk and listened impassively to the alibi of his ambassador.

"I tell ya, Rick, I couldn't do anything about it. The Saint musta been tipped off. He had four guys with him, and they was all heeled."

"I don't believe you," Lansing said contemptuously. "But even if it's the truth, what did you come straight back here for? How do you know one of 'em didn't tail you?"

"Honest, Rick, I shook 'em clean."

This was when Simon Templar quietly opened the door and stepped into the room.

"That's right, Rick," he corroborated gravely. "He shook all of 'em except me . . . Just don't do anything reckless, boys, and I won't hurt you either."

The position of his left hand in the side pocket of his coat made his proposition especially persuasive.

Lansing kept his hands on top of the desk and considered the situation without a change of expression.

"Good evening, Mr Templar," he said at length.

"Good evening, Rick," said the Saint amiably. "I believe you wanted to see me. So here I am. You didn't need to make a production of it. I'm only too anxious to hear what's on your mind. Shall we talk it over in private, or does Sonny Boy here make you feel safer?"

Lansing sat still for a moment, and then made a slight movement of his hand.

"Beat it, Joe."

"That's better," said the Saint. "Now he can collect the rest of the mob outside the door, which will make you feel really comfortable, but they know I've got you here, so I haven't a thing to worry about. We can let our hair down and enjoy it."

Lansing suddenly smiled, displaying a wide row of perfect white teeth.

"And I thought you were supposed to be smart," he said. "You're wasting yourself, Saint. Listen, with your talents you're just the guy I need for a partner. Petty blackmail isn't big enough for you. And what if you do tell the D.A. that Jake Hardy didn't commit suicide? You couldn't prove a thing."

A slight frown touched the Saint's brow.

"Jake Hardy?" he repeated. "You mean your last partner?"

"Go on—kid me."

The Saint's memory, which missed very little of the underworld news that reached the papers or circulated through the grapevine, responded again. Jake Hardy, for reasons unknown, had plunged from a penthouse window to his death several months before, leaving Rick Lansing in sole control of a cartel which, while it was not rated by Dun & Bradstreet and had little standing with the Better Business Bureau, was one of the richest enterprises of the Windy City.

"Let me make a guess," said the Saint slowly. "Do I gather that someone claiming to be me is trying to shake you down for a certain amount of moola on account of they know that Jake's high dive wasn't Jake's own idea?"

"Look," Lansing said impatiently. "The comedy belongs outside with the floor show. Why, even if you hadn't given your name on the phone, I can recognize your voice."

"My voice?"

"Yes, your voice."

"And that's why you sent Sonny Boy to bring me in?"

Lansing made a clipped gesture.

"I was upset. So now I'm sorry. No hard feelings, Saint. Believe me, a partnership with me will pay you a lot more than the lousy ten grand you're asking for hush money. It wouldn't be just this joint. I could give you a cut in everything, all over town—sports areas, bookies, numbers—the works."

Simon fished out a cigarette with his right hand and arched an eyebrow over his lighter.

"Even in the Shakespearean drama too?"

The other man blinked.

"Huh? Oh—that." He smiled again, deprecatingly, with the corners of his mouth turned down. "Just a present for my wife. If she wants to play Shakespeare she can play Shakespeare. I can afford it. It might even make money. There aren't many things I can't afford, and most of 'em make money sometime. I can afford you, and make money for both of us. The two of us together could really clean up."

"I appreciate the compliment," said the Saint. "But there's one hitch."

"What's that?"

"I wasn't the guy who tried to blackmail you."

A slight scowl settled over Lansing's black eyes.

"I told you before—the comedy belongs outside."

"I don't doubt the show could use it," said the Saint. "Only whether you like it or not, the comedy is right here. Because I give you my word that I've never spoken to you on the phone in my life, and I don't have the least idea how to start proving that Jake was helped out of his window."

Lansing stared at him for several seconds.

"Is that on the level?"

"Absolutely."

"Then who is this guy who's pretending to be you?"

"That," said the Saint, "is what I'd like to know. I'll have to try and find out." He took the hand out of his left side pocket. "Now that we understand each other, I guess you won't mind if I leave."

Rick the Barber stood up and came around the desk. He opened the door.

The first gunman, reinforced by two others, stood watchfully in the corridor outside.

"It's okay," Lansing said. "The Saint is okay."

Simon strolled through the goon squad, and Lansing followed him out to the bar.

"Will you let me know if you find out anything, Saint?"

"I will if you will," Simon agreed. "By the way, how was this dough to be paid?"

"In an envelope addressed to Cleve Wentz at the Canal Street Post Office, general delivery. I can have the boys keep an eye on the window."

"It might take a long time," said the Saint. "And it still wouldn't be easy to spot the pickup. But there's no harm trying . . . I'll be seeing you, Rick. Give my regards to Lady Macbeth."

Nevertheless, he had no more brilliant ideas himself, and even the nest morning found him without inspiration. The problem of locating an anonymous impersonator who had just spoken to somebody once on the telephone made the proverbial needle in the haystack look simple.

He was brooding over the impasse after a late breakfast when there was a knock on the door, and when he opened it he was confronted by a pair of rather prominent eyes in a lean dyspeptic face which he recognized instantly. Taken in conjunction with the recent trend of his thoughts, the recognition gave him a premonitory qualm which no one could have guessed from the cordiality with which he renewed an old acquaintance.

"Why, Alvin!" he exclaimed. "This is a pleasant surprise. Come in and tell me about your latest triumphs."

Lieutenant Alvin Kearney came in without a responding smile, but there was a certain amount of smugness in the lines of his normally unhappy countenance.

"I don't know what sort of a triumph you'd call it," he said. "But this time I've really got the goods on you, my friend."

The Saint looked puzzled.

"The goods, Alvin?"

"Yeah," Kearney said grimly. "Although frankly I never thought I'd get you for common blackmail."

Simon realized that he had been unduly despondent. He didn't think for a moment that Rick the Barber would have gone to the police, but what he had overlooked was that the impostor was not likely to stop with one victim.

"A lot of people seem to be going nuts these days," he remarked almost cheerfully. "Who says I'm blackmailing him now?"

"Vincent Maxted."

"The meat packer?"

"You ought to know," Kearney said. "You claim to be able to prove that he made a nice piece of change during the war out of black-market steaks."

Simon lighted a cigarette.

"I keep being amazed by the things I know," he said. "It's a little startling to be credited with clairvoyance all of a sudden. The embarrassing thing is that I don't really deserve it. I assure you, Alvin, this is the first I've heard about Maxted's illegal butchery."

"Is that so?" Kearney was unimpressed. "Then I guess you'd figured he'd just be scared enough to pay up rather than go through an investigation. It doesn't make any difference. You made the threat anyhow, and he'll be able to identify your voice."

"My voice? On the telephone?" Simon scoffed.

"That's for your lawyer to fight about. It's good enough for me to hold you. Let's go, Saint. I've got a nice cozy room reserved for you at headquarters."

Simon thought for a few moments.

"Okay," he said at last. "If you want to stick your neck out I suppose I can't stop you. Do you mind if I throw a few things in a bag?"

"Make it snappy," Kearney said.

He followed Simon into the bedroom. The Saint pulled out a suitcase and opened it. He took out a crumpled piece of paper, glanced at it, and gave a guilty start. Rather clumsily, he tried to get rid of it under the bed. "What's that?" Kearney snapped.

"Nothing," said the Saint unconvincingly. "Just an old bill."

"Let me see it."

Simon hesitated, without moving.

Kearney came around the bed, pushed the Saint aside, and went down on his knees to grope underneath.

Simon stepped out of the bedroom, closed the door, and turned the key in the lock, in one fluid sweep of co-ordinated movements. He was out of the suite so quickly that he did not even hear the detective's roar of rage.


By day, the Blue Paradise had an uninviting drabness which contrasted significantly with its neon-lighted nocturnal glitter. The doors were inhospitably closed and locked, but Simon found a bell to ring, and after a while a beady eye peered out through a two-inch opening and was sufficiently satisfied to let him in.

"Greetings, Sonny Boy," said the Saint. "Is Rick around yet?"

"I guess he'll see you," conceded the gunsel gloomily, and Simon went through the dim deserted bar and down the back corridor to Lansing's office.

"I've got news for you, Rick," he said. "You're in good company."

Lansing looked up from the accounts he was studying. "What does that mean?"

"Someone else I don't have anything on is being blackmailed by the Saint."

"Who's that?"

Simon skipped the question for a moment. "Did you buy any black-market meat during the war?"

"Maybe you really want a job in the floor show," Lansing said. "I'll buy the gag. So I had to stay in business. So what?"

"Did you get anything through Vincent Maxted?"

Lansing's eyelids flickered. "What about him?"

"Only this," said the Saint. "The first job of blackmail that we met over referred to something which only you or someone very close to you should have known. Maybe the same can be said about this new job. I've got an idea it can. And if that's true, we may be getting somewhere. We don't want to miss something that might be right under our nose."

Lansing's eyes were flat and hard like jet. "I can only think of one guy who might be liable to know as much as I know myself, including about what happened to Jake," he said. "But don't ask me how he'd know. I just say I could believe it because I know the kind of guy he is. This guy always seems to know too much about everything that goes on."

"And who's that?"

"Some people call him the Saint." Simon smiled.

"You give me too much credit, Rick. As a matter of fact, I never suspected anything about Jake Hardy until you practically told me yourself. I'd never even given it a thought. From what I hear, he was no great loss to the community, so why should I worry about how he was moved on? I couldn't have cared less if it had been the other way around, and when somebody does get you one of these days, as they probably will, it still won't bother me."

"Then what are you wasting your time here for?"

"Because I hate people taking my name in vain, and because I'm beginning to think it's someone quite close to you. Someone who knows much more about your affairs than I do," said the Saint thoughtfully. He went to the door. "Think it over, chum."

There was a drugstore on the corner of the block, and he stopped there to phone Patricia.

"No doubt you've seen Kearney," he said.

"And heard him." She was trying to keep the anxiety out of her voice but he still felt it. "What on earth did you do it for?"

"It was the only thing I could do, baby. I couldn't run down this character who's impersonating me if Alvin had me in the hoosegow, and if I don't run him down I can't clear myself. It's a stock situation straight out of any pulp detective story, but it can happen."

"But what's this now about Vincent Maxted?"

"Well, apparently my alter ego is expanding his business."

"Can't I meet you somewhere?" she said.

"Darling, it's a sure bet that Kearney'll have you followed, hoping for just that."

"Then you don't really think any of the tricks you've taught me for losing a shadow are any good."

The Saint sighed.

"All right," he said. "I'll meet you at the Delphian theater."

There was a perceptible pause before she said, "Have you gone out of your mind?"

"No," said the Saint. "But I was invited to a rehearsal, and I happened to remember that Iris Freeman was once Mrs Vincent Maxted."

He took a taxi to the theater and turned on the radio. He found a local news broadcast, and had the ambiguous satisfaction of hearing his own name on a last-minute flash just before the commercial.

"Must be quite a guy, that Saint," said the driver chattily.

"He'd better be," Simon agreed.


There was no janitor at the stage door, and he found his way unchallenged to the stage. Voices grew louder as he approached it, and presently he stopped in the shadow of some stacked scenery and listened.

The rehearsal seemed to be justifying some of Stratford Keane's gloomy prognostications. The voice of Macbeth, declaiming, did not even have the lush rotundity of Keane's:

> *"Is this a dagger which I see before me,*
> *The handle toward my hand?*
> *Come, let me clutch thee.*
> *I have thee not, and yet I see thee still.*
> *Art thou not, fatal vision, sensible*
> *To feeling as to sight—"*

There was a soft footfall behind him, and he turned and saw Patricia at his shoulder.

"Hullo," she whispered. "What's going on?"

"Hush," he said. "This is what Stratford was weeping about."

*" . . . Now o'er the one-half world*
*Nature seems dead, and wicked dreams abuse*
*The curtain'd sleep; now witchcraft celebrates*
*Pale Hecate's offerings, and withered murder,*
*Alarum'd by his sentinel—"*

"No, no, no!" moaned the anguished voice of Stratford Keane, further off in the hollow of the empty auditorium. "I can't stand it! Belden, you're beating those lines with a club! A bludgeon!"

"Oh, dry up," Iris Freeman said, from the stage. "I think Mark is doing wonderfully."

Stratford Keane's groan reverberated like the plaint of a wounded bull.

"You think! Ye gods, what have I done to deserve this? I, Stratford Keane, who have striven all my life to learn understanding and patience! Even Job was at last tried too far, and I am not Job . . . You think Belden is doing wonderfully.

"That is too much. You may direct this play, Miss Freeman." His voice was louder but still further off. "I resign. I'm through!"

In the distance a door slammed.

There was an uneasy silence on the stage for a few moments, and then Iris Freeman said with weary disgust, "Oh, for crying out loud! Again?"

"Exit Stratford, pursued by a bear," Belden said sepulchrally.

And then suddenly the voice of Stratford Keane boomed out again with remarkable verisimilitude. "Ye gods, what have I done to deserve this? I, Stratford Keane, who have striven all my life to learn understanding and patience!"

There was a general chorus of laughter.

Patricia's fingers tightened on the Saint's arm.

"Simon! Did you notice—"

"Stratford didn't really do him justice," said the Saint.

On the stage, Iris Freeman was saying, "Better run along kids. You'll probably be called back as usual after Mr Keane cools off."

In a little while the footsteps and voices of the rest of the cast died away and the theater was silent again. The Saint held Patricia motionless in the shadows. Then Iris Freeman spoke again with a rather tired relaxation.

"You know, Mark, this sometimes seems like doing it the hard way."

"Don't worry, honey," Belden said. "As soon as I collect a few more touches with the dope you're giving me about the people who've used Rick in their various operations—why, I'll be all set to back the show myself. Then you can divorce him and we can be married."

"But suppose something goes wrong. And if Rick ever finds out—"

"How can he? And if anything ever does go wrong, the Saint gets it in the neck. Don't forget we've got that piece of paper now with his signature and his fingerprints all over it. We can type anything we like over his name and plant it where it'll do the most good."

Simon Templar gently released Patricia and strolled out onto the stage. He was cool and unhurried, putting a cigarette in his mouth and lighting it as he moved, so easy and natural that the shock of his entrance only held the other two in a kind of misty trance.

"That's a great idea, children," he murmured, "only it doesn't solve any of my problems." His voice sharpened suddenly as Belden started to come out of his freeze. "Don't try anything, Mark. I want you to be able to talk when Lieutenant Kearney gets here. Pat, do you think you could find a phone?"

"Don't bother," Kearney said.

His angular figure emerged from the shadows on the other side of the stage, and Mark Belden watched him approach in a new and even deeper trance from which even the click of a handcuff on his wrist did not arouse him.

Iris Freeman was less ready to give up. She struggled furiously for one hectic moment before Kearney snapped the other cuff on her wrist, where it made a tasteful contrast with her jewel bracelets.

"You can't do this to me," she panted.

"I can try my best," said the detective. "From what I heard, it sounds like a clear case of conspiracy to me."

"Don't let it get you down, darling," said the Saint. "Cross your legs on the witness stand, and the jury will probably see everything your way. On the other hand, I'm afraid Rick may not be so easy."

What Iris Freeman said cannot be printed without grave risk to the publisher.

Simon and Patricia strolled south on Michigan Avenue in a rather noticeable silence.

"Kearney was pretty nice about you, wasn't he?" said Patricia at last.

"He's not a bad guy," Simon agreed. "And he's got something to thank me for. Getting the real blackmailers ought to be worth more to him than trying to hang a shaky rap on me . . . Of course, it started to be obvious as soon as Iris showed up as a connecting link. It would have been too much for her to imitate my voice, but the only thing left was to identify her stooge. It occurred to me at once that we couldn't rely on Stratford Keane's definition of Belden. A ham like Keane wouldn't know the difference between one vaudeville performer and another, but I'll bet Belden wasn't a hoofer. I'll bet he was one of those dreadful acts which start, 'I would like to give you my impression of . . .' I always wanted to see something unpleasant happen to that kind of artist, but I never hoped I should have the chance to arrange it."

There was a further silence.

"Now," said Patricia with difficulty, "I suppose you're only waiting to tell me that you knew all along I wouldn't shake Kearney off."

"I was betting on it," said the Saint blandly. "And I owe you a lot for your co-operation." He turned and hailed a passing taxi. "However, I shall let Rick the Barber contribute to your reward. Things may not be too happy for him when Iris blows her top, as she probably will, and I think Rick ought to pay us quite well for a tip-off."

LIDA

The moon was a paste-up job. True, it had come up dripping out of the sea two hours before, but now it hung in the Florida sky like a cut-out from golden paper, and looked down with a bland open countenance on the denizens of Miami Beach and all the visiting firemen therein.

Including wives whose husbands were busy in their offices from Chicago to Boston providing the wherewithal for their helpmeets to fritter around; certain characters who went around with thousand-dollar bills in their pockets but never paid any income tax; touts, pimps, and prostitutes; hopeful gents and girls who felt that one more throw of the dice would get them even with the board again, and Simon Templar and Patricia Holm.

Simon, known as the Saint in varying degrees of love, hate, and envy, lounged behind the wheel of a long low convertible, and pushed that rented job up Collins Avenue at ten miles more than the law allowed. Patricia, her golden head making the moon look like a polished penny, sat easily beside him.

"Simon," she said, "look at that moon. It can't be real."

"Strictly a prop, Pat," the Saint said. "The president of the Chamber of Commerce hangs it up each night."

"If you had any romance in what you call your soul," Patricia complained, "you'd admit it was pretty lush."

"And when we get to the Quarterdeck Club, the atmosphere will be even lusher."

After a contemplative silence, the girl said, "There must be something beyond that, Simon—something that scared Lida Verity half out of her mind. Otherwise she wouldn't have been so desperate on the phone."

"You know her better than I do. Is she the hysterical type?"

"Not even in the Greek meaning of the word," Pat said. "She's a swell gal. Nice family, nice husband in the Navy, plenty of money, and she has her head screwed on tight. She's in trouble, all right."

"Then why didn't she call Sheriff Haskins? . . . Ah, I see things."

"Things" were a neon sign which read "The Quarterdeck" and a driveway which led through an avenue of royal palms, past a doorway labeled "Gangplank," to a vista of macadam which could have served as the flight deck of an aircraft carrier, but appeared to be used as a parking lot. On this bit of real-estate development were parked Cadillacs, Chryslers, Chevrolets, and cars further along in the alphabet, all with gleaming paint jobs and, as far as could be seen in the advertisable moonlight, good tires.

In case any patron might be arriving without a perfectly clean conception of the atmospheric motif of the joint, the requisite keynote was struck immediately by the resplendent personage who advanced to greet them as they pulled up alongside the "gangplank."

"Get a load of the Admiral," Simon observed, as he set the hand brake.

The "Admiral" was one to arouse exclamations. He had more gold braid than an Arabian-nights tapestry, his epaulets raised his shoulder height three inches, his cocked hat probably had John Paul Jones spinning in his grave, and the boots were masterpieces of dully gleaming leather. His face was square, and hearty and red as fresh beefsteak.

He eyed the Saint and Patricia, resplendent in evening dress, with limited approbation.

"Ahoy there!" he hailed them, in a restrained bellow. "Have you arranged for your moorings?"

"If by that corny seagoing salutation you mean do we have reservations," the Saint replied, "no. We do not."

"Then I'm sorry, skipper," the admiral boomed. "You can't drop anchor."

"But, Admiral," Pat said, "we drove all the way from—"

"Very sorry, miss. But the harbor's overcrowded already."

"This is Patricia Holm," the Saint said, "and I am Simon Templar."

"Sorry, sir, but it doesn't matter if—" The man gulped, and peered at them more closely. "Templar, did you say?"

"Yes, Simon Templar."

The Admiral removed his hat, mopped at his pink forehead.

"Whew! That was a shot across the bow. I've heard about you, Mr . . . er . . . Sss . . ."

"Call him Saint," said Patricia. "He likes it."

"But I still can't let you in the Quarterdeck, sir."

"You aren't letting us," the Saint said gently. "But you aren't stopping us, either."

"I wouldn't want to cause any unpleasantness, sir, but—"

"No," the Saint agreed, not so gently. "I wouldn't, if I were you. It might be more unpleasant for you than you'd bargained for. Now if you'll just slip anchor and drift to the northwest a trifle—"

"For another thing," Pat put in, "we were invited here."

The Admiral removed his uneasy eyes from the Saint's blue stare. His face broke into a mass of uplifting wrinkles.

"Invited?" he said genially. "Why didn't you say so?"

"You didn't ask," the Saint said. "Mrs Verity asked us to join her."

This name impressed the Admiral. His eyes widened.

"Mrs Verity? Then come aboard!"

"We intended to," the Saint said. "Ready, Pat?"

"Aye, aye, sir. Boarding party, forward."

The Admiral fawned on the Saint more than befitted his dignified dress.

"I hope you'll pardon me, sir, for— Oh!" Somehow, his hand was convenient for the Saint to reach. His white glove closed around what the Saint put there. "Thank you, sir!"

Simon took the girl's arm and steered her along a short companionway, brass-railed on either side, to a doorway which bore a small brass plate: "Lounge."

The big room fanned out to impressive dimensions in three directions, but it was stocked with enough tables and patrons to avert any impression of bleakness.

On the tables were numbers in patterns, pertaining to dice, roulette, and faro. On the feminine patrons were the fewest glittering scraps permitted by current conventions. Bare backs and white ties made a milling chiaroscuro backgrounded by hushed murmurs and the plastic chink of chips.

The cash customers, in fact, were the only discrepancy in an otherwise desperately consistent decor. The roulette wheels were set in a frame intended to be a ship's wheel. The crap table was a lifeboat, its deck the playing surface. Everywhere was the motif of the sea, polished and brazen. Waiters were dressed as stewards, with "Quarterdeck" embroidered on their gleaming jackets. The cigarette girl was dressed in white shorts, a sailor's cap, and two narrow straps that crossed over her pneumatic bosom. The croupiers wore three-cornered hats emblazoned, aptly, with the Jolly Roger.

Patricia's blue eyes took in the big room one customer at a time.

"I don't see Lida," she said presently. "She said she'd be waiting."

"Probably she's just late," Simon answered. "It has happened to women before." He ignored the daggered glance which his lady launched at him. "Shall we mingle with the elite, and lose a fortune in the well-bred fashion of wealthy suckers?"

"The next time I have to wait for you—" Patricia began, and then Simon stopped her with a hand on her arm.

"Don't look now," he said in a low voice, "but something tall, dark, and rancid is coming up on our starboard quarter."

The newcomer wasn't really tall. He stood several inches below the Saint's seventy-four, but he gave the impression of height by his manner: suave, completely poised.

"Good evening," he said, his dark eyes flickering up and down Pat in appreciation. "Permit me to introduce myself. I am Esteban. Welcome to the Quarterdeck."

"How do you do, Esteban?" said the Saint. "Quite well, I guess, from the looks of things."

Esteban smiled, and made a comprehensive gesture at the crowd.

"Always there are many people at the Quarterdeck Club. We conduct honest games. But what will you play? Roulette, faro, blackjack?"

"None but the brave *chemin de fer*," murmured the Saint. "It's nice of you to give us a choice of weapons. But as a matter of fact, we're looking for a friend. A Mrs Verity."

The dark eyes went flat.

"Ah," Esteban said without expression. "Mrs Verity."

Pat said, "You know her?"

"Who does not, señorita? Of course."

"She's here, isn't she?"

"I am afraid you are to be disappointed. I think Mrs Verity has gone."

"You *think*?" Simon repeated pointedly. "Did you see her go?"

Esteban shrugged, his face still blank and brown.

"There are so many. It is hard to say."

Simon's stare could have been fashioned in bronze. "You wouldn't be stalling, would you, Esteban?" he asked with gentle deadliness.

"She told us she'd wait for us," Pat said. "When did she leave?"

Esteban smiled suddenly, the accommodating host.

"I try to find out for you. Mrs Verity like to play the big, big stake, take the big risk. Maybe she hit too many times wrong at the blackjack; perhaps she went for more money . . . Please, will you have a drink on the promenade deck while I make inquiries? Out here . . ."

He ushered them towards French doors that opened on one side of the gaming room, and bowed himself away. The patio was dappled with moonlight and the shadows of palm fronds, but it seemed to have no appeal for the other customers. Simon lighted a cigarette, while Patricia walked to a rail trimmed with unnecessary life belts, and gazed out at the vista of landscaped ground sloping gently to the moongladed sea.

She caught her breath at the scene, and then shivered slightly.

"It's so beautiful it hurts," she said. "And yet it seems every time we find a romantic spot like this, there's something . . . I don't know, but this place gives me the creeps."

"Inside," the Saint said, "the creeps are giving to Esteban. I don't know if you'd call that a fair exchange."

He looked up as a waiter arrived.

"Esteban's compliments, sir. Would you and the lady care for anything?"

"Very handsome of Esteban," the Saint said. "We'll have double Manhattans made with a good bourbon, and—"

He broke off as a flat *splat!* broke the silence off in the direction of the sea, seeming to come from a clump of magnolia trees.

"What was that?" Patricia breathed.

"Probably a backfire, miss," the waiter said. "Somebody having trouble with a car."

"On account of driving it into the sea?" Simon said, and swung a leg over the rail.

"Could a motorboat do that?" Pat asked.

"No, darling. Come on."

"About your drinks, sir—"

"Don't put any cherries in them," said the Saint.

He sped down a winding path to the deeply shadowed little grove of trees, white with blossoms that were like wax in the moonlight, and Patricia was only a stride behind him.

It took no searching at all to find the body. It lay sprawled under a tree, half in shadow, staring upward with glazed eyes that would never see again. It was—had been—Lida Verity. She held an automatic pistol in one hand, and under the swell of her left breast was a small dark hole and a spreading stain.

The Saint made a brief examination, and knew while he did it that he was only deferring to a conventional routine. There was no doubt now that Lida Verity had had reason to call him, and the line of his mouth was soured by the recollection of his earlier flippancy.

He knew that Patricia was only obeying the same inescapable conventions when she said, "Simon—is she—"

He nodded.

"Now she isn't scared anymore."

Lida Verity had lived—gaily, indifferently, passionately, thoughtfully, frantically. Her life had echoed with the tinkle of champagne glasses, Mendelssohn's solemnity, the purr of sleek motors, the chatter of roulette frets, before the final sound of a gun in the night had changed the tense of the declarative sentence "I am."

The Saint stood quietly summarizing the available data: the body, the wound, the gun, the time, the place. And as he stood, with Patricia wordless beside him, a whisper of footsteps announced the coming of Esteban.

Simon's eyes hardened as they moved up the proprietor of that palace of chance in which only the guests took the chance.

"Welcome to the wake, comrade," he said coldly.

Esteban looked over the situation. His expression was impassive, yet his dark eyes were sharp as he added the factors and came up with an answer.

"The waiter told me there was some trouble," he said, exactly like one of his headwaiters dealing with some trivial complaint. "You found her—like this?"

"We did."

"Is she—"

"You've lost your place in the script," Simon said patiently. "We've already read that line."

"I am sorry," Esteban said bloodlessly. "She was a lovely lady."

"Somebody didn't share your opinion," the Saint said.

The words hung in the quiet night, as if they were three-dimensional, to be touched, and turned, and examined. The pause lengthened while the Saint lighted a cigarette without taking his eyes off Esteban. His meaning seemed to materialize slowly during the silence.

"But—" Esteban gestured at the body, face upward, black hair glinting in the wash of moonlight. "The gun is in her hand. Surely you cannot mean—"

"She was murdered."

"But that is impossible!" Esteban protested. "It is so obvious, Mr Templar. It is suicide."

"Lida wouldn't have killed herself!" Patricia said hotly. "She was so—so alive. She wouldn't, I tell you!"

"Madame," Esteban said sadly, "you do not know. She lose much money tonight at the gaming table. Perhaps more than she should."

"How much?" Simon asked bluntly.

Esteban shrugged.

"We do not keep accounts. She buy many chips for the roulette table."

"A few minutes ago you thought 'perhaps' she had been losing at blackjack. Now you seem to know different."

Esteban's shoulders rose another inch.

"You ask me to find out, I accommodate you. And now I go call the sheriff. I must ask you not to disturb anything."

"I think," the Saint said softly, "that before the evening is out we shall disturb many things, my friend."

Esteban went back up the path, and the Saint took Patricia's arm and led her off at a tangent to pass around the outside of the building. He had several more questions to ask, and he thought he knew where to start asking them.

In front of the club, the Admiral was admitting new customers on a froth of salt-water argot. He greeted the Saint and Pat with his largest smile.

"Ahoy, mates! Enjoying the trip?"

"That is hardly an accurate description of our emotions at the moment," Simon said. "We're after a little information about an incident that occurred a few moments ago."

"I keep an accurate log, sir. Fire away."

"Did you see Mrs Verity come out of the club?"

"Aye, that I did, not more than fifteen minutes ago. Fact is, I'd just sounded four bells when she went ashore."

"Why didn't you stop her?" Simon asked sharply. "You knew we were waiting for her."

"Why, shiver my timbers, sir, I supposed she'd already seen you. It's hardly my place to stop the passengers."

"Hmm. I see."

"Did you miss her, sir?"

"We did, but somebody else didn't. They got her dead center."

The Admiral blinked, and seemed to examine the remark for some time. A puzzled frown formed on his round face.

"Blow me down, sir, but your message isn't clear."

"She's dead."

The Admiral's jaw dropped.

"No! Why, she was smiling pretty as pretty when she passed me, sir. Give me a dollar, too. If I'd known she was going to scuttle herself, I'd have made her heave to."

Simon gave him a long speculative stare.

"That's an interesting deduction, chum," he murmured. "When did I say that she killed herself?"

The man blinked.

"Why, what else, sir? Surely nobody would harm a fine lady like Mrs Verity. Tell me, sir, what did happen?"

"She was shot." The Saint pointed. "On the other side of the building, down towards the beach. Did you notice anyone wandering about outside?"

The Admiral thought, chin in gloved hand.

"No, sir. Only Mrs. Verity. She went off that way, and I supposed she was going to her car."

"But you didn't see her drive out."

"I didn't notice, sir. There were other passengers arriving and leaving at the same time, and I was pretty busy."

"But you noticed that no one else was wandering around."

"That's just my impression, sir. Of course, there's the back way out to the promenade deck too."

The Saint's cigarette glowed brightly again to a measured draw.

"I see. Well, thanks . . ."

He took Patricia back into the club and located the bar. They sat on high stools and ordered bourbon. Around them continued the formless undertones of the joint, the clink of chips, the rattle of dice, the whir of wheels, the discreet drone of croupiers, the tinkle of ice and glass, a low-key background broken from time to time by the crash of a cocktail mixer or a burst of high excited laughter. For the other guests of the Quarterdeck Club, life went on unaware of the visit of Death, and if the employees had heard anything of it, their faces were trained to inscrutability.

"Do you think I'm nuts?" Simon asked presently. "Do you think it was suicide?"

"It doesn't seem possible," Patricia said thoughtfully. "I keep thinking of the dress she was wearing."

Simon regarded her.

"That," he said, with some asperity, "would naturally be the key to the whole thing. Was she correctly dressed for a murder?"

"You idiot," said his lady, in exasperation. "That was a Mainbocher, an original! No pretty girl in her right mind would ruin an expensive dress like that by putting a bullet through it. I wouldn't have believed it if I hadn't seen it."

"But we didn't see it, darling," Simon reminded her gently. "Not with our own eyes."

He put down his glass and found the silent-moving Esteban at his elbow again.

"The sheriff is here, Mr Templar. You will please come this way?"

It could have been suspected, from his appearance, that Sheriff Newt Haskins had spent all his life in black alpaca. One must admit that his first article of apparel was probably three-cornered, but he wore the tropical-weight black as if he had never changed his clothes since he got any. He sat with his well-worn but carefully shined black shoes on Esteban's polished maple desk and welcomed Simon with a mere flick of his keen gray eyes, and Patricia Holm with the rather sad faint smile of a man long past the age when the sight of such beauty would inspire any kind of activity—

"Can't say I'm exactly pleased to see you again, Saint, said Haskins.

"How do, Miss Holm." The amenities fulfilled, he turned to Esteban. "Well?"

Esteban shrugged.

"I tell you on the phone. You have seen the body?

"Yep, I saw it. And I'm sure curious"—he looked at the Saint— "Mr Templar."

"So am I, Sheriff," Simon said easily, "but possibly not about the same thing."

"You admit you came here lookin' for the dead woman, son?"

"Now, daddy," the Saint remonstrated. "You know I'd be looking for a live woman."

"Hum," Newt Haskins said. "Reckon so. But the law's found plenty o' dead people around right after you been in the neighborhood. So when I see you here right next to a death that's just happened, I kinda naturally start wonderin' how much you know about it."

"I hope you're not suggesting that I murdered her?"

"You done the suggestin', son. That she was murdered, that is. Everything else points to the lady's takin' the hard way out of a jam."

"You don't really believe that, do you?"

"Will you excuse me?" Esteban said. "My guests . . ."

Sheriff Newt Haskins waved a negligent hand.

"Go ahead, Esteban. Call you if I want ya." To the Saint, after Esteban had gone, he said, "He ain't much help."

"Are you sure he couldn't be if he wanted to?"

"Wa'al—" Newt Haskins shrugged his thin shoulders noncommittally. "Let's get back to your last question. Nope, I don't think Mrs Verity shot herself. Seems how good-lookin' dames like her hate to disfigure themselves. It's generally gas, or sleepin' tablets. Still, you can't say it's never happened."

Pat said, "Think of that little evening bag. Lida wouldn't have carried a gun in that."

Haskins pulled his long upper lip.

"It ain't exactly probable, ma'am," he agreed. "But on the other hand, it ain't impossible, either."

"Permit me to call your attention," Simon said, "to one thing that is impossible."

"The white thread caught in the trigger guard?" Haskins anticipated blandly. "Yup, I saw that, son."

"You've got good eyes for your age, daddy. It's a white cotton thread. Lida Verity was wearing a green silk dress. She didn't have anything white on her that I noticed. On the other hand, if someone had wiped the gun with a handkerchief to get rid of fingerprints—"

Haskins nodded, his eyes on Patricia.

"You're wearin' a white jacket thing, Miss Holm."

"This bolero? You can't suggest that I—"

"Don't get excited darling," said the Saint. "The sheriff is just stirring things up, to see what comes to the top."

Haskins held the creases in his leathery face unchanged.

"Any reason, son, why you and Miss Holm shouldn't lay your cards on the table?"

"We always like to know who's staying in the game, daddy. Somebody around this place has a couple of bullets, back to back."

The lanky officer sighed. He picked up a glass paperweight, turned it in bony fingers, gazed into it pensively.

"I guess I'll have to put it to you straight, then."

"A novelty," the Saint said, "from the law. You're going to say that Mrs Verity was loaded down with moola."

"An' might have been shaken down for some of it. Your crystal ball's workin' almost as good as mine, son . . ."

The Saint looked out into space, poising puppets with a brown hand.

"If you'll just concentrate . . . concentrate . . . I may be able to do more— I have it!" He might have expected to get his palm crossed with a silver dollar. "My record leads you to suspect me of a slight tendency towards—"

"Bein' interested in other folks' money."

"Your confidence touches me."

"That ain't all that may be touchin' you soon, son."

"Now you've broken the spell," said the Saint reproachfully. "We are no longer in tune with the infinite. So—it seems as if we may have to leave you with your problem. Unless, of course, you propose to arrest me now and fight it out with my lawyers later."

"Not right away, son. We don't none of us want to be too hasty. But just don't get too far away, or the old police dog might have to start bayin' a trail."

"We'll be around," said the Saint, and ushered Patricia out.

As the murmurous inanities of the public rooms lapped around them again, she glanced up and found his eyes as blue and debonair as if no cares had ever crossed his path. The smile he gave her was as light as gosling down.

"I hardly think," he drawled, "that we have bothered Señor Esteban enough. Would'st you care to join me?"

"Try and lose me," said the girl.

They found Esteban keeping a weather eye on the play of his guests, and followed his politely lifted brows to the patio.

"The moonlight, she is so beautiful," Esteban said, with all the earnestness of a swing fan discussing Handel. "Did the sheriff let you go?"

"Like he let you—on probation," Simon answered cheerfully. "He just told us to stick around."

The man formed insolent question marks with the corners of his mouth.

"I did not think you would care to stay here after your friend kill herself."

"I heard you the first time, Esteban. I'm sure if your customers have to die on the premises, you'd much rather have a Monte Carlo suicide than a murder. It wouldn't scare half so many suckers away. But we happen to know that Mrs Verity wasn't the sort to be worried about being blackjacked out of a few hundreds, or even thousands, in this kind of clip joint."

There was no reaction in the dark lizard eyes.

"You hint at something, maybe?"

"I hint at nothing, maybe. I'm still asking questions. And one thing I've been wondering is, who did she come here with?"

Esteban repeated, without inflection, "Who she come here with?"

"She wouldn't have come here alone," said Patricia. "She didn't come with her husband, because he's still in Tokyo. So—who?"

"A little while ago, madame, you tell me she come here to meet you."

"Tonight, perhaps," Simon admitted patiently. "But this wasn't her first visit. The Admiral of the watch seemed to know her quite well. So who did she usually come with?"

Esteban shrugged.

"I do not inquire about these things."

The Saint's voice became rather gentle.

"Comrade, you don't seem to get the point. I'm a guy who might make a great deal of trouble for you. On the other hand, I might save you a lot."

Esteban took note of the steady blue eyes, the deceptive smile that played across the Saint's chiseled mouth. He forced a laugh.

"You frighten me terribly, Señor Templar."

"But you don't frighten me, Don Esteban. Because whatever Sheriff Haskins may think, I have the advantage of knowing that I had nothing to do with killing Mrs Verity. Which leaves me with a clear head to concentrate on finding out who did. So if you don't co-operate, I can only draw one conclusion."

There was silence, save for the rustle of palm fronds and the thud and hiss of the surf—and the muffled sounds of the Quarterdeck doing business as usual.

At last Esteban said craftily, "What will you do if I help you?"

"That depends on how much you know and how much you tell. I don't mind admitting that Miss Holm and I are slightly allergic to people who kill our friends. Also, it wouldn't bother me a bit if the sheriff closed your Parcheesi parlor. You ought to know how much you've really got to be scared of."

Esteban seemed to give him the same poker-faced assessment that he would have performed on a new customer who wanted to cash a check. And with the same impenetrable decisiveness he said, "Mrs Verity come here with Mr Maurice Kerr. He is what you call a—ah, playboy. A leetle old, perhaps, but most charming. Perhaps you should ask him your questions. If you wait, I tell you where he lives."

The address he came back with was only a half mile south, on a side street off Collins Avenue. There were still lights in the house when the Saint's car pulled up outside a mere matter of minutes later, and a man who could only have been Kerr himself, in white tie and a smoking jacket, opened the door to the Saint's casual knock. His somewhat florid face peered out under the porch light with strictly reasonable ineffusiveness.

He said, "What do you want? Who are you?" But his tone was still genial enough to be described as charming.

"A moment with you, Mr Maurice Kerr," the Saint answered. "You may call me the Saint—temporarily. Before we're through with you, you may think of some other names. And this is Miss Holm."

Kerr's eyebrows rose like levitating gray bushes.

"I don't pretend to understand you."

"May we come in? This is a matter of life and death."

Kerr hesitated, frowned, then swung the door wide.

"Do. In here, in the library."

The library was lighted for the benefit of those who liked to read comfortably at the least expense to their eyesight. The walls were lined with books, an artificial fire flickered in the fireplace, and chairs, lovingly fashioned to fit the human form, were spaced at tasty intervals.

"Sit down," Kerr invited graciously. "What is this all about?"

Simon remained standing. He put his lighter to a cigarette and said, "Our spies tell us that you went to the Quarterdeck Club with Lida Verity tonight."

He risked the exaggeration intentionally, and saw it pay off as Kerr paused to pick up the highball which he had obviously put down when they knocked.

Kerr sipped the drink, looked at the Saint. "Yes?"

"Why did you leave the club without her?"

"May I ask what that has to do with you?"

"Lida was a friend of mine," Patricia said. "She asked us to help her."

"Just before she died," the Saint said.

Kerr's soft manicured hand tightened around his glass. His dark eyes swung like pendulums between the Saint and his lady. He didn't catch his breath—quite, and the Saint wondered why.

"But that's ghastly!" Kerr's voice expressed repugnance, shock, and semi-disbelief. "She—she lost too much?"

"Meaning?" the Saint asked.

"She killed herself, of course."

"Lida," Simon explained, "was shot through the heart in the grounds of the Quarterdeck Club."

"You're trying to frighten me," Kerr said. "Lida couldn't have been—"

"Who said so? Who told you she committed suicide?"

"Why, why—it was just a—" Kerr broke off. "I don't know what you're talking about."

The Saint did not actually groan out loud, but the impulse was there.

"I can't understand why this is always happening to me," he complained. "I thought I spoke reasonably good English. The idea should be easy to grasp. All I told you was that Lida Verity was dead. You immediately assumed that she'd committed suicide. Statistics show that suicide is a helluva long way from being the most common way to die. Therefore the probability is that something or someone specifically gave you that idea. Either you knew that she might have had good reason to commit suicide, or somebody else has already talked to you. Whichever it is, I want to know about it."

Kerr licked his lips.

"I fail to see what right you have to come here and cross-examine me," he said, but his voice was not quite as positive as the words.

"Let's not make it a matter of rights," said the Saint easily. "Let's put it down to my fatal bigness of heart. I'm giving you the chance to talk to me before you talk to the sheriff. And you'll certainly have to talk to the sheriff if the gun that Lida was shot with happens to be registered in your name."

It was a shot in the dark, but it seemed to be worth taking, and Simon felt an inward leap of optimism as he saw that at least he had come close to his mark. Kerr's hand jumped involuntarily so that the ice in his highball gave a sharp tinkle against the glass, and his face turned a couple of shades lighter in color.

"What sort of gun was she shot with?"

"A thirty-two Colt automatic."

Kerr took it with his eyes. There was a long moment's silence while he seemed to search either for something to say or for the voice to say it.

"It could have been my gun." He formed the words at last. "I lent it to her this evening."

"Oh?"

"She asked me if I had a gun I could lend her."

"Why did you let her have it if you thought she was going to shoot herself?"

"I didn't think so at the time. She told me she was going to meet someone that she was scared of, but she didn't tell me who it was, and she wouldn't let me stay with her. She was rather overwrought and very mysterious about it. I couldn't get anything out of her. But I never thought about suicide—then."

Simon's blue eyes held him relentlessly through a cool drift of cigarette smoke.

"And that," said the Saint, "answers just half my question. So you weren't thinking about suicide. So somebody told you. Who?"

Muscles twitched sullenly over Kerr's brows and around the sides of his mouth.

"I fail to see—"

"Let me help you," said the Saint patiently. "Lida Verity didn't commit suicide. She was murdered. It wasn't even a planned job to look like suicide. This unanimous eagerness to brush it off as a suicide was just an afterthought, and not a very brilliant one either. The sheriff doesn't believe it and I don't believe it. But there's one difference between the sheriff and me. I may be a red herring to him, but I'm not a red herring to myself. I know this is one killing I didn't do. So I've got a perfectly clear head to concentrate on finding out who did it. If anyone seems to be stalling or holding out on me, the only conclusion I can come to is that they're either guilty themselves or covering up for a guilty pal. In either case, I'm not going to feel very friendly about it. And that brings us to another difference between the sheriff and me. When I don't feel friendly about people, I'm not tied down by a lot of red tape and pettifogging legal procedures. As you may have heard. If you are covering up for a pal he must mean a lot to you, if you're willing to let me hang you for him."

Kerr took another sip of his drink. It was a long sip, turning gradually into a gulp. When he set down his glass, the last pretense of dignified obstinacy had gone out of him.

"I did have a phone call from one of the men at the club," he admitted.

"Who was it?"

"I don't know exactly. He said, 'The Saint's on his way to see you. Mrs Verity just shot herself here. Esteban says to tell you not to talk.'"

"Why should this character expect you to do what Esteban told you?"

Kerr fidgeted.

"I work for Esteban, in a sort of way."

"As a shill?" Simon inquired.

The other flushed.

"I bring people to the club and I get a small commission on the business. It's perfectly legitimate."

"It would be in a legitimate business. So you shill for the joint. You latch on to visiting pigeons around town and steer them in to be plucked." Simon studied him critically. "Times must be getting tough, Maurice. I seem to remember that you used to do much better marrying them occasionally and getting a nice settlement before they divorced you."

"That's neither here nor there," Kerr said redly. "I've told you everything I know. I've never been mixed up with murder, and I don't want to be."

The Saint's cigarette rose to a last steady glow before he let it drop into an ashtray.

"Whether you want it or not, you are," he said. "But we'll take the best care we can of your tattered reputation."

He held out his hand to Patricia and helped her up, and they went out and left Maurice Kerr on his own doorstep, looking like a rather sullen and perturbed penguin, with an empty glass still clutched in his hand.

"And that," said Patricia, as the Saint nursed his car around a couple of quiet blocks and launched it into the southbound stream of Collins Avenue, "might be an object lesson to Dr Watson, but I left my dictionary at home."

The Saint dipped two fingers into the open pack in his breast pocket for another Pall Mall, and his smile tightened over the cigarette as he reached forward to press the dashboard lighter.

"Aside from the fact that you're much too beautiful to share an apartment safely with Mr Holmes," he said, "what seems to bother you now?"

"Why did you leave Kerr like that? He was working for Esteban. He told you so himself. He was telling you the story that Esteban told him to tell you—you even made him admit that. And Lida seems to have been shot with his gun. It's all too obvious."

Simon nodded, his eyes on the road.

"That's the whole trouble," he said. "It's all too obvious. But if she really was shot with Kerr's gun—which seems to be as certain as any guess can be—why did the guy leave it behind to lay a trail straight to his doorstep? He may be a poop, but can you believe that he's that half-witted? There's nothing in his record to show that he had softening of the brain before. A guy who can work his way through four rich wives in ten years may not be the most desirable character on earth, but he has to have something on the ball. Most of these over-bank-balanced broads have been around too."

Patricia fingered strands of golden hair out of her eyes.

"He doesn't sound like the dream-boy of all time," she said. "I can imagine how Dick Verity would like to hear that Lida and Maurice were a steady twosome." Her eyes turned to him with a sudden widening. "Simon, do you think—"

"That there was blackmail in it?" The Saint's face was dark and cold. "Yes, darling, I think we're getting closer. But I don't see the fine hand of Maurice in it. A man with his technique doesn't suddenly have to resort to anything so crude as murder. But you meet all kinds of types at the Quarterdeck Club—and I think we belong there."

The moon was the same, and the rustle of palm fronds along the tall dark margins of the road, but the night's invitation to romance had turned into something colder that enclosed them in a bubble of silence which only broke on the eventually uprising neons of the Quarterdeck Club and the hurricane voice of the Admiral.

"Avast there!" he bellowed, as the car came to a stop. "My orders are to repel boarders."

Simon opened the door and swung out a long leg.

"A noble duty, Horatio," he murmured, "but we belong here—remember? The sheriff wouldn't like it if he thought we'd jumped ship."

The Admiral stood firmly planted in his path. His face was no longer ruddily friendly, and his eyes were half shuttered.

"I'm sorry, sir. I don't know how you were able to disembark, but my orders—"

That was as far as he got, for at that moment the precise section of his anatomy known to box-fighting addicts as the button came into unexpected violent contact with an iron fist which happened at that moment, by some strange coincidence, to be traveling upwards at rocket speed. For one brief instant the Admiral enjoyed an entirely private fireworks display of astonishing brilliance, and thereupon lost interest in all mundane phenomena.

The Saint caught him as he crumpled and eased his descent to the gravel. There was no other movement in the parking lot, and the slow drumming of the distant surf blended with a faint filtration of music from inside the club to overlay the scene with the beguiling placidity of a nocturne. Simon took another grip and heaved the Admiral quite gently into the deeper shadows of some shrubbery, where he began to bind and gag him deftly with the Admiral's own handkerchief, necktie, and suspenders.

"You, too, can be a fine figure of a man, bursting with vibrant health and super strength," recited Patricia. "Send for our free booklet, *They Laughed When I Talked Back to the Truck Driver*."

"If Mary Livingstone ever loses her voice, you can get a job with Jack Benny," said the Saint. "Now while I finish this up, will you be a good girl and go in and engage Esteban in dulcet converse—with his back to the door. I'll be with you in two seconds."

To be drearily accurate, it was actually sixty-eight seconds later when the Saint entered the gaming room again. He found Esteban facing a vivacious Pat, and it was clear from his back that it would take something rather important to drag him away from her.

The Saint was able to provide this. It manifested itself as a pressure in the center of Esteban's spine.

"This isn't my pipe, Esteban," he breathed in the entrepreneur's ear. "Shall we adjourn to your private office, or would you like bits of your sacroiliac all over the joint?"

Esteban said nothing. He led the way, with the Saint walking apparently arm in arm with him, and Pat still chattering on the other side.

"—and I am going to write to my mother, Mr Esteban, and tell her what a romantic place you—"

"Now we can wash this up," the Saint said.

He closed the door behind them. Esteban stood very still.

"What do you expect this to get you, Mr Templar?"

"A peek in your safe," said the Saint softly.

"The safe is locked."

"This is still the Society for the Prevention of Cruelty to Sacroiliacs," Simon reminded him. "The safe can be unlocked."

"You wouldn't dare to shoot!"

"Not until I count to three, I wouldn't. It's a superstition with me. One . . . two . . ."

"Very well," Esteban said.

Little beads of sweat stood on his olive brow as he went to the wall safe and twirled the dial.

Simon handed his gun to Pat.

"Cover him. If he tries anything, shoot him in his posterity." He added to Esteban, "She will, too."

Esteban stood to one side as the Saint emptied the safe of bundles of currency, account books, and sheaves of business-like papers. He was pleased to find that Esteban was a neat and methodical man. It made the search so much quicker and easier. He had known before he started what kind of thing he was looking for, and there were not too many places to look for it. He was intent and efficient, implacable as an auditor, with none of the lazy flippancy that normally glossed his purposes.

Another voice spoke from the doorway behind him.

"So we're havin' a party. Put that gun down, Miss Holm. What would this all be about, son?"

"Come on in, daddy," Simon said. "I was just deciding who you were going to arrest."

Esteban's sudden laugh was sharp with relief. "I think, my friend, the sheriff knows that already. Mr Haskins, I shall be glad to help you with my evidence. They stick me up in my own club, bring me in here, and force me to open the safe. Fortunately you catch them red-handed."

"That's the hell of a way to talk about a guy who's just going to save your worthless neck," said the Saint.

Newt Haskins pushed his black hat onto the back of his head.

"This had shuah better make a good story, son," he observed. "But I'm listenin'."

"It wasn't too hard to work out," Simon said seriously. "Lida Verity was being blackmailed, of course. That's why she told us she was in trouble, instead of calling on you. Blackmail has been a side line in this joint for some time—and a good hunting ground this must be for it, too. This town is always full of wives vacationing from their husbands, and vice versa, and the climate is liable to make them careless. Somebody stooging around this joint could build up interesting dossiers on a lot of people. In fact, somebody did."

He took a small notebook from his pocket.

"Here it is. Names, dates, details. Items that could be plenty embarrassing if they were used in the wrong way. I'm going to rely on your professional discretion to see that it's destroyed when you're through with it."

"He's trying to pull the fast one!" Esteban burst out. "He never found such a book in my safe—"

"I didn't say I did," Simon responded calmly. "I found it on somebody else. But since you were the most obvious person to be behind the operation, I wanted to nose around in your safe to see if there was anything in it that would confirm or deny. I'm afraid the results let you out. There doesn't seem to be anything that even remotely connects you. On the other hand, I found this."

He handed Haskins a slip of paper, and the sheriff squinted at it with his shrewd gray eyes.

"Seems to be a check made out to Esteban," Haskins said. "It says on the voucher 'January installment on car-park concession.' What do you figger that means, son?"

"It means that if the Admiral was paying Esteban for the car-park concession, Esteban could hardly have been using him as part of a blackmail racket. Otherwise the pay-off would have gone the other way. And certainly it would if the Admiral had been doing Esteban's dirty work when he killed Lida Verity."

"The Admiral!" Patricia exclaimed.

Simon nodded.

"Of course. Our corny nautical character. He never missed anything that went on here—including Mrs Verity's rather foolish affair with a superior gigolo and shill named Maurice Kerr. Only she didn't sit still for blackmail. I guess she told the Admiral she was going to have me take care of him, and she may even have tried to scare him with the gun she'd borrowed. He got mad or lost his head and grabbed the gun and shot her." The Saint dipped in his pocket again. "Here are the white gloves he always wore. You'll notice that there's a tear in one of them. I'm betting that the thread you found in that trigger guard can be proved to have pulled out of that glove."

Haskins turned the gloves over in his bony hands, and brought his eyes slowly back to the Saint.

"Reckon you done another good job, Saint," he conceded peacefully. "We'll soon know . . . An' this heah Esteban, he ought to stake you with blue chips all night for lettin' him out."

"Letting me out!" Esteban echoed indignantly. The enormity of the injustice done to him grew visibly in his mind, finding voice in a crescendo of righteous resentment. "I tell the world I am let out! That Admiral, he makes agreement with me to pay me half of everything he makes from the concession. And he never tells me—the peeg!—he never tells me anything about this blackmail at all!"

# JEANNINE

# INTRODUCTION

Before you have ploughed very far into this episode, it is bound to become manifest even to the most obtuse of you that you are reading a sort of sequel to the one before. So I am going to take the edge off it and admit it before you start.

But this was not anything I planned. There was a lapse of many years between the writing of the stories. The fact that the same girl turned out to be involved was almost a surprise even to me. But the story called for a character that the Saint had matched wits with before, and while I suppose it wouldn't have been too difficult to invent one, it seemed a lot simpler to dig one out of the Saint's recorded past, where the previous encounter was fully documented.

This is one of the sordid advantages of writing such an unconscionable number of stories. You don't have to keep on creating new characters indefinitely. The time comes when you only have to reach back into the half-forgotten past, pick up some personality that once flashed across your screen, and figure what might have happened to him or her (and how tediously grammatical I must be getting) since the earlier encounter.

If any aspirant authors among you want to exploit this simplified system of story-concocting, I bequeath it to you gladly with my blessing. All you have to do is to put in fifteen or more creative years, and from then on everything is on the house.

*—Leslie Charteris (1951)*

"*Wine, that maketh glad the heart of man,*" quoted Simon Templar, holding his glass appreciatively to the light. "The Psalmist would have had things to talk about."

"It would have been a love match," said Lieutenant Wendel, like a load of gravel.

"Up to a point," Simon agreed. "But then he goes on: *And oil to make him a cheerful countenance.* Here we start asking questions. Is the prescription for internal or external application? Are we supposed to swallow the oil, or rub it on the face? . . . I am, of course, quoting the Revised Version. The King James has it *Oil to make his face to shine,* but the revisers must have had some reason for the change. Perhaps they wanted to restore some element of ambiguity in the original, dividing the plug equally between mayonnaise and Max Factor."

The detective stared at him woodenly.

"I've wondered a lot of things about you, Saint. But what a guy like you wants with that quiz stuff is beyond me."

Simon smiled.

"A man in my business can never know too much. A brigand has to be just a little ahead of the field—because the field isn't just a lot of horses trying to win a race with him, but a pack of hounds trying to run him down. Quite a lot of my phenomenal success," he said modestly, "is due to my memory for unconsidered trifles."

Wendel grunted.

They sat in a booth in Arnaud's, which Simon had chosen over the claims of such other temples of New Orleans cuisine as Antoine's or Galatoire's because the oak beams and subdued lights seemed to offer a more propitious atmosphere for a meal which he wanted to keep peaceful.

For Simon Templar was in some practical respects a devout lover of peace, and frequently tried very hard to vindicate the first person who had nicknamed him the Saint, in spite of all the legends of tumult and mayhem that had collected about that apparently incongruous sobriquet. Because a modern buccaneer in the perfect exploit would cause no commotion at all, even if this would make singularly dull reading; it is only when something goes wrong that the fireworks go off and the plot thickens with alarums and excursions, hues and cries, and all the uproar and excitement that provide such entertainment for the reader.

"Besides which," Simon continued at leisure, "I like civilized amenities with my crime—or wine. Both of them have a finer flavor for being enriched with background." He raised his glass again, passing it under his nostrils and admiring its ruby tint. "I take this wine, and to me it's much more than alcoholic grape juice. I think of the particular breed of grapes it was made from, and the dry sunny slopes where they ripened. I think of all the lore of wine-making. I think of the great names of wine, that you could chant like an anthem—Chambertin, Romanée-Conti, Richebourg, Vougeot . . . I think of great drinkers— *buveurs très illustres*, as Rabelais addresses us—of August the Strong of Saxony, who fathered three hundred and sixty-five bastards and drank himself to death on Imperial Tokay, doubtless from celebrating all their birthdays—or of the Duke of Clarence who was drowned in a butt of malmsey wine . . . Or, perhaps, I might think of pearls . . ."

Wendel suddenly stiffened into stillness.

"I was wondering how to bring pearls into it."

"Did you ever hear that wine would dissolve pearls?" asked the Saint. "If you collected these items, you'd have read about how the decadent Roman emperors, in their lush moments, would dissolve pearls in the banquet wine, just to prove that money was no object. And then there's a story about Cleopatra's big party to Caesar, when she offered him wine with her own hands, and dropped a priceless pearl in his goblet. Now if you knew—"

"What I want to know," Wendel said, "is how much you're interested in Lady Offchurch's pearls."

The Saint sighed.

"You're such a materialist," he complained. "I arrive in New Orleans an innocent and happy tourist, and I've hardly checked into a hotel when you burst in on me, flashing your badge and demanding to know what the hell I want in town. I do my best to convince you that I'm only here to soak up the atmosphere of your historic city and incidentally absorb some of your superb cooking with it. I even persuade you to have dinner with me and get this epicurean picnic off to a good start. We are just starting to relax and enjoy ourselves, with poetic excursions into history and legend, when suspicion rears its ugly head again and you practically accuse me of planning to swipe some wretched dowager's jewels."

"I'll go further than that," Wendel rasped, with the raw edges of uncertainty in his voice. "I'm wondering what made you choose this place to eat in."

"It seemed like a good idea."

"It wasn't because you expected Lady Offchurch to choose it too."

"Of course not."

"So it's just a coincidence that she happens to be here."

Simon raised unhurried eyebrows.

"Behind you, on your left," Wendel said, trap-mouthed.

The Saint drank some wine, put down his glass, and looked casually over his shoulder.

He did not need to have Lady Offchurch more specifically pointed out to him, for her picture had been in the papers not long before, and the story with it was the sort of thing that made him remember faces. The late Lord Offchurch had, until his recent demise, been the British Government's official "adviser" to a certain maharajah, and this maharajah had bestowed upon the departing widow, as a trivial token of his esteem, a necklace of matched pink pearls valued at a mere $100,000. Lady Offchurch had provided good copy on this to receptive reporters in Hollywood, where she had been suitably entertained by the English Colony on what was supposed to be her way "home." She had also expressed her concern over the fate of an Independent India, abandoned to the self-government of a mob of natives which even the most altruistic efforts of the British raj had been unable in two centuries of rule to lift above the level of a herd of cattle—except, of course, for such distinguished types as the dear maharajah.

She was a thin, bony, tight-lipped woman with a face like a well-bred horse, and Simon could construct the rest of her character without an interview. There was no need even to look at her for long, and as a matter of fact, he didn't.

What kept his head turned for quite a few seconds more than identification called for was Lady Offchurch's companion—a girl half her age, with golden hair and gray eyes and a face that must have launched a thousand clichés.

"Well?" Lieutenant Wendel's voice intruded harshly, and Simon turned back. "Beautiful," he said.

"Yeah," Wendel said. "For a hundred grand, they should be."

"Oh, the pearls," Simon said innocently. "I didn't notice. I was talking about her daughter."

Wendel squinted past him.

"She doesn't have a daughter. I guess that's just a friend. Maybe came with her from Hollywood—she's pretty enough." His eyes snapped back to Simon with a scowl. "Now quit tryin' to head me off again. When I read this Offchurch was in town, I naturally start wondering if any big operators have checked in about the same time. I'm a lazy guy, see, and it's a lot easier to stop something happening than try to catch a crook after he's done it . . . And the first register I go through, I see your name."

"Which proves I must be up to something, because if I wasn't planning a Saint job I'd obviously use an alias."

"It wouldn't be out of line with the kind of nerve I hear you've got."

"Thank you."

"So I'm tellin' you. I'm having Lady Offchurch watched twenty-four hours a day, and if my men ever see you hanging around they'll throw you in the can. And if those pearls ever show up missing, whether anybody saw you or not, you better be ready with all the answers."

Simon Templar smiled, and it was like the kindling of a light in his keen, dark, reckless face. His blue eyes danced with an audacity that only belonged with cloaks and swords.

"Now you're really making it sound interesting."

Wendel's face reddened.

"Yeah? Well, I'm warning you."

"You're tempting me. I wish policemen wouldn't keep doing that." Simon beckoned a waiter. "Coffee—and how about some crêpes Suzette?"

The detective bunched his napkin on the table.

"No, thank you. Let me have my check—separately."

"But I invited you."

"I can take care of myself, Saint. I hope you can too. Just don't forget, you had your warning."

"I won't forget," said the Saint softly.

He lighted a cigarette after the police officer had gone, and thoughtfully stirred sugar into his coffee.

He was not affronted by Wendel's ungraciousness—that sort of reaction was almost conventional, and he hadn't exactly exerted himself to avoid it. But it was a pity, he thought, that so many policemen in their most earnest efforts to avert trouble were prone to throw down challenges which no self-respecting picaroon could ignore. Because it happened to be perfectly true that the Saint had entered New Orleans without a single design upon Lady Offchurch or her pearls, and if it was inept of the law to draw his attention to them, it was even more tactless to combine the reminder with what virtually amounted to a dare.

Even so (the Saint assured himself), his fundamental strength and nobility of character might still have been able to resist the provocation if Destiny hadn't thrown in the girl with the golden hair . . .

He didn't look at her again until Lady Offchurch passed his table, on her way to the special conveniences of the restaurant, and then he turned again and met the gray eyes squarely and timelessly.

The girl looked back at him, and her face was as smooth and translucent as the maharajah's pearls, and as brilliantly expressionless.

Then she lowered her eyes to a book of matches in front of her, and wrote inside the cover with a pencil from her bag.

The Saint's gaze left her again, and didn't even return when a passing waiter placed a match booklet somewhat ostentatiously in front of him.

He opened the cover and read:

*27 Bienville Apts.*
*St Ann Street*
*at 10:30*

Lady Offchurch was returning to her table. Simon Templar paid his check, put the matches in his pocket, and strolled out to pass the time at the Absinthe House.

This was the way things happened to him, and he couldn't fight against fate.

So after a while he was strolling down St Ann Street, until he found the Bienville. He went through an archway into a cobble-stoned courtyard, and there even more than in the narrow streets of the Vieux Carré it was like dropping back into another century, where cloaks and swords had a place. Around him, like a stage setting, was a chiaroscuro of dim lights and magnolia and wrought-iron balconies that seemed to have been planned for romantic and slightly illicit assignations, and he could make no complaint about the appropriateness of his invitation.

He found an outside stairway that led up to a door beside which a lantern hung over the number 27, and she opened the door before he touched the knocker.

He couldn't help the trace of mockery in his bow as he said, "Good evening."

"Good evening," she said calmly, and walked back across the living room. The front door opened straight into it. There were glasses and bottles on a sideboard in the dining alcove across the room. As she went there she said, "What would you like to drink?"

"Brandy, I think, for this occasion," he said.

She brought it to him in a tulip glass, and he sniffed and sipped analytically.

"Robin, isn't it?" he remarked. "I remember—you had a natural taste." His eyes ran up and down her slender shape with the same candid analysis. "I guess there's only one thing you've changed. In Montreal, you were pretending to be Judith Northwade. What name are you using here?"

"Jeannine Roger. It happens to be my own."

"A good name, anyway. Does it also belong to the last man I saw you with?"

For an instant she was almost puzzled.

"Oh, him. My God, no."

"Then he isn't lurking in the next room, waiting to cut loose with a sawed-off shotgun."

"I haven't seen him for months, and I couldn't care less if it was years."

Simon tasted his brandy again, even more carefully.

"Then—are you relying on some subtle Oriental poison, straight from the pharmacopoeia of Sherlock Holmes?"

"No."

"This gets even more interesting. In Montreal—"

"In Montreal, I tried to pull a fast one on you."

"To be exact, you set me up to pull a job for you, and I was damn nearly the sucker who fell for it."

"Only instead of that you made a sucker out of me."

"And now all of a sudden I'm forgiven?"

She shrugged.

"How can I squawk? I started the double-cross, so how can I kick if it backfired? So now we're even."

Simon sat on the arm of a chair.

"This is almost fascinating," he said. "So you sent me that invitation so we could kiss again and be friends?"

A faint flush touched her cheekbones.

"When you saw me with Lady Offchurch, I knew I'd have to deal with you sooner or later. Why kid myself? So I thought I'd get it over with."

"You thought I was after the same boodle."

"If you weren't before, you would be now."

"Well, what's the proposition?"

"Why don't we really team up this time?"

Simon put a cigarette in his mouth and struck a match.

"It's a nice idea," he said. "However, you may be overlooking something. How do you see the split?"

"Fifty-fifty, of course."

"That's the trouble."

"That's how it has to be. You can't turn it down. If you can louse me up, I can do the same to you."

The Saint smiled.

"That isn't the point. You're forgetting something. Remember when you were the damsel in distress, and I was all set up to be the knight in shining armor? You had the right idea then."

"You hijacked me," she said sultrily, "like any other crook.

"But I didn't keep the spoils, like any other crook, he said imperturbably. "I found out how much Northwade had under paid that young inventor, and I sent him the difference—anonymously. Minus, of course, my ten-per-cent commission."

She was not quite incredulous.

"I've heard stories like that about you, but I didn't believe them."

"They happen to be true. Call me crazy, but that's my racket . . . Now in this case, it seems to me that most of the value of that necklace ought to go back to the poor bloody Indians who were sweated by the maharajah to pay for it while the British Government, as represented by Lord and Lady Offchurch, were benevolently sipping tea in the palace. So if you helped, I might let you have another ten per cent for yourself, but that's all. And you can't turn it down. Don't forget you can louse me up, I can do the same to you."

She sat down in another chair and looked upwards at him under lowered brows, and her gray eyes had the darkness of storm clouds.

"You certainly make it tough—stranger," she said, and her smile was thin.

"Can't I sell you a good cause, just once?"

"I think your cause stinks, but I have to buy it. You don't give me any choice. Damn you."

The Saint laughed. He crossed to her and held out his hand.

"Okay, Jeannine."

She put her cool fingers firmly in his, and he knew, he knew quite surely, that the handshake was as false as the way her eyes cleared. The certainty was so real that it was a fleeting chill inside him, and he knew that now they were committed to a duel in which no tricks could be ruled out. But his gaze matched hers for frankness and straightforwardness, and he said, "Well now, pardner, let's know what track you were on."

"I was on the Coast when she arrived. I was working out on a producer. He took me to a party that she was at. I knew I couldn't risk her in Hollywood, but I found out that New Orleans was the first place she wanted to stop over in on her way. So right away this was my home town. I took the next plane here and got hold of this apartment, and don't ask how. Then I wired her the address and said I was sorry I'd been called away suddenly but she must look me up and let me show her the town. Then I spent my time with a guidebook finding out what to show her."

"As an inspirational worker, it's an honor to know you," Simon murmured approvingly. "Of course, you can't belong to an old Creole family, because you can't introduce her around. So what are you—an artist?"

"A writer. I'm getting material for a novel."

"Which the producer was interested in."

"Exactly."

"And how did you figure the job?"

She was silent for a few moments, her eyes turned to a corner but not looking at anything.

"I've been able to get the necklace in my hands long enough to count the pearls while I was admiring them, and take a wax impression of one of them for size. I'm having an imitation made in New York. As soon as it gets here, I've only got to make the switch."

Simon showed his respect.

"You can write scripts for me, any time," he said.

"Now tell me your angle," she responded.

"Darling, I never had one."

She stared.

"What?"

"I didn't even know Lady Offchurch was here, until that guy I was having dinner with pointed her out and practically dared me to steal her necklace. He just happens to be the local Gestapo."

Gun metal glinted in the gray eyes.

"Why, you chiseling . . ." Then she laughed a little. "So you do it to me again. Why do you always have to be bad news, stranger? It could have been so much fun."

"It still could be," he said impudently, but she stood up and slipped past him towards the sideboard. He strolled lazily after her and said, "By the way, when do you expect to get that imitation?"

"Maybe the day after tomorrow."

And again he felt that tenuous cold touch of disbelief, but he kept it to himself, and held out his glass for a refill.

"On account of Wendel—that's the name of the gendarme—I'd better not risk being seen with you in public." He looked across the alcove into the kitchen, and said as the idea struck him, "Tell you what—if we can't eat out together, we can still dine. I'll bring some stuff in tomorrow and start fixing. I forgot to tell you before, but I'm as good as any chef in this town."

"You just got a job," she said.

He went back to his hotel in a haze of thought. The cool drafts of skepticism which had whispered around him began to reward him with the exhilaration of walking on the thin ice which they created. He was a fool for danger, and he always would be.

This was danger, as real as a triggered guillotine. It was true that she had no choice about accepting his terms—out loud. But it wasn't in keeping with her character as he knew it to accept them finally. And she had been just a little too evasive at one point and too acquiescent at another. It didn't balance. But when the catch would show was something he could only wait for.

He went to her apartment the next afternoon, laden with the brown paper bags of marketing. She made him a drink in the kitchen while he unpacked and went to work with quick and easy efficiency.

"What are we having?"

"Oxtail." He smiled at her lift of expression. "And don't despise it. It was always destined for something rarer than soup."

He was slicing onions and carrots.

"These—browned in butter. Then we make a bed of them in a casserole, with plenty of chopped parsley and other herbs. Then, the joints packed neatly in, like the crowd at a good fire. And then, enough red wine to cover it, and let it soak for hours."

"When does it cook?"

"When you come home tonight. I'll drop in for a nightcap, and we'll watch it get started. Then it cools overnight, and tomorrow we take off the grease and finish it . . . You'd better let me have a key, in case you're late."

"Why don't you just move in?" He grinned.

"I guess you forgot to invite me. But I'll manage." He trimmed fat from the joints, while the frying pan hissed gently with liquescent butter. "Did the mailman deliver?"

"It didn't come today."

And once again it was like a Geiger counter clicking to the intrusion of invisible radioactivity, the way his intuition tingled deep down at her reply.

He said, pleasantly, "I hope you really do know as much about me as you indicated once."

"How do you mean?"

"I shouldn't want you to be worrying about whether I'm going to double-cross you again. I made a deal with you, and when I make deals they stay made. It's only when someone else starts dealing from the bottom that all bets are off."

"Obviously," she said, with cool indifference.

She let him take a key to the apartment when he left, and that alone told him to save himself the trouble of returning for a search while she was out. If there was anything she didn't want him to find, it would certainly not be there.


He had taken routine precautions against being followed when he went to the Bienville, but as he turned into the lobby of the Hotel Monteleone the chunky figure of Lieutenant Wendel rose from an armchair to greet him.

"Had a nice afternoon, Saint?"

"Very nice, thank you," Simon replied calmly, and the detective's face began to darken.

"I thought I warned you to stay away from Lady Offchurch."

The Saint raised his eyebrows.

"I wasn't aware that I'd been annoying her. She is at the St Charles, which is very grand and metropolitan, but the French quarter is good enough for me. I can't help it if our hotels are only a few blocks apart. Perhaps you ought to have the city enlarged."

"I'm talking about this gal Jeannine Roger. What are you cooking up with her?"

"Oxtails," said the Saint truthfully.

Lieutenant Wendel did not seem to be the type to appreciate a simple and straightforward answer. In fact, for some reason it appeared to affect him in much the same way as having his necktie flipped up under his nose. His eyes became slightly congested, and he grasped the Saint's arm with a hand that could have crumbled walnuts.

"Listen, mister," he said, with crunching self-control. "Just because I spotted you right off didn't mean I figured my job was done. When I found Lady Offchurch was going around with this Roger twist, I had her investigated too. And it comes right back from Washington that she's got a record as long as your arm. So I put a man on to watch her. And whaddaya know, first thing I hear is that you're spending time over in her apartment."

Simon Templar's stomach felt as if a cold weight had been planted in it, but not the flicker of a muscle acknowledged the sensation. As though the grip on his arm hadn't been there at all, he conveyed a cigarette to his mouth and put a light to it.

"Thanks for the tip, chum," he said gravely. "I just happened to pick her up in a restaurant, and she looked like fun. It only shows you, a guy can't be too careful. Why, she might have stolen something from me!"

The detective made a noise something like a cement mixer choking on a rock.

"What you'd better do is get it through your head that you aren't getting away with anything in this town. This is one caper that's licked before it starts. You're washed up, Saint, so get smart while you've got time."

Simon nodded.

"I'll certainly tell the girl we can't go on seeing each other. A man in my position—"

"A man in your position," Wendel said, "ought to pack his bags and be out of town tomorrow while he has the chance."

"I'll think that over," Simon said seriously. "Are you free for dinner again tonight?—we might make it a farewell feast."

He was not surprised that the offer was discourteously rejected, and went on to the bar with plenty to occupy his mind.

One question was whether Wendel would be most likely to challenge Jeannine Roger openly, as he had challenged the Saint, or whether in the slightly different circumstances he would try to expose her to Lady Offchurch, or whether he would pull out of the warning business altogether and go out for blood.

The other question was whether Jeannine knew the score already, and what was brewing in her own elusive mind.

At any rate, he had nothing to lose now by going openly to the Bienville, and he deliberately did that, after a leisured savoring of oysters Rockefeller and *gumbo filé* at Antoine's, while the young officer who was following him worried over a bowl of onion soup and his expense account. The same shadow almost gave him a personal escort into the courtyard off St Ann Street, and Simon thought it only polite to turn back and wave to him as he went up the outside stairs to Number 27.

From the window, he watched the shadow confer with another shape that emerged from an obscure recess of the patio. Then after a while the shadow went away, but the established watcher sidled back into his nook and stayed.

Simon crossed the living room and peered down from a curtained window on the other side. The back overlooked an alley which was more black than dark, so that it was some time before the glimmering movement of a luminous wrist-watch dial betrayed the whereabouts of the sentinel who lurked patiently there among the garbage cans.

Simon put on the kitchen lights and inspected his casserole. He added a little more wine, lighted the oven, and put the dish in. He hummed a gentle tune to himself as he poured a drink in the dinette and settled down in the living room to wait.

The apartment was very effectively covered—so effectively that only a mouse could possibly have entered or left it unobserved. So effectively that it had all the uncomfortable earmarks of a trap . . .

The question now was—what was the trap set for, and how did it work?

It was a quarter to midnight when the girl came in. He heard her quick feet on the stone steps outside, but he only moved to refill his glass while her key was turning in the lock. She came in like a light spring breeze that brought subtler scents than magnolia with it.

"Hullo," she said, and it seemed to him that her voice was very gay. "I hope you haven't been waiting too long."

"Just long enough. There's a bolt on the inside of the door—you'd better use it," he said, without looking up. He heard the bolt slam, after a pause of stillness, and turned with an extra glass in his other hand. "Here's your nightcap, baby. You may need it."

He thought of a foolish phrase as he looked at her—"with the wind and the rain in your hair." Of course there was no rain, and her hair was only just enough out of trim to be interesting, but she had that kind of young, excited look, with her cheeks faintly freshened by the night and her gray eyes bright and arrested. The incongruity of it hurt him, and he said brusquely, "We don't have any time to waste, so don't let's waste it."

"What's happened?"

"The joint is pinched," he said bluntly. "The Gestapo didn't stop at me—they checked on you too, since you were Lady Offchurch's mysterious pal, and they know all about you. Wendel told me. They've got both sides of the building covered. Look out the windows if you don't believe me."

"I believe you," she said slowly. "But—why?"

"Because Wendel means to catch somebody with the goods on them."

It was only an involuntary and static reaction, the whitening of her knuckles on the hand that held her purse, but it was all he needed. He said, "You had the imitation necklace today. You pulled the switch tonight. You made a deal, but you kept your fingers crossed."

"No," she said.

Now there were heavy feet stumping methodically up the stairway outside.

"You were followed every inch of the way back. They know you haven't ditched the stuff. They know it has to be here, and they know you can't get it out. What are you going to do—throw it out of a window? There's a man watching on both sides. Hide it? They may have to tear the joint to shreds, but they'll find it. They've got you cold."

"No," she said, and her face was haggard with guilt.

A fist pounded on the door.

"All right, darling," said the Saint. "You had your chance. Give me your bag."

"No."

The fist pounded again.

"You fool," he said savagely, in a voice that reached no further than her ears. "What do you think that skin we love to touch would be like after ten years in the pen?"

He took the purse from her hand and said, "Open the door." Then he went into the kitchen.

Lieutenant Wendel made his entrance with the ponderous elaboration of a man who knew that he had the last ounce of authority behind him and nothing on earth to hurry for. Certainty smoothed down the buzz-saw edges of his voice and invested him with the steam-roller impermeability of an entire government bureau on two feet.

"I'm from the Police Department, Miss Roger. I'm sure Mr Templar has told you about me. I've come to trouble you for Lady Offchurch's pearl necklace."

"I don't know what you're talking about," she said.

"Of course not." His confidence was almost paternal. "However, it hasn't gone out by the front since you came in, and I don't think it's gone out by the back. We'll just make sure."

He crossed the room heavily, opened a window, and whistled.

This was the moment that Simon Templar chose to come back.

"Why, hullo, Lieutenant," he murmured genially. "What are you doing—rehearsing *Romeo and Juliet* for the Police Follies?"

Wendel waved to the night and turned back from the window.

"Ah, there you are, Mr Templar. I knew you were here, of course." His eyes fastened on the purse that swung negligently in Simon's hand. "This may save us a lot of trouble—excuse me."

He grabbed the bag away, sprung the catch, and spilled the contents clattering on the dining table.

After a few seconds the Saint said, "Would anyone mind telling me what this is all about?"

"All right," Wendel said grimly. "Where is it?"

"Where is what?"

"You know what I'm talking about. The necklace."

"The last time I saw it," Jeannine Roger said, "it was on Lady Offchurch's neck."

The detective set his jaw.

"I work regular hours, Miss Roger, and I don't want to be kept up all night. I may as well tell you that I talked to Lady Offchurch before you met her this evening. I arranged for her to give one of my men a signal if you had been suspiciously anxious to handle the necklace at any time while you were together. She gave that signal when she said good night to you. That gives me grounds to believe that while you were handling the necklace you exchanged it for a substitute. I think the original is in this apartment now, and if it is, we'll find it. Now if one of you hands it over and saves me a lot of trouble, I mightn't feel quite so tough as if I had to work for it."

"Meaning," said the Saint, "that we mightn't have to spend quite so much of our youth on the rock pile?"

"Maybe."

The Saint took his time over lighting a cigarette.

"All my life," he said, "I've been allergic to hard labor. And it's especially bad"—he glanced at the girl—"for what the radio calls those soft, white, romantic hands. In fact, I can't think of any pearls that would be worth it—particularly when you don't even get to keep the pearls . . . So—I'm afraid there ain't going to be no poils."

"You're nuts!" Wendel exploded. "Don't you know when you're licked?"

"Not till you show me," said the Saint peaceably. "Let's examine the facts. Miss Roger handled the necklace. Tomorrow a jeweler may say that the string that Lady Offchurch still has is a phony. Well, Lady Offchurch can't possibly swear that nobody else ever touched that rope of oyster fruit. Well, the substitution might have been made anywhere, anytime, by anyone—even by a chiseling maharajah. What's the only proof you could use against Jeannine? Nothing short of finding a string of genuine pink pearls in her possession. And that's something you can never do."

"No?" Wendel barked. "Well, if I have to put this whole building through a sieve, and the two of you with it—"

"You'll never find a pearl," Simon stated.

He made the statement with such relaxed confidence that a clammy hand began to caress the detective's spine, neutralizing logic with its weird massage, and poking skeletal fingers into hypersensitive nerves.

"No?" Wendel repeated, but his voice had a frightful uncertainty.

Simon picked up a bottle and modestly replenished his glass.

"The trouble with you," he said, "is that you never learned to listen. Last night at dinner, if you remember, we discoursed on various subjects, all of which I'm sure you had heard before, and yet all you could think of was that I was full of a lot of highfalutin folderol, while I was trying to tell you that in our business a man couldn't afford to not know anything. And when I told you this afternoon that Jeannine and I were cooking up oxtails, you only thought I was trying to be funny, instead of remembering among other things that oxtails are cooked in wine."

The detective lifted his head, and his nostrils dilated with sudden apperception.

"So when you came in here," said the Saint, "you'd have remembered those other silly quotes I mentioned—about Cleopatra dissolving pearls in wine for Caesar—"

"Simon—no!" The girl's voice was almost a scream.

"I'm afraid, yes," said the Saint sadly. "What Cleopatra could do, I could do better—for a face that shouldn't be used for launching ships. "

Lieutenant Wendel moved at last, rather like a wounded carabao struggling from its wallow, and the sound that came from his throat was not unlike the cry that might have been wrung from the vocal cords of the same stricken animal.

He plunged into the kitchen and jerked open the oven door. After burning his fingers twice, he took pot holders to pull out the dish and spill its contents into the stoppered sink.

Simon watched him, with more exquisite pain, while he ran cold water and pawed frantically through the debris. After all, it would have been a dish fit for a queen, but all Wendel came up with was a loop of thread, about two feet long.

"How careless of the butcher," said the Saint, "to leave that in."

Lieutenant Wendel did not take the apartment apart. He would have liked to, but not for investigative reasons. For a routine search he had no heart at all. The whole picture was too completely historically founded and cohesive to give him any naïve optimism about his prospects of upsetting it.

"I hate to suggest such a thing to a respectable officer," said the Saint insinuatingly, "but maybe you shouldn't even let Lady Offchurch think that her necklace was switched. With a little tact, you might be able to convince her that you scared the criminals away and she won't be bothered any more. It may be years before she finds out, and then no one could prove that it happened here. It isn't as if you were letting us get away with anything."

"What you're getting away with should go down in history," Wendel said with burning intensity. "But I swear to God that if either of you is still in town tomorrow morning, I'm going to frame you for murder."

The door slammed behind him, and Simon smiled at the girl with rather regretful philosophy.

"Well," he said, "it was one way of giving those pearls back to the Indians. One day you'll learn to stop being so smart, Jeannine. Can I offer you a ride out of town?"

"Whichever way you're going," she said with incandescent fascination, "I hope I'll always be heading the other way."

It was too bad, Simon Templar reflected. Too bad that she had to be so beautiful and so treacherous. And too bad, among other things, that his crusade for the cultivation of more general knowledge seemed to make so few converts. If only there were not so much ignorance and superstition in the world, both Wendel and Jeannine Roger would have known, as he did, that the story of pearls being dissolved in wine was strictly a fable, without a grain of scientific truth . . . Nevertheless, the pearls in his pocket were very pleasant to caress as he nursed his car over the Huey Long Bridge and turned west, towards Houston.

# LUCIA

Simon Templar might easily have passed the "hotel." For reasons known only to itself, it stood outside the town, perched aloofly on a stony slope that rose above the rudimentary road. But as he went by he saw the girl on the veranda, and admitted to himself that he was thirsty. He climbed the rough path and unslung his pack in the shade.

"If I were a millionaire," he said, smiling at her, "I might offer you half my fortune for a drink."

She had a rather pale, thoughtful face, delicately featured, almost too classically oval to have a character of its own, like one of those conventionalized portraits of the Italian seventeenth-century school. The sunlight struck blue-black glints from her hair as she wiped the table.

"What would you like?" she asked.

"What would you recommend?"

"We have some beer."

"It was revealed to me in a vision," said the Saint.

He leaned back and lighted a cigarette while he waited for her to bring it, gazing out across the sun-baked vista of granite and sandstone, ramshackle houses slumbering in the midday heat with their boards cracked and scarred and the tinted plaster peeling from their walls like the skin of a Florida sun-worshiper; sage, mesquite, violet-shadowed mesas, sparse trees powdered with dust, and the blue hint of mountains in the far distance. The same dust was thick on his bare brown arms, and the narrowing of his gaze against the glare creased dry wrinkles into the corners of his eyes. His clothes made no attempt to hide the fact that they had seen many weeks of vagabondage, and yet in some indefinable way they still rode his lean, wide-shouldered frame with a swashbuckling elegance that matched the gay lines of his face, for Simon made an adventure of all journeys.

"There you are." The girl set a beaker of liquid gold before him, and watched while he drank. "Where are you from?" she asked.

Simon gestured toward the south.

"Cuautia," he said. "Before that, Panama. A long time before that, Paris. And once upon a time I was in a place called Pfaffenhausen."

"Looking for work?"

He shook his head.

"I'm an outlaw," he said, with that smiling veracity which sometimes was so immeasurably more deceptive than any untruth. "I steal from the rich and wicked, and give to the poor and virtuous. I'm quite poor and virtuous myself," he remarked parenthetically. "There has been some talk of making me a Saint."

She laughed quietly, and left him as a man's voice called her testily from indoors. Simon took another draught of the cool beer and stretched out his long legs contentedly.

He was in the state of happy vagueness in which an artist may find himself when confronted with a virgin canvas: for a modern privateer who modestly rated himself a supreme technician in the art of living, the situation was almost identical. Anything might take shape—dragons, murder, green hippopotami, bank robbers, damsels in distress, blue moons, or an absconding company promoter. Straight ahead of him as he sat there, if he cared to take that direction, he might come at last to Denver. He could turn east and follow the coast round to New Orleans and Miami. Or, in the fullness of time, he could wake up to the excitements of Chicago, New York, or San Francisco. Or he could stay right where he was with his beer in this forgotten border town of Saddlebag, and as a matter of fact, he was just preparing to discard the last alternative when he was privileged to witness the arrival of Mr Amadeo Urselli.

Urselli came on the bus, which went rattling past in a cloud of dust while Simon sat on over his refreshment. The same cloud of dust, halting to poise itself aridly over the roofs of the houses below, indicated that the bus had stopped somewhere in the village, and a few minutes later Mr Urselli himself came into view, toiling up the road toward the hotel with three or four inquisitive urchins following in his wake and apparently offering comment and counsel. Simon immediately admitted that there was some excuse for them—in his own early youth he would probably have been their ringleader. For Mr Urselli—whose name the Saint had yet to learn—was indeed a remarkable and resplendent sight in that setting.

His gray check suit fitted him so tightly, particularly around the waist, that he would probably have found it necessary to take his coat off in order to tie his shoelaces. His pearly hued felt hat looked as if it had come straight from a shop window; his tie had the gorgeous flamboyance of a tropical sunset; the pigskin suitcase which he carried in his right hand shone with a costly luster. The gesticulations which he made with his left hand in the attempt to rid himself of his juvenile escort flashed iridescent gleams of jewelry on his fingers.

He crested the slope leading up to the veranda and dumped his bag with a sigh. The escort gathered round him in an admiring circle while he mopped his brow with a large silk handkerchief.

"Say, will you sons of bandmasters scram?" he rasped—not, Simon gathered, for anything like the first time.

"Give them their fun, brother," murmured the Saint. "They don't get many chances to see the world."

The newcomer turned toward him, and his sallow face slowly lightened to the gregarious gleam with which the exile in foreign climes recognizes another who speaks the same language.

"This is a helluva place," he said emotionally.

It may be acknowledged at once that Simon Templar did not like the face, which was thin and pointed like a weasel's, with flat brown eyes that shifted restlessly in their orbits, but Simon nodded amiably, and the traveler sank into a chair beside him.

"My name's Urselli," he volunteered. "I came out here to look at the neck of the woods where I was born. Ain't there anyone around in this jernt?"

Simon glanced casually round, and was answered by the reappearance of the girl in the doorway. Mr Urselli stood up.

"Where's Mr Intuccio?"

The girl turned and called, "Papa!" into the dark room behind her, and presently the innkeeper clumped out—a big black-bearded man in grimy shirt sleeves. Urselli held out a white manicured hand.

"You may not remember me, Salvatore," he said in halting Italian. "I am Amadeo."

The innkeeper's sunken eyes surveyed him impassively, and held the hand with a callused paw.

"I remember. You will drink something?"

"Thank you," said Mr Urselli.

He flopped back in his chair as the other left them after dispersing the enraptured audience with a hoarse "Git outside!" and a menacing lift of his arm which sent the urchins scampering. The girl followed the old man in.

"What I call a royal welcome," observed Mr Urselli, when they were alone. He winked, craning his neck, "But the girl ain't so bad, at that. It mightn't be so dull here. If she calls him Papa she must be some kinda cousin of mine—Intuccio is. Since I'm here I guess I better like it."

"Are you on a pleasure trip?" asked the Saint, turning his glass reflectively.

"You might call it that. Yes, I thought I might come back and take a rest in the old home town. I haven't seen it for twenty years, and I guess it ain't changed at all." Urselli studied his expensive-looking hands. "I'm in the joolry trade. Look at that piece of ice."

He slipped a ring from one of his fingers and passed it over. "Very nice," Simon remarked casually, examining it.

"I'll say it's nice," affirmed Mr Urselli. "There ain't a flaw in it, and it was a cheap buy at five grand. You gotta know your business with diamonds."

Simon handed the ring back, and Mr Urselli replaced it on his finger. There was a tinge of mockery in the depths of the Saint's sea-blue eyes, unperceived by Mr Urselli. It seemed a fantastic place for any practitioner of that ancient spiel to come with his diamonds, and Simon Templar's curiosity never slept. He debated within himself, lazily interested, whether he should offer some ingenuous lead which would help the sales talk into its next phase, or whether he should leave the whole onus of its development on Mr Urselli's doubtless capable shoulders, but at that moment the black-bearded innkeeper returned with a bottle and two glasses.

He poured out two drinks in silence, and sat down. Every movement he made was heavy and stolid, as his greeting had been. He raised his glass with a perfunctory mutter, and drank. His daughter came and leaned in the frame of the door. "What brings you home, Amadeo?"

The voice was dull and apathetic, and Urselli seemed to make an effort to retain his full expansiveness of geniality.

"I felt I needed a holiday. After all, there's no place like home. And what's home without a woman?" Urselli jerked his thumb slyly towards the girl. "I didn't know you had a family."

"There is only Lucia. Her mother died when she was born."

"Pretty girl," said Urselli approvingly.

Intuccio drank again, moving only his arm. "This is a long way from Chicago," he said. "Where do you go now?"

"I thought I'd stay here for a while," said Urselli comfortably. "It looks restful. Can you find room for me?" He looked at the girl as he spoke.

"There is always room," she said.

Intuccio raised his deep-set eyes to her face, and lowered them again.

"What we have is yours," he said formally.

"Then that's settled," said Urselli jovially. "It'll be great to sit around and do nothing, and talk over old times." He unbuttoned his coat and fanned himself energetically. "Jeez, is it always as hot as this? I'll have to copy your costume if I'm making myself at home."

Intuccio shrugged, watching him dispassionately, and Urselli took off his tight-waisted coat and hung it over the back of his chair. Something clunked solidly against the wood as he did so, and the Saint's eyes turned absently towards the sound. One pocket was gaping under an unusual weight, and Simon looked into it and saw the gleaming metal of a gun butt.

Mr Urselli remembered him as his glass was refilled.

"Are you stayin' here too?" he asked.

"I think I will," said the Saint.

There was something bizarre about the home-coming of Amadeo Urselli. During the afternoon, with no more effort than was called for by attentive listening, Simon learned that both men were the scions of local families, immigrants to the United States at the beginning of the century. Not long afterwards their paths had separated. The Ursellis had taken to the big cities, merging themselves flexibly into the pace and turmoil of a rising civilization; the Intuccios, unyielding peasants for as many generations as the oldest of them could remember, had naturally sent down their roots into the soil, preferring to find their livelihood in the surroundings to which they had been born. The divergence was summed up almost grotesquely in the two men; if the Saint's hypersensitive intuition had not been startled into alertness by the other oddities that had struck him about Urselli, he might have found himself staying on for nothing but the amusement of the human comedy which they were acting.

It was not until dinner was half finished that Intuccio's rock-like taciturnity unbent at all. They ate in the smoky oil-lighted kitchen, the four of them together round a stained pine table, in the incense of garlic and charring wood.

Urselli prattled on in a kind of strained desperation, as if the mighty silence that welled in on them whenever he stopped was more than his nerves could stand. The older man answered only with grunts and monosyllables; the girl Lucia spoke very little, whether from shyness or habit Simon could not decide, and the Saint himself felt that he was a spectator rather than a player—at least for those early scenes. It was as a spectator that Simon watched Intuccio wind the last reel of spaghetti dexterously round his fork, and heard him interrupt Urselli's recital of the delights of Broadway to ask, "You have done well in your business, Amadeo?"

They were speaking in Italian, the language on which Intuccio stubbornly insisted, and which Simon spoke as easily as he.

"Well enough," Urselli answered. "It was easy for me. I must have been born for it. Buy and sell, the same as any other business—there is only the one secret—and know what you can sell before you buy."

He slapped his waist. "Here in my belt I have twenty thousand good American dollars. And you, Salvatore?"

The other drank from his wineglass and wiped his matted black beard.

"I also have no complaints. Five years ago I have much land and everyone is paying the highest prices, but I have the intelligence to see that it will not always be like that. *Ebbene*, I sell the farm, and presently when the prices have gone down I buy this place. It is something for me to do, and I like to stay here. I have perhaps thirty thousand dollars, perhaps a little more. We are thrifty people, and we do not have to spend money on fine clothes."

The meal was completed with some grudging attempts at graciousness on the part of Intuccio at which Urselli gave Simon a covert grimace of relief and turned his attentions more openly to Lucia. When it was over the girl picked up a pail and went out to draw water from the well to wash the dishes, and Urselli followed her out with an offer of help. The old man's shadowed eyes gazed after them fixedly.

"You have an attractive daughter," Simon observed, with a touch of humorous significance.

Intuccio's face turned slowly back to him, and the Saint was surprised by its darkness. There was a hunted flicker of fear and suspicion at the back of the innkeeper's eyes, the same look that Simon might have expected if he had burst into the solitude of a hermit.

"Perhaps I should not have told that Amadeo that I had so much money," he said, with an equal significance in the harshness of his reply.

"Why worry," asked the Saint gently, "when it was not true?"

For the first time the semblance of a smile touched the innkeeper's grim mouth.

"Amadeo does not know that. But I had to say it. I have not three hundred dollars, signor, but I have pride. Why should I let Amadeo boast against me?"

He raised himself from the table and stumped out of the kitchen. Simon went out and smoked a cigarette in the fresh air on the veranda. Later he found the old man serving the scanty orders of his evening customers in the big gloomy outer room, moving about his work in the same heavy unsmiling manner.

Simon drifted into a place at the long communal table which occupied the center of the room. The four customers were at the other end of it, grouped over a game of poker. Simon ordered himself a drink and listened abstractedly to the scuff of cards and the expressionless voices of the players. Intuccio called for the girl to come out and take over the serving; she came, composed and silent, and the old man joined Simon at the table. He sat there with his brawny arms spread forward and his glass held clumsily between his huge hands, without speaking, and the Saint wondered what thoughts were passing through the dark caverns of that heavy impenetrable mind. There was a sense of menace about that somber immobility, a dreadful inhumanity of aloofness, that sent an eerie ripple of half-understanding up Simon Templar's spine. Suddenly he knew why so few men came to the inn.

Amadeo Urselli entered jauntily, and pulled out a chair beside them.

"This is a dandy spot," he said fluently. "You know, when I first dropped in here I nearly got straight back on the bus and went out again. Seemed like a guy would go nuts sittin' around here with nothing to look at but a lot of mesquite. Well, now I guess movies and cabarets don't mean so much compared with real home life. I could settle down in a town like this. Say, Salvatore, what's the hunting around here?"

Intuccio lifted his eyes under their dense black brows. "Hunting?"

"Yeah. You got a swell rifle hangin' on the wall outside. I took it down to have a look at it, and it was all cleaned and erled. Or is it in case the bandits come this way?"

The innkeeper sat motionless, as if he had not heard, staring at the glass cupped between his hands. The voices of the poker players muttered a pizzicato background to his stillness: "Two to come in."

"And four."

"Make it four more."

"I'll raise that ten." The chips slithered and spilled across the board and hands were turned face downwards and sent spinning over the table to join the discard.

Intuccio, detached as a statue, turned his head as the game fell into the lull of a fresh deal.

"Mr Jupp, have you seen any bandits here?"

One of the players looked up.

"Since Roosevelt became President there have been no more bad men," he said solemnly.

Another of the men leaned round in his chair.

"Yo're new to these parts, I guess," he drawled. "You oughta know that them stories belong back in the days of your grandfather. This is a peaceful country now."

"By hookey," erupted the third man, who wore a sheriff's badge, "it had better be! You won't see any bad men here while I'm responsible."

Intuccio nodded. He turned to Urselli again, his eyes dispassionately intent, gleaming motionlessly in their hollow sockets like deep pools of stagnant water in a cave.

"You see, Amadeo?" he said. "At one time there were bad men and bandits here. Even now, sometimes, little things have happened. There are some who believe that the bad men are not altogether stamped out. But the times have changed." The craglike head, inscrutable as a mask of rugged wax, held itself squarely in the field of Urselli's shifting eyes. "Today you will find more robbers in the big cities of America than you will find here."

Simon could still hear every intonation of the slow rough-hewn voice when he went up to bed, and he ran over it again and again in his mind while he smoked the last cigarette of the day. In spite of the recollection he lost no sleep. A glimpse of a pretty girl leads to an inn, and to the same inn comes an Americanized Italian who is not quite everything that an Americanized Italian should be, and all at once there is a mystery; that is how these things happen, but the Saint was still waiting for his own cue. Then he woke up late the next morning, and suddenly it dawned upon him, with dazzling simplicity, that the most elementary and obvious solution would be to lure Amadeo personally into a secluded spot, scratch him tactfully, and see what his subcutaneous ego looked like to the naked eye.

He went down to breakfast in the same exuberant spirits to which any promise of direct action always raised him. Simon Templar's conception of a tactful approach was one which nobody else had ever been able to comprehend.

The girl asked him what he proposed to do that day.

"You will remember that I am an outlaw," said the Saint. "I am going to make a raid."

Through the kitchen window he caught sight of Mr Urselli, an earlier riser, sitting on the edge of the well at the back and filing his nails meditatively. He went out as soon as he had finished his coffee and nailed his fellow guest with every circumstance of affability.

"What cheer, Amadeo," he said.

Mr Urselli jerked round sharply, identified him, and relaxed. "Morn'n'," he said.

His manner was preoccupied, but it took more than that to deter Simon once he had reached a decision. The Saint traveled round and sank cheerfully onto a reach of parapet at his victim's side. In a similar fashion one of Nero's lions might have circumnavigated a plump martyr.

"Amadeo," said the Saint, "will you tell me a secret? Why do you carry a gun?"

Urselli stopped filing abruptly. For a couple of seconds he did not move, and then his eyes slewed round, and they were narrowed to brown slits.

"Whaddaya mean?"

"I know you carry a gun," said the Saint quietly.

Urselli's gaze shifted first. He looked down at his hands.

"You gotta be able to take care of yourself in my business," he explained, and if his voice was a shade louder than was necessary, many ears less delicately tuned than the Saint's might not have noticed it. "Why, it was nothing to travel about the country with fifty grand worth of ice on me. Suppose I hadn't packed a roscoe—hell, I'd of been heisted once a week!"

Simon nodded.

"But can you shoot with it?"

"I'm telling you I can shoot with it."

"That tin can up on the slope, for instance," Simon persisted innocently. "Do you think you could hit that?"

Urselli squinted upward.

"Sure."

"I'd like to see you do it," said the Saint airily.

The barb in his words was subtly smooth, but the other shot a quick glance sideways, his underlip jutting.

"Who says I'm a liar?" he questioned aggressively.

"Nobody I heard." The Saint was as suave as velvet. Out of the corner of his eye he saw Intuccio standing in the door of the kitchen, watching them in silence, but he had no aversion to an audience. He put a hand in his pocket. "All the same, I've got a double saw that wonders whether you can."

"And I've got a century that says I'm telling you I can."

"Call it a bet."

Urselli drew out his automatic fumblingly, as though he had started to regret his rashness, and then he caught the Saint's blue gaze resting on him in gentle mockery, and snapped back the jacket with vicious resolution. He aimed carefully, and his first shot kicked up a spurt of dust six inches to the left of the target. His second was three inches to the right. Urselli cursed under his breath, and the third shot fell short. Intuccio drew nearer, and stood behind them with folded arms.

At that range it was reasonably good shooting, but the Saint smiled, and covered the weapon with a cool hand before Urselli could fire again.

"I mean like this," he said.

He took the gun and fired without appearing to aim, but the tin leaped like a grasshopper; the third shot caught it in the air and spun it against the side of the hill. Urselli stared at him while the echoes rattled and died, and the can rolled tinkling down toward them till an outcrop of stone checked it.

"By the way," Simon said, recalling the other's peculiarly localized pronunciation of *jernt* and *erled*, "I thought you came from Chicago."

"Well?"

"You wouldn't have noticed it," Simon said kindly, "but your accent betrays you. You spent some time in the East, didn't you—on your jewelry business?" He was casually slipping the empty magazine out of the automatic while he talked, and then he suddenly let out an exclamation of dismay and peered anxiously down into the well. A faint splash came up from far below. "It slipped right through my fingers," he said, looking at Urselli blankly.

The other sprang up, swiftly tearing the now useless weapon out of Simon's hands.

"You did that on poipose!" he grated.

The Saint seemed to ponder the accusation.

"I might have," he conceded. "You handle that rod just a little too well, and you wouldn't want to be tempted to commit murder, would you? Now suppose you happened to run into the guy who told you that that white sapphire in your ring was a real diamond, and charged you five grand for it?"

Urselli's eyes dilated incredulously towards the scintillation on his left hand.

"Why, the son of a—" He pulled himself together. "What's the idea?" he snarled. "Are you tryin' to put me on the spot?"

Simon shook his head.

"No," he answered. "But maybe you left Chicago because you were already on it."

Intuccio came up between them.

"You like shooting?" he said in his deep harsh voice.

"I'm always ready for a bit of fun," said the Saint lightly. "Maybe Amadeo would like some hunting, too. D'you think we could find anything worth shooting around here?"

The innkeeper nodded hesitantly.

"Yesterday morning I saw the tracks of a mountain lion. If you like, we will go out and see what we can find."

An hour later Intuccio halted his horse in an arroyo two miles away. He laid a rifle across Urselli's saddlebow. "You will wait here," he said. "We go round the other side of the mountain and drive him down."

Urselli's glance flickered at him.

"How long do I wait?"

The innkeeper shrugged.

"Perhaps three hours, perhaps four. It is a long way. But if we find him, he will come down here." He turned calmly to the Saint. *"Andiamo, signor!"*

Simon was contented enough to follow him. Intuccio set a tiring trot, but it was easy for the Saint, who was as iron-hard as he had ever been. A coppery sun baked the air out of a sky of brilliant unbroken blue, one of those subtropical skies that are as flat and glazed as a painted cyclorama. Little whirls of dust floated up behind them as they rode, dancing a phantom veil dance to the irregular tom-tom of swinging hoof beats. Intuccio made no conversation, and Simon was left to ruminate over his own puzzle. To be out under the blazing daylight in that ridged and castled wilderness of mighty boulders piled against steep scarps of rock, with such an enigma on his mind, gave him the exact opposite of the feeling which he had had the night before. Then he had been a spectator; now he was an actor, and he was ready, as he always was, to enjoy his share in the play.

Three hours later, as they rode down the barren slopes again toward the place where they had left Urselli, he felt very much at peace. He had settled quite a number of things in his own mind during the ride, and about Amadeo Urselli's own exact position in the cosmic scale he had removed all doubts even before they set out. He knew the rats of the big cities too well to be mistaken about Amadeo.

But the setting for the encounter was what made it so ineffably superb. To have met him in the city would have been ordinary enough, but to meet the city gunman out here in the great open spaces was a poem which only the Saint's impish sense of humor could realize to the full.

Glancing down at the rifle carried ready across his pommel, the Saint even asked himself the wild question whether Amadeo Urselli might conceivably be mistaken in a moment of well-staged excitement for a mountain lion. Almost regretfully he dismissed the idea, but when a turn of the trail brought him a sight of Urselli sitting disconsolately on a rock slapping at the indefatigable flies, he felt genuinely distressed to think that such an ideal opportunity had to be passed by. They rode down into the gulch, and Intuccio leaned over in the saddle with his forearm on his thigh.

"You have seen nothing, Amadeo?"

"Nothing but flies," said Urselli sourly.

He was pinkly sun-broiled and very bad-tempered, and the sight of his misery almost made up for the fact that they had not seen so much as a toe print of the mountain lion which they had set out to look for.

They arrived back at the hotel a few minutes after four. Urselli was the first to dismount, moving stiffly from the exertion of the day. He stopped to read a message that was nailed to the door; Simon, coming up behind him, saw the conventional black hand at the head of the letter before he could distinguish the words, and then Intuccio's arm drove between them and ripped it down.

Urselli spoke from the side of a thin hard mouth.

"I thought there were no more bad men."

Intuccio did not answer. The paper crumpled in his grasp, and without a word he thrust them both aside and crashed through the door. He stumbled over an upturned chair in the gloom as he went in, and then they stood on either side of him surveying the wreck of the kitchen. The center table was tilted drunkenly against the range of the far end, and two other chairs were flung into different corners, one of them broken. A saucepan lay at their feet, and little splashes of shattered china and glass winked up at them from the floor.

Intuccio dragged himself across the room and detached a fragment of gaily printed cotton stuff from the back of the broken chair. He stared at it dumbly. Then, without speaking, he held out the message from the door.

Simon took it and smoothed it out.

*If you wish to see your daughter again, bring $20,000 in cash to the top of Skeleton Hill by midnight tonight. Come*

*alone and unarmed. We shall not send a second warning.*
*Death pays for treachery.*

"You gotta pay, Salvatore," Urselli was saying. "I'm tellin' ya. You can't fool with kidnappers. A gang that snatches a girl won't stop for nothin'. Say, I remember when Red McLaughlin put the arm on Sappho Lirra—"

Intuccio straightened up lifelessly, like a stunned giant.

"I must find the sheriff," he said.

The Saint's hand crossed his path, barring it, in a gesture as lithe and vivid as the flick of a sword.

"Let me go."

He went down the short road to the town with a light step. This was adventure as he understood it, objective and decisive, like a blast of music, and the Saint smiled as he went. Far might it be from him to deny the home-coming of Amadeo Urselli any of its quintessential poetry. He walked into the sheriff's office and found Saddlebag's solitary representative of the law at home.

"Lucia Intuccio has been kidnapped," he said. "Will you come up?"

The man's eyes bulged.

"Kidnapped?" he repeated incredulously.

"There was a note calling for twenty thousand dollars ransom nailed to the door," said the Saint, and the sheriff took down his gun belt.

"I'll be right along."

Simon went with him. The news spread like an epidemic, and a dozen men had gathered in the back room when they arrived.

Intuccio told the story. He seemed to have shaken off some of his first numbness, and at intervals his eyes veered towards Urselli with an ugly soberness. When he had finished, the sheriff's gaze leveled in the same direction.

"So," he said slowly, "while Urselli knew that you'd be gone at least three hours, there wasn't anybody to see what he was up to."

"What of it?" protested Urselli grittily. "You got no—"

Simon interposed himself.

"We're wasting time," he said coolly. "I guess we ought to make a search."

"Mebbe we will." The sheriff's gaze did not shift. "You'll come as well, Urselli—and stay with me."

The group of men filed out quickly, splitting up outside into two and threes, for there were less than five hours of daylight left—an almost hopeless time in which to find and follow a cold trail in that wild country. Simon joined them.

The sun went down in a riot of gold and crimson, and the search parties began to filter back through the gray-blue dusk. By ten o'clock, when the night was a vaulted bowl of dark glass studded with silver pin points, they were all gathered together at the inn, and the sheriff, with Intuccio and Urselli, came in last while they were all waiting.

There was no need for questions. A silence that was its own answer hung in the room, mirroring itself in the glazed tension of the yellow highlights smeared by the single oil lamp on the circle of leathery faces. The angles of black shadow in the far corners held the strained heaviness of a mounting thunderstorm.

The sheriff read through the ransom notice again, and raised his eyes to Intuccio's face. The nervous scrape of a man's feet on the bare floor rasped a nerve-stabbing discord into the stillness before he spoke.

"You wasn't aimin' to pay this money, was you, Salvatore?"

The old man stared back at him haggardly. Before he came in, the alternatives had been discussed by the reassembled search parties in measured low-pitched voices that scarcely ruffled the texture of the air. Organized help could not come from the nearest big town before midnight—it might not come before morning. What would the sophisticated city police think of Black Hand threats?

"*Buon Dio!*" said Intuccio, in a terrible voice, "I have not so much money in the world."

Urselli started.

"But you said yesterday—"

"I lied."

The innkeeper's great fists were clenched at his sides, his powerful shoulders quivering under his soiled shirt.

"I have always failed. Everything I touched has been under a curse. You all know how the farm ate up my money until it was nearly all lost, and the land was sold for the mortgages. You all know how I bought this inn to try and make a living, but none of you came here. Perhaps you were afraid of me because I never laughed with you. *Dio mio*, as if a man who has suffered as much as I have could laugh! You thought I had the evil eye, some black secret that made me unfit to be one of you. Yes, I had. But the only secret was one which you all knew—that I had failed . . . But when that cousin of mine came back from Chicago, with his fine clothes and his jewels, and boasted of the money he made—I lied. I did not want to see him despise me. I told him I had thirty thousand dollars. I have not got five hundred."

Urselli lighted a cigarette mechanically.

"That looks bad," he said. "I tell you, those guys mean business."

"You know a great deal about them, Amadeo? You speak from experience?"

The innkeeper's burning eyes were bent rigidly on the smaller man's face. There were red notes glinting in them, hot swirling sparks from a fire that was breaking loose deep within them. In the core of the soft voice was a deep vibrant note like the premonitory rumble of a volcano. "Perhaps you know more than any of us?"

Urselli looked right and left, with a sudden widening of his rat-like eyes. Not one of the ring of faces painted in the lamplight moved an eyelash. They waited.

He sucked at his cigarette, the tip flickering abruptly to the uncertain inhalation.

"In the cities, you hear things," he gabbled shakily. "You read newspapers. I'm only tellin' you—"

"Now I will tell you!"

Intuccio's restraint broke at last; the fire that was in him seethed through in a jagged roar. His iron hands crushed into the other's shoulders, half lifting, half hurling him round.

"I said last night that you would find more robbers in the big cities of America than you would find here. I was right. Here is one of them! A dog who has come back to the home where he does not belong any longer!"

The voice sank again, only momentarily. "This very morning you were exposed. The stranger here did it. He challenged you. I was listening. He made you show your gun. Does an honest man need a gun? And you could shoot. I watched. He told you that you were a liar when you said you traded in jewelry—because you did not know that the diamond on your finger was not real. And he said that perhaps the true reason why you left Chicago was because you were—on the spot. Perhaps you thought I did not understand. But we are not so ignorant. We also read newspapers. I know you, Amadeo! You are a gunman!"

He turned to the Saint.

"Is that not so?"

Simon nodded.

"That would be my guess."

"So you thought you could swindle me," Intuccio went on mercilessly. "But then you were exposed. You knew that after what I had seen and heard I should never trust you. You had to be quick, before I denounced you to the sheriff. This afternoon you were alone. You came back here. You! You took Lucia away! You wrote that letter! You are the man we want!"

Urselli's gasp of fright as he was shaken as if he were a doll in the convulsive grasp of the huge hands that held him sobbed out against the fearful low-pitched growl of wrathful men. As the innkeeper's voice rose uncontrollably, the murmur beat upwards like an angry sea. Other voices clanged against it, echoing clearer and louder in the vengeful cry of a wolf pack, soaring to drown every other sound, shouting against each other. The circle narrowed in, creeping out of the shadows into the full yellow of the smoking lamp, hands reaching out, throats snarling gutturally. "Lynch him! Lynch the swine!"

"Stop!"

The sheriff's command boomed like a gunshot through the din. He turned to Urselli grimly.

"Reckon you better say something quick, friend," he drawled.

Urselli's face twisted and twitched, his hunted eyes swiveling frantically over the bank of remorseless faces. He shrank away like a cornered animal.

"It's not true!" he blubbered. "I ain't done nothing. Ya can't frame this on me! This won't help ya. That ransom's gotta be paid by midnight—an' if it ain't there—"

The clamor which had been hushed began again. Fingers plucked at him. Red eyes glowered into his whichever way he turned. And all the time the innkeeper's inexorable hands held him as helpless as a struggling child. Urselli screamed.

"Don't touch me!" he gasped, writhing away from them. "You're all wrong. You don't know what you're doing. Gimme a break. Don't touch me! Salvatore—you wouldn't let them do this to me? I'll do anything—anything. Here, look. I told you I had twenty thousand bucks. You can have them. I'll give them to you. Take them and pay the ransom!"

"What do you think, Salvatore?" asked the sheriff steadily.

Silence came down again, raw-edged and expectant. Intuccio turned. He shrugged, and the slobbering object in his grip rose and fell like a puppet with the heave of his shoulders.

"It is easy enough to pay ransom to oneself," he said skeptically. "But I can take his money. If they will give Lucia back to me—if she is safe—afterwards we shall see."

"We can all go with you," spoke up one of the bystanders, and there was a chorus of assent. "If we can catch one o' them thar coyotes—"

Others chimed in.

"Fools!" cried the old man bitterly. "If it were as easy as that, should I not have asked your company long ago? Lucia will not be there. They will keep her until the money is paid." The fire smoldered again in his dark eyes. "But when I return, you, Amadeo, will still be here. And death pays for treachery. If Lucia does not come home, I will kill you myself."

He tore off Urselli's belt and flung it to the sheriff. Pack after pack of new crisp bills came from it, and the sheriff counted the pile and stacked it together.

"It is my duty to forbid this," he said gravely. "But it's—your daughter."

Intuccio nodded stonily.

"Yes," he said. "It is my daughter."

He scanned their faces once, his eyes resting last on the trembling figure of Urselli held by two pairs of strong hands, and then he passed through them to the door, with the circle opening to let him through. And again the stillness began to be broken, voice by voice.

"I have an idea," said the Saint.

He stood by the wall, a little apart from them, cigarette poised between lean brown fingers. The very quiescence of his lounging suppleness had the electric quality of a smoothly humming dynamo, but the light was too dim for them to see the reckless blue twinkle of his eyes. Yet they all looked at him.

"All of you couldn't go," he said quietly. "But one man might. I've done plenty of night hunting. I could follow—and see where the money was taken."

"Could you be sure no one would know?" asked the sheriff, and Simon smiled.

"Anyone who heard me, or saw me, would be a living miracle."

He had a way about him.

They listened to him.

He went through the night toward Skeleton Hill with a blithe softness. The country before him and on either side was an earthly sleeping wilderness, ragged and obscure in the shrouded darkness of a night without a moon. The cry of a hunting coyote somewhere in the distance wailed faintly through the veiled space, and the Saint smiled again. Presently, ahead of him, he heard the monotonous scrunch of plodding boots going down the dirt road. He came up swiftly with the sound, till he could see the ghostly bulk of the walker blotting out the stars.

He himself made no sound. He came up until his hand could stretch out and grip the man's shoulder, and he spoke in a sudden gentle whisper of Italian.

"One moment, Salvatore. You know as well as I do that there is no hurry to reach Skeleton Hill."

The man halted with a jerk, and turned. His black-bearded face bent forward till he could recognize the Saint in the vague starlight. Then the shaggy black head bowed.

"*Lai fatto molto bene*," said the old man gruffly. "I thought we should meet here."

For a moment even Simon was startled. "You guessed, did you?"

"I knew that Amadeo could never have been so stupid as to try anything like that immediately after you had shown him up. And the hunting trip that left him alone for nearly four hours was your idea. Also you knew that I had no money, so I knew that I had nothing to fear from you. Where is Lucia?"

"She went and hid in the woodshed as I told her to," answered the Saint shamelessly. "I told her to slip out as soon as it was dark and come along here. You'll probably find her a little way along the road. But if you knew, why did you help me?"

"I did not see why that Amadeo should have so much money," said Intuccio calmly. "You will be content with half?"

Simon laughed softly.

"From the very beginning," he said, "I always meant you to have three quarters."

Intuccio took out the money and divided it.

"Do we go back?" he asked.

"I think we shall have to make some ingenious explanations," said the Saint. "If Lucia says it was Amadeo, he will probably be lynched. As far as I'm concerned, the probability leaves me unmoved, but since he's still your cousin you may feel differently. If she says it was me, I'm not likely to have such a good time either. Perhaps she had better invent somebody."

"Let us decide about that on the way," agreed Salvatore Intuccio, and they walked on, arm in arm.

# TERESA

# INTRODUCTION

One more story that stems from long ago. From 1931, to be quite exact—although I didn't write it for a longish while afterwards.

This is another story in which the locale, and only that, was changed for contemporary geopolitical reasons, between the time it was first written and published in a magazine and the time when it ended up in a book collection.

I can make no more apologies for the liberties I have taken with times and places in the reprinting of stories such as this.

The way I see it, nothing is so dated as last year—at least in fiction. Put your setting back a century, and anything goes: any apparent anachronism, any unfamiliarity, is acceptable because it is said to have occurred in an era about which the reader happily admits his ignorance. Things were different in those days—that's all. But let the period fall within the theoretical scope of his faulty memory, and the reader is at once a dissecting critic: anything that seems as if it could have happened yesterday must be submitted to the awareness of today. If a story uses a telephone, this kind of telescoping consciousness requires that it should also take cognizance of television.

This story was first written around a Corsican bandit whom I had the pleasure of meeting on his home ground in very similar circumstances to those I have used in this narrative. But they caught him eventually, although it took several regiments of the French Army to do it, and today Corsican bandits are just an old wives' tale. Mexican bandits, however, for some reason, are still exotic currency. So let the story go there. If it is considered legitimate to disguise names, why not places?

*—Leslie Charteris (1951)*

"Bandits?" said Señor Copas. He shrugged. "*Sí, hay siempre bandidos.* The Government will never catch them all. Here in Mexico they are a tradition of the country."

He looked again at the girl in the dark hat, appreciatively, because she was worth looking at, and he was a true Latin, and there was still romance in the heart that beat above his rounded abdomen.

He chuckled uncertainly, ignoring the other customers who were sitting in various degrees of patience behind their empty plates, and said, "But the señorita has nothing to fear. She is not going into the wilds."

"But I want to go into the wilds," she said.

Her voice was low and soft and musical, matching the quiet symmetry of her face and the repose of her hands. She was smart without exaggeration. She was Fifth Avenue with none of its brittle hardness, incongruously transported to that standstill Mexican village, and yet contriving not to seem out of place. To Señor Copas she was a miracle.

To Simon Templar she was a quickening of interest and a hint of adventure that might lead anywhere or nowhere. His eye for charm was no slower than that of Señor Copas, but there was more in it than that.

To Simon Templar, who had been called the most audacious bandit of the twentieth century, the subject was always new and fascinating. And he had an impish sense of humor which couldn't resist the thought of what the other members of the audience would have said and done if they had known that the man who was listening to their conversation about bandits was the notorious Saint himself.

"Are you more interested in the wilds or the bandits?" he asked, in Spanish as native as her own.

She turned to him with friendly brown eyes in which there was a trace of subtle mockery.

"I'm not particular."

"*No es posible*," said Señor Copas firmly, as he dragged himself away to his kitchen.

"He doesn't seem to like the idea," said the Saint.

He was sitting beside her, at the communal table which half filled the dining room of the hotel. She broke a roll with her graceful, leisurely moving hands. He saw that her fingers were slender and tapering, delicately manicured, and one of them wore a wedding ring.

Fifth Avenue in the Fonda de la Quinta, in the shadow of the Sierra Madre, in the state of Durango in Old Mexico, which was a very different place.

"You know a lot about this country?" she asked.

"I've been here before."

"Do you know the mountains?"

"Fairly well."

"Do you know the bandits too?"

The Saint gazed at her with precarious gravity. He looked like a man who would obviously be on visiting terms with bandits. He looked rather like a bandit himself, in a debonair and reckless sort of way, with his alert tanned face and clean-cut fighting mouth and the unscrupulous gay twinkle in his blue eyes.

"Listen," he said. "Once upon a time I was walking between San Miguel and Gajo, two villages not far from here. I saw from my map that the road led around in a great horseshoe, but they told me at an inn that there was a short cut, straight across, down into the canyon and up the other side. I climbed down something like the side of a precipice for hours—the path was all great loose stones, and presently one of them turned under my foot and I took a spill and sprained my ankle. When I got to the bottom I was done in. I couldn't move another step, particularly climbing. I hadn't any food, but there was a stream running through the bottom of the canyon, so I had water. I could only hope that someone else would try that short cut and find me . . . At the end of the third day a man did find me, and he looked like one of your bandits if anyone ever did. He did what he could for me, gave me food from his pack—bread and sausage and cheese—and then he said he would go on to San Miguel and send help for me. He could have taken everything I had, but he didn't. He was insulted when I offered to pay him. 'I am not a beggar,' he said, and I've never seen anything so haughty in my life— 'I am El Rojo.'"

"Then why is Señor Copas so frightened?"

"They're all frightened of El Rojo."

Her finely penciled brows drew together.

"El Rojo?" she said. "Who is El Rojo?"

"'The greatest bandit since Villa. They're all scared because there's a rumor that he's in the district. You ought to be scared, too. They're all offended if you aren't scared of El Rojo . . . He really is a great character, though. I remember once the Government decided it was time that something drastic was done about him. They sent out half the Mexican army to round him up. It was the funniest thing I ever heard of, but you have to know the country to see the joke."

"They didn't catch him?"

The Saint chuckled.

"One man who knew the country could laugh at three armies."

For a little while the girl was wrapped in an unapproachable solitude of thought. Then she turned to the Saint again.

"Señor," she said, "do you think you could help me find El Rojo?"

Even south of the border, he was still a Saint errant, or perhaps a sucker for adventure. He said, "I could try."


They rode out on the dazzling stone track that winds beside the river—a track which was nothing more than the marks that centuries of solitary feet had left on the riot of tumbled boulders from which the hills rose up.

The Saint lounged in the saddle, relaxed like a vaquero, letting his mount pick its own way over the broken rock. His mind went back to the café where they had sat together over coffee, after lunch, and he had said to her, "Either you must be a journalist looking for an unusual interview, or you want to be kidnapped by El Rojo for publicity, or you've been reading too many romantic stories and you think you could fall in love with him."

She had only smiled in her quiet way, inscrutable in spite of its friendliness, and said, "No, señor—you are wrong in all your guesses. I am looking for my husband."

The Saint's brows slanted quizzically.

"You mean you are Señora Rojo?"

"Oh, no. I am Señora Alvarez de Quevedo. Teresa Alvarez."

Then she looked at him, quickly and clearly, as if she had made up her mind about something.

"The last time I heard of my husband, he was at the Fonda de la Quinta," she said. "That was two years ago. He wrote to me that he was going into the mountains. He liked to do things like that, to climb mountains and sleep under the stars and be a man alone, sometimes—

it is curious, for he was very much a city man . . . I never heard of him again. He said he was going to climb the Gran Seño. I remembered, when I heard the name, that I had read of El Rojo in the newspapers about that time. And it seemed to me, when I heard you speak of El Rojo, that perhaps El Rojo was the answer."

"If it was El Rojo," said the Saint quietly, "I don't think it would help you to find him now."

Her eyes were still an enigma.

"Even so," she said, "it would be something to know."

"But you've waited two years—"

"Yes," she said softly. "I have waited two years."

She had told him no more than that, and he had known that she did not wish to say any more, but it had been enough to send him off on that quixotic wild-goose chase.

He had been leading the way for two hours, but presently, where the trail broadened for a short distance, she brought her horse up beside his, and they rode knee to knee. "I wonder why you should do this for me," she said.

He shrugged.

"Why did you ask me?"

"It was an impulse." She moved her hands puzzledly. "I don't know. I suppose you have the air of a man who is used to being asked impossible things. You look as if you would do them."

"I do," said the Saint modestly.

It was his own answer, too. She was a damsel in distress—and no damsel in distress had ever called on the Saint in vain. And she was beautiful, also, which was a very desirable asset to damsels in distress. And about her there was a mystery, which to Simon Templar was the trumpet call of adventure.

In the late afternoon, at one of the bends in the trail where it dipped to the level of the river, the Saint reined in his horse and dismounted at the water's edge.

"Are we there?" she said.

"No. But we're leaving the river."

He scooped water up in his hands and drank, and splashed it over his face. It was numbingly cold, but it steamed off his arms in the hot dry air. She knelt down and drank beside him, and then sat back on her heels and looked up at the hills that hemmed them in.

A kind of shy happiness lighted her eyes, almost uncertainly, as if it had not been there for a long time and felt itself a stranger.

"I understand now," she said. "I understand why Gaspar loved all this, in spite of what he was. If only he could have been content with it . . ."

"You were not happy?" said the Saint gently.

She looked at him.

"No, señor. I have not been happy for so long that I am afraid."

She got up quickly and put her foot in the stirrup. He helped her to mount, and swung into his own saddle. They set off across the shallow stream; the horses picked their way delicately between the boulders.

On the far side, they climbed, following a trail so faint that she could not see it all, but the Saint rarely hesitated. Presently the trees were thicker, and over the skyline loomed the real summit of the hill they were climbing. The valley was swallowed up in darkness, and up there where the Saint turned his horse across the slope the brief subtropical twilight was fading.

Simon Templar lighted a cigarette as he rode, and he had barely taken the first puff of smoke into his lungs when a man stepped from behind a tree with a rifle leveled and broke the stillness of the evening with a curt, "*Manos arriba!*"

The Saint turned his head with a smile.

"You've got what you wanted," he said to Teresa Alvarez. "May I present El Rojo?"

The introduction was almost superfluous, for the red mask from which El Rojo took his name, which covered his face from the brim of his sombrero down to his stubble-bearded chin, was sufficient identification. Watching the girl, Simon saw no sign of fear as the bandit came forward. Her face was pale, but she sat straight-backed on her horse and gazed at him with an unexpected eagerness in her eyes. Simon turned back to El Rojo.

"*Qué tál, amigo?*" he murmured genially.

The bandit stared at him unresponsively.

"*Baje usted*" he ordered gruffly. He glanced at the girl. "You too—get down."

His eyes, after that glance, remained fixed on her, even after she was down from the saddle and standing by the horse's head. The Saint wondered for the first time whether he might not have let his zest for adventure override his common sense when he deliberately led her into the stronghold of an outlawed and desperate man.

El Rojo turned back to him.

"The señorita," he said, "will tie your hands behind you."

He dragged a length of cord from his pocket and threw it across the space between them. The girl looked at it coldly.

"Go on," said the Saint, "Do what the nice gentleman tells you. It's part of the act."

He could take care of such minor details when the time came, but for the present there was a mystery with which he was more preoccupied.

When the Saint's hands had been tied, El Rojo pointed his rifle.

"The señorita will lead the way," he said. "You will follow, and I shall direct you from behind. You would be wise not to try and run away."

He watched them file past him, and from the sounds that followed, the Saint deduced that El Rojo had taken the horses by their bridles and was towing them after him as he brought up the rear.

As they moved roughly parallel with the valley, the slope on their right became steeper and steeper until it was simply a precipice, and the rocks on their left towered bleaker and higher, and they were walking along a narrow ledge with the shadow of one cliff over them and another cliff falling away from their feet into a void of darkness. The path wound snake-like around the fissures and buttresses into which the precipice was sculptured, and presently, rounding one of those natural breastworks, they found themselves at a place where the path widened suddenly to become a natural balcony about twenty feet long and twelve feet deep—and then stopped. A natural wall of rock screened it from sight of the valley or the hills on the other side.

El Rojo followed them into the niche, leading the two horses, which he tied up to an iron ring by the mouth of a cave that opened in the rock wall at the end.

There was a dull glow of embers close by the mouth of the cave. The bandit stirred them with his foot, and threw on a couple of mesquite logs.

"Perhaps you are hungry," said El Rojo. "I have little to offer my guests, but you are welcome to what there is."

"I should like a cigarette as much as anything," said the Saint. "But I'm not a very good contortionist." The bandit considered him.

"I could untie you, señor, if you gave me your word of honor not to attempt to escape. It is, I believe, usual in these circumstances."

His speeches had an elaborate theatricalism which came oddly out of his rough and ragged clothing.

"I'll give you my word for two hours," said the Saint, after a moment's thought. "It can be renewed if necessary."

*"Es bastante. Y usted, señorita?"*

*"Conforme."*

*"Entonces, por dos horas."*

El Rojo laid down his rifle and untied the Saint's hands, but Simon noticed that he picked up the gun again at once, and that he kept it always within easy reach. The Saint understood the symptom well enough not to be disturbed by it. He lighted a cigarette and stretched himself out comfortably beside the fire and beside Teresa Alvarez, while the night closed down like a purple blanket and El Rojo brought out the bread and cheese and sausage and coarse red wine which are the staple fare in the mountains.

He said presently, "I take it that you have ideas about ransom."

The bandit shrugged.

"I regret the necessity. But I am a poor man, and you must be charitable. Let us say that it was unlucky that you chose to travel this way."

"But we were looking for you," said Teresa.

El Rojo stopped with a knife-load of cheese halfway to his mouth.

"For me?"

"Yes," she said. "I wanted to see you, and this gentleman was good enough to help me. We were not unlucky. We came here on purpose."

"You pay me an unusual compliment, señorita. Could one ask what I have done to deserve such a distinguished honor?"

"I am looking for my husband," she said simply.

He sat watching her.

*"No comprendo.* It is true that I often have the pleasure of entertaining travelers in the mountains. But, alas, they never stay with me for long. Either their friends are so desolate in their absence that they bribe me to ensure their safe and speedy return—or their friends are so unresponsive that I am forced to conclude that they cannot be very desirable guests. I am incapable of believing that a gentleman

who had won the heart of the señora can have belonged to the latter category."

"It is possible," she said, without bitterness. "But I knew nothing of it."

She was silent for a moment.

"It was two years ago," she said. "He came here to Durango, to La Quinta. He was going into the mountains. No one ever heard of him again. I know that you were here then, and I wondered if you might have—entertained him. Perhaps I was foolish . . ."

El Rojo dug his knife in the cheese.

"*Por Dios!*" he said. "Is it like that that one lives in Mexico? You have lost your husband for two years, and it is not until today that you want to find him?"

"I don't want to find him," she said. "I want to know that he is dead."

She said it quietly, without any force of feeling, as if it was a thought that she had lived with for so long that it had become a commonplace part of her life. But in the very passionlessness of that matter-of-fact statement there was something that sent an electric ripple up the Saint's spine.

He had finished eating, and he was sitting smoking with his feet towards the warmth of the fire and his back leaning against the rock. On his left, Teresa Alvarez was looking straight ahead of her, as if she had been alone, and El Rojo's eyes were riveted on her through the slits in his mask, so that the Saint almost felt as if he were an eavesdropper. But he was too absorbed in the play to care about that.

"I was very young," said the girl, in that quiet and detached way that left so much emotion to be guessed at. "I was still in the convent school when I was engaged to him. I knew nothing, and I was not given any choice. I was married to him a few weeks later. Yes, these things happen. It is still the custom in the old-fashioned families. The parents choose a man they think will make their daughter a good husband, and she is expected to be guided by their wisdom."

Her face was impassive in the firelight.

"I think he was unfaithful to me on our honeymoon," she said. "I know he was unfaithful many times after that. He boasted of it. I might have forgiven that, but he boasted also that he had only married me for my dowry—and for what pleasure he could have out of me before he wanted a change. I found out that he was nothing but a shady adventurer, a gambler, a cheat, a petty swindler, a man without a shadow of honor or even common decency. But by that time I had no one to go to . . . My father and mother died suddenly six months after we were married, and I had never had any friends of my own. It will seem strange to you—it seems strange to me, now—but I never realized that I could leave him myself. I had never been brought up to know anything of the world. So I stayed with him. For four years . . . and then he came here, and I never saw him again." The Saint could feel the suffering and humiliation and disillusionment of those four years as vividly as if she had told the story of them day by day, and his blue eyes rested on her with a new and oddly gentle understanding.

She went on after a while: "At first I was only glad that he had gone, and that I could have some peace until he returned. He had told me that he was going away for a holiday, but one day a man from the police came to see me, and I found out that he had gone away because for once he had not been so clever as he had been before, and there was a charge against him.

"Then I hoped that the police would catch him and he would go to prison, perhaps for many years, perhaps forever. But they never found him. And I hoped that he might have fallen over a precipice in the mountains, or that he had escaped to the other end of the world, or anything that would mean he would never come back to me. I didn't mind very much what it was, so long as I never saw him again. But I was happy. And then, six months ago, I fell in love. And my happiness was finished again."

"Because you were in love?" El Rojo asked, incredulously.

"Because I was not free. This man is everything that my husband never was, and he knows everything that I have told you. He wants to marry me. Before, I never cared where my husband was, or what had happened to him, but now, you see, I must know."

El Rojo looked up toward the Saint.

"And the señor," he said, "is he the fortunate man with whom you fell in love?"

"No. He is in Mexico City. He is in the government service, and he could not leave to come with me."

"He is rich, this man?"

"Yes," she said, and her voice was no longer cold.

There was silence for a long time—for so long that the dancing firelight died down to a steady red glow.

Teresa Alvarez gazed into the dull embers, with her arms clasped around her knees, absorbed in her own thoughts, and at last she said, "But I have only been dreaming. Even in such a small territory as this, why should anyone remember one man who was here two years ago?"

El Rojo stirred himself a little.

"Was your husband," he said, "a man of middle height, with smooth black hair and greenish eyes and a thin black mustache?"

Suddenly she was still, with a stillness that seemed more violent than movement.

"Yes," she said. "He was like that."

"And his name was Alvarez?"

"Yes. Gaspar Alvarez de Quevedo."

Her voice was no more than a whisper.

The bandit drew a gust of evil-smelling smoke from his cheap cigarette.

"Such a man was a guest of mine about two years ago," he said slowly. "I remember him best because of the ring, which I gave to a girl in Matamoros, and because he was the only guest I have had here who left without my consent."

"He escaped?"

The words came from the girl's lips with a weariness that was too deep for feeling.

"He tried to," said El Rojo. "But it was very dark, and these mountains are not friendly to those who do not know them well."

He stretched out his arm, toward the black emptiness beyond the rock wall that guarded the niche where they sat.

"I buried him where he fell. It was difficult to reach him, but I could not risk his body being seen by any goatherds going up the valley. In the morning, if you like, I will point you out his grave. It is below the path we followed to come here—more than a hundred meters down . . . The señora may go on without fear to the happiness that life has kept waiting for her."

It was very dark, but Simon could see the tears rise in the girl's eyes before she hid her face in her hands.

The morning sun was cutting hot swaths through the fading mist when El Rojo followed the Saint and Teresa along the winding ledge between cliff and cliff that led out of his eyrie high above the river. Where the slope of the mountain opened clear before them he called to them to stop, and held the bridle of the horse which the girl was to ride while she climbed into the saddle.

"I give you—*buen viaje*," he said. "You can make no mistake. Follow the side of the hill until you come to a belt of trees, and then go downwards. To find your way back here—that is another matter. But if you keep going downwards you must come to the river, and on the other side of the river is the road to La Quinta. I will meet you somewhere on that road in three days from now, at about four o'clock in the afternoon."

"I can never thank you," she said.

"You have no need to," he answered roughly. "You are going to bring me—how much did we agree?—one hundred thousand pesos, and the señor remains as my guest as a surety for our meeting. I regret that I have to be commercial, but one must live, and if your lover is rich he will not mind." She held out her hand to the Saint.

"I shall be there to meet him in three days," she said. "And then I shall be able to thank you again."

"This was nothing," he answered with his lazy smile. "But if you ever meet any dragons I wish you'd send for me."

He kissed her fingers, and watched her ride away until the curve of the hill hid her from sight. It was true that he had done very little, but he had seen the light in her eyes before she went, and to him that was reward enough for any adventure.

He was thoughtful as he walked back along the cliff edge track towards the bandit's cave with El Rojo just behind his elbow, and when they were halfway along it he said casually, "By the way, I ought to warn you that the parole I renewed last night is just running out."

The muzzle of the bandit's rifle pressed into his chest as he turned.

"In that case señor, you will please put up your hands. Unless, of course, you prefer to renew your parole again." Simon raised his hands to the level of his shoulders. "My friend," he said, "have you forgotten the Arroyo Verde?"

"*Perdone?*"

"The Arroyo Verde," said the Saint steadily. "Between San Miguel and Gajo. Where there was a man with a sprained ankle who had been there for three days without food, and who might have stayed there until he starved if a brigand with a price on his head had not stayed to help him."

"I have not the least idea what you are talking about."

"I thought not," said the Saint softly. "Because you weren't there."

He saw the bandit's hands go rigid around the gun, and the blue steel was as sharp as knife points in his eyes.

"I didn't think this brigand would have forgotten me so completely that we could spend an evening together without him recognizing me. You see, we got quite friendly down in that forsaken canyon, and when my ankle was better I paid him a visit here. That's why I was able to find my way so easily yesterday. I came to Durango because I hoped to meet him again. And yet this brigand's name was El Rojo, too. How do you explain that—Señor Alvarez?"

For a moment the bandit was silent, standing tense and still, and Simon could feel the shattering chaos whirling through the man's mind, the wild spin of instinctive stratagems and lies sinking down to the grim realization of their ultimate futility.

"And suppose I am Alvarez?" said the man at last, and his natural voice was quite different from the way he had been speaking before.

"Then you should tell me more about what you said last night—and about El Rojo. Where is he?"

"I found him here by accident, but he thought I was looking for him. We fought, and he fell over the precipice. He lies in the grave which I said was mine."

"And because you wanted to disappear, and because you loved the mountains, you thought that the best way for you to hide would be to take his place. No one had ever seen the face of El Rojo, no one ever knew who he was. You took his mask and became El Rojo."

"*Eso es.*"

Alvarez had not moved. Simon could sense the taut nerves of a man who held death in his hands and was only waiting for one word to turn the scale of his decision.

Simon Templar was also waiting for the answer to one question. He said, "And last night?"

"*A usted que más le da?*"

"The answer is in your hands," said the Saint.

His eyes were as clear and unclouded as the sky over their heads, and there was something as ageless and unchangeable as justice in the even tones of his voice.

"Perhaps in these two years you might have changed," he said. "Perhaps you were glad that you could never go back to the old life. And perhaps you told that lie to cut the last link with it, and you were glad to set your wife free for the happiness which you never gave her. If that was so, your secret will always be safe with me. But I've never seen a man like you change very much, and I wondered why all you asked about your wife's lover was whether he was rich. I wondered if it had occurred to you that if you let her believe you were dead, so that she would marry this man, you could go back to Mexico City and charge a price for your silence. And if that was so—"

"You will never tell her," said Alvarez viciously, and the rifle jerked in his hand.

The crack of the shot rattled back and forth, growing fainter and fainter, between the hills, and something like fire struck the Saint's chest. He smiled, as if something amused him.

"You're wasting your time," he said. "I took all the bullets out of the shells in your gun while you were asleep last night. But you've told me what I wanted to know. I said that the answer was in your own hands—"

Alvarez came out of the superstitious trance which had gripped him for a moment. He snatched the rifle back and then lunged with it savagely. Simon stepped to the right, and the thrust passed under his left arm. Then he swung his right fist to Alvarez's jaw. Alvarez was on the very edge of the path, and the force of the blow lifted him backwards with his arms sprawling . . .

Simon Templar stood for some time gazing down into the abyss. His face was serene and untroubled, and he felt neither pity nor remorse. His mind went on working calmly and prosaically. There was no need for Teresa Alvarez to know. Nothing would disturb her conscience if she went on believing what she had been told the night before. And she would think well of El Rojo, who to her would always be the real El Rojo whom Simon had called his friend.

He would have to think up some story to account for El Rojo deciding to waive his claim to the hundred thousand pesos she had promised. He went thoughtfully back to collect his horse.

# LUELLA

Mr and Mrs Matthew Joyson had never heard of Paolo and Francesca, but in certain ways they could have given serious competition to those classic lovers. It would be unkind of the chronicler to suggest that this resemblance may even have extended to the technical morality of their bedded bliss, although when questioned Mrs Joyson tended to be somewhat hazy about the details of the ceremony by which she acquired the name. We prefer instead to refer to the intensity of Mr Joyson's jealous devotion, a feature which he frequently had occasion to emphasize, and which paid him much better dividends than ever stuck to the wad of the late Paolo Malatesta.

Matt Joyson was a man of about fifty with the solidly impressive bearing that one would associate with a banker or an attorney, which had been a certain asset to him in the days when he had played parts of that type in second and third road companies. Unfortunately his thespian talents were somewhat less distinguished than his appearance, and the rigors of cheap rooming houses between jobs and even worse accommodations on the road were uncongenial to a temperament conditioned by the stage-sets in which he usually appeared, so that when he met a kindred soul in the very nubile shape of the fair Luella, an ambitious ingénue who tried to pawn a watch which he unguardedly left in his dressing room, it seemed like a good time to branch out into a more comfortable career.

They adopted into their design for living a third party, one Tod Kermein, a photographer who had fallen upon evil days on account of certain exposures to which the United States Post Office adopted a rather puritanical attitude, and Matt Joyson proceeded to develop for the troupe a cameo drama which played to extremely limited houses, but with more profit to the performers than any production in which they had previously appeared. It was still necessary to travel from time to time, but the runs in any given town were usually longer than the engagements to which they had been accustomed, and by mutual co-operation and keeping a watchful eye on each other's sleight of hand in the division of the spoils they had achieved a very pleasant and profitable way of life by the time they reached Los Angeles and the purview of Simon Templar.

The Saint (as he was known to his friends, most of whom were still alive, and just as well to his enemies, many of whom were not so lucky) was not looking for trouble at the time. He was, as a matter of fact, looking for something a lot harder to find.

"I'm sorry, Mr Templar," said the assistant manager at the Hollywood Plaza, "but we daren't make any exceptions. Your five days are up tomorrow, and we must have your room."

"Who are you going to give it to?" Simon protested.

"Probably to somebody who's just being thrown out of the Roosevelt," answered the manager philosophically, and added hastily, "but I don't think it would help you to rush over there. They've certainly got somebody waiting who's just being thrown out of the Ambassador."

Patricia Holm, with her shining golden head at the Saint's shoulder, brought her blue eyes into play.

"Isn't there anything you could do," she pleaded, "to let a couple of nice people into this private game of musical chambers?"

The man swooned but was helpless.

"If I could solve that one," he said, "I wouldn't have to work here."

The Saint took her arm.

"Leave us drink some lunch," he said, "and brood about life in this nation of nomads."

The adjoining restaurant was cool and surprisingly quiet. They sat in a booth and ordered drinks. The Saint lighted cigarettes for them both.

"Well, old darling," he said, "I suppose we could always get several reservations on the night train to San Francisco, and a lot more reservations on the train back. We could spend every second day there and every other day here, and live in a compartment. After a month, it'd be the same as spending two weeks in each place."

"We could plant a potato in a pot," said the girl wistfully, "and in six months we'd have vines trained over the window."

The Saint sighed.

It was, he thought, an unjustly humiliating complication in the life of any self-respecting buccaneer. There had been other times when it had been difficult for him to stay in sundry towns, but those repulses had always been sponsored either by the police, who disapproved of him on principle, or by certain citizens who preferred to have only the police to contend with. Here he had done no harm and planned none—so far . . . He gazed moodily about the room, and it was at that moment, although neither of them thought anything of it at the time, that he made his first contact with the life of Luella Joyson.

She happened to be sitting at an adjoining table with an Air Force top sergeant, whose voice carried clearly to Simon's ears.

"These real-estate prices have lost their altimeters," the sergeant was saying. "But what's a guy gonna do? This climate agrees with my kid, and my wife's nuts about it. I've gotta give 'em a roof if it takes all my mustering-out and accrued pay."

His companion smiled, and the Saint's eyes focused on her. Her smile was one of Luella's most valuable assets. It was fashioned with wide, fun lips exquisitely accented in a shade of shocking pink which matched the hue of her Adrian suit. The smile crinkled bewitchingly in the corners of long dark eyes. Between the red lips gleamed small even teeth, and a man instinctively wondered how it would feel to be bitten by them—lightly and without passion. This pleasing prospect was framed in shining black hair rippling to sleek square shoulders, and topped by an attractive but unnecessary scrap of hat.

When she spoke, the lazy promise in her voice brought the Saint to full attention.

"I know the spot you're in, Sergeant—er, Bill—I can call you Bill, can't I? The price is too high. I didn't set it; I can't do anything about that. But I'll tell you what I can do. For you, Bill. I'll knock my commission off the price."

She laid a small white hand over the sergeant's muscular brown paw for one brief instant, in a gesture compounded charmingly of propitiation and appeal.

A frown dwelt momentarily on the sergeant's rugged young features. Then his gray eyes softened, and a corner of his straight-across mouth twisted upward.

"That's pretty damned sweet of you, Miss, uh, Luella—"

"Just plain Luella, Bill."

"Okay, Luella. It's swell of you, but I can't let you do it. You've got to make a living."

"Let me worry about that, Bill. I'll just add it on to my next sale, to somebody who made his pile while you were out there on a Fortress."

"If you put it like that—you're sweet to do it, though."

"It's a pleasure—Bill." Abruptly she became businesslike. "Finished? Then let's go on up to my place and get the forms made out and signed."

The Saint watched them go, not failing to note that Luella's legs tapered to slim ankles which would have wrung a whistle from a real timber wolf.

"That's quite a gal," he observed, in a fatherly way.

"I noticed you taking in her personality," retorted his lady. "Beautiful, weren't they?"

Simon tossed her a sad sweet smile.

"It's the artist in me. I see pretty women simply as interesting masses of light, shadow, and line."

"Curved lines, of course."

"Of course. Did you notice, darling Pat, that there was a certain note in that conversation, on which we so shamelessly eavesdropped, which didn't quite belong?"

Patricia frowned.

"Well . . . I . . . she was flirting with the sergeant—a little. But who wouldn't? He's nice-looking, in a craggy sort of way. His kind of crisp curly hair always gives women itchy fingers."

"I always wondered what did it," murmured the Saint. "Ah, the patter of little fingers through one's locks . . . !" He dropped his bantering tone for one laced with puzzlement. "But there was something off key. Her 'place'? That usually means an apartment. Why her apartment? She's a female real-estate agent—why not an office? Oh well . . ." He shrugged. "The sergeant is a lucky character, Pat. He has—or will shortly have—a place to lay his head, and those of his family. Which he most certainly deserves, but which doesn't help us. However, it does give me an idea."

"Don't let it run away with you," said Patricia tartly. "You haven't seen his wife yet."

The Saint ran a hand over his dark head.

"Darling, my thoughts would get a special award from the Hays office. It only occurred to me that there may be a solution to this hotel business. Why do we have to go through this routine with the hotels? Why don't we just take an apartment, and when we're tired of the place we'll just rent it and move on."

This was an interesting idea while it lasted, which was for some three hours after lunch. In that time they had an intensive refresher course in the topography of Hollywood and Beverly Hills, made the acquaintance of a couple of dozen real-estate agents and twice that many apartment managers, and came painfully to the conclusion that several thousand other people had had the same idea first.

"You'd better do something about those train reservations," Patricia said finally. "I'm going to sink myself in a bubble bath and think about the life of a traveling salesman."

"Make yourself beautiful, and we'll go dancing somewhere," Simon told her. "I'll go over to the Brown Derby and drown a sorrow, and catch up with you."

There was just one vacant place at the bar, and as the Saint slid into it and ordered a Peter Dawson he recognized the soldier on the next stool, and felt the first premonitory flutter of psychic moth wings as the pattern of coincidence began to build. For his neighbor was the sergeant to whom his attention had been indirectly drawn at lunch time.

Only it was a very different-looking sergeant with the same face. His eyes stared a light-year into space, his straight lips were frozen into a white line, and his fingertips also were white from the force with which they pressed on the bar. He looked less like a man with a beautiful piece of real estate and a beautiful realtress thrown in than anything the Saint could imagine.

Simon Templar's reflexes of observation and curiosity were automatic. The form of his response was just as spontaneous even when it seemed most theatrical, for his sense of drama had a fundamental impishness that was as natural to him as breathing. He managed to corner the sergeant's blank stare for an instant, and said, "Did you lose out on the house or the babe—or both?"

The soldier's eyes came stiffly into focus. "What's that?"

"You don't," said the Saint with a smile, "look like a man who's found a place to live ought to look, in this day and age."

He was expecting a reaction, but nothing like what he got.

The head which Pat had admired a few hours earlier swung towards him with an expression that only seemed to belong with a gunsight. One of the hands on the bar balled into a white-knuckled fist, and the shoulder muscles tensed under the olive drab.

"Who're you?" the young mouth snarled. "Whadda you know about it?"

"Take it easy," drawled the Saint softly. "I'm just the innocent bystander and I'd like to avoid his traditional fate. I just happened to be sitting at the next table to you at lunch—remember?—And I couldn't help overhearing your conversation with the lovely Luella."

"That ——!" The sergeant used a one-syllable expletive and inventoried the dregs of his vocabulary for kindred honorifics reflecting variously on her character, morals, charms, and ancestry—which was, one inferred, dubious.

The bartender brought a drink. The Saint tasted it, and felt the moth wings of anticipation grow firmer. Like fingers on his spine.

"Then you didn't buy a house?" he asked mildly.

The soldier reached into one of his blouse pockets, his face still frozen, but the deadliness gone from his eyes. He produced a film holder of the type and size used in a Speed Graphic camera. He tossed it onto the bar.

"There's my house," he said viciously. "How do you like the color scheme? Isn't it swell, with all the pepper trees around it? And the closed back yard for the kid to play in, just like the doctor said. But what I like best is the view—Baldy, Mount Wilson, and Catalina on a clear day. That's my house, whoever you are, fourteen hundred bucks' worth, by God!"

The Saint's chiseled features developed set lines of their own. He picked up the film holder, turned it over in his hands.

"There's a negative in this, of course?"

"Sure. A picture of Luella. A keepsake!"

"In—er—underthings?"

"Underthings, hell. In practically nothing."

"And you?"

The boy blushed, the rich red visibly flooding up his neck and ears in the low-lit bar, and the Saint saw that he really was quite young.

"The badger game," Simon remarked.

"I guess so." The sergeant wrung the miserable words from deep inside him. "I knew it, the minute these two guys broke in. One of 'em was a 'private detective'—they said—with a camera. Sure—I was a dope. But she's a sexy, good-looking babe, and I'm human." He laughed briefly and bitterly. "So I was a sucker, and I figured she saw a big healthy guy and a chance to make beautiful music. A chance to make beautiful money, I would say. Well, she did."

He drained the rest of his drink and beckoned the bartender.

"So after she got your name, and address, and your wife's first name—" prompted the Saint.

"Well, then it was time to draw up a bill of sale. And she said, 'Excuse me, Bill, I have something to do in the bedroom for a minute.' Well, you heard her voice. You know what she can promise you, just talking about the weather."

The Saint felt a familiar anger growing within him. He saw the picture clearly—a not very complicated picture: the soldier, his pockets crammed with accumulated pay, home to his wife and son from the wars. Probably the wife had come to the Coast to wait for him, moved in with Aunt Mabel pending his return. Probably she was named something like Lola May.

"What's your wife's name?" the Saint asked irrelevantly.

"Lola May. Why—"

"Nothing at all."

And so, "ruptured duck" conspicuous on his blouse, his six stripes heralding relative solvency, his candid gray eyes clean of suspicion, he was the ideal candidate for one of crook-dom's oldest and dirtiest rackets—with a new and up-to-date come-on.

"So then," said the Saint, "she came out of the bedroom in something that was next to nothing and in less time than it takes to tell it you were in a, shall we chastely say, compromising position."

The sergeant glared.

"It wasn't quite that way," he amended. "She launched herself at me like a runaway steam roller."

"I see. In any event, when the door opened—"

"They came in through the window. Off the fire escape."

"Um. Authentic touch, that. When the window opened to admit her—'husband' and the 'detective' with his little camera, the exploding flash bulb illumined a scene in which one and one added up to a very damning two."

"You ain't just whistling 'Dixie.'"

"And now, the Outraged Husband has the floor. For a long time, and I quote, he has suspected that this Abandoned Woman is up to just this sort of thing. Here, at long last, is pictorial evidence to convince the most skeptical judge. The fact that it involves you, Bill, is unfortunate, but—"

"That's just what he said." The sergeant's bitter voice took it up. "'I hate to mix you up in something like this, soldier, but it's already cost me more than I can afford to get the goods on her.'"

"Luella has withdrawn to the bedroom, weeping," supplied the Saint.

"She did a runout, all right. Well, by that time I knew I'd been had. It's been three years since I saw my wife and the little guy; I couldn't start off with something like this, could I? So the next move was up to me. I asked him how much it would take to keep the detectives going till he got some other evidence."

"Which amount," Simon observed, "by a strange coincidence, was exactly the sum Luella had been prepared to accept as a down payment on a house."

"It was a smooth act," agreed the veteran miserably.

"So you paid him the money, the 'detective' handed you an exposed negative, and—exit one sergeant."

"You seem to know an awful lot about these things," observed the soldier, a thin edge of his earlier truculence creeping back into his voice. "Just who the hell are you?"

"My name," said the Saint, "is Simon Templar."

"Templar!" The sergeant took a long look. "But you're not—you mean . . ."

Simon nodded.

"The Saint! The . . . the Robin Hood of Modern Crime!"

"As the headline writers say," Simon confessed wryly.

"Well—uh, glad to meet you." They shook hands, the sergeant rather bemused, it seemed. He gulped at his drink. "Where do you fit into this?" he blurted.

"That is what I'm wondering," said Simon Templar, and the banter was gone from his voice, the blue eyes tempered to damascene hardness. "But I know I belong somewhere." He emptied his glass thoughtfully and signaled for a refill. "I think you and I had better get serious about Operation Luella, Sergeant. Brief me on where she hangs out and how the pickup works."

The prime tactical problem was hardly a problem at all to a pirate of Simon Templar's experience. Nor was the role which he selected for the immediate performance. With one or two subtle changes to his appearance that could hardly be called make-up, and one or two props that were scarcely props at all, and a change of voice and bearing that was a matter of infinitesimal modulations, he could put on another personality as a man might put on a coat, and only an audience that knew he was acting would even appreciate the masterpieces that he created.

"This one shows the two boys in front of my summer place at Carmel," the Saint was saying late the next afternoon. "Oldest one's twelve. Little devil, but smart as a whip." He beamed with fatherly pride.

"The young one looks like you, Mr Taggart," said the lady known as Luella.

"Well, thanks, Miss, uh—"

"My friends call me Luella. And I'm sure you're a friend."

Without moving a muscle, the Saint conveyed the impression of bashfully digging a toe into the bar carpet.

"That's mighty nice of you, ma'am—Luella. It's a right pretty name. Sort of bell-like—or something."

Luella touched the snapshot with a long red-tipped finger. "Your summer place looks wonderful."

"Cost twenty thousand," the Saint said modestly, "but worth every cent. Wife's up there with the boys. And I'm here in Hollywood. Tendin' to some business, o' course, but—" His glance was a work of genius. It reminded you of a timid bather sticking a dainty toe in a pool of water before wading—not plunging—in. It reminded you of a nice boy playing hooky for the first time. It reminded you of a professor of Sanskrit about to consign a single quarter to a gaudy slot machine. "—but havin' a little fun, too, if we tell the truth."

Seated on a stool at the Beverly Wilshire bar, the Saint looked the part of a conservative businessman who could stick twenty grand into a summer place. His blue serge suit was of excellent cloth, but by a tailor who must have hated London. His high collar and tightly knotted dark tie placed him as a man who served on civic committees. And his hair, sleekly parted in the middle, added the final touch of authenticity to his characterization of Mr Samuel Taggart, Vice-President of the Stockmen's National Bank of Visalia, California.

And that was what his business card, freshly printed earlier that same day, said. The name Taggart appeared on the back of the snapshot, bought earlier from a photographer's shop.

"And are you having fun, Mr—uh—"

"Call me Sam, Luella," the Saint simpered. "Wife calls me Samuel most of the time, but I like Sam. Sorta friendly, I think."

"Are you having fun, Sam?"

"Well, I got a feelin' I'm about to, Luella. Say, could I buy you somethin' to drink? I been tellin' you all about myself, seems the least I could do. Say, bartender! Uh, give the young lady what she wants. Me, I'll have a lemonade." He cupped one hand alongside his mouth, whispered to the bartender, who was eyeing him stonily, "Put some gin in it." To Luella he said apologetically, "I like gin in 'em."

"Aren't you a one, though, Sam."

"Shucks," the Saint said, "man's got a right to have a little fun. Kind of hard for me, though, not knowin' these places people're always talkin' about in Hollywood. Don't know my way around very well yet."

He put a hundred-dollar bill on the bar, replaced the roll in his pants pocket, and looked moodily into his lemonade with gin.

Luella's manner became more animated. She clinked glasses. "Here's to an evening of fun, Sam. I'll tell you what, Sam. I have an engagement for the evening, but I can break it. I'll be your pilot."

"Well, say, that's mighty fine of you, Luella. But I don't like to bust up anything. Course a nice-lookin' lady like you must keep awful busy, and an old duffer like me couldn't expect you to—"

"Poo!" Luella said lightly. She laid a hand on the Saint's sleeve. "Excuse me while I make a phone call."

She went away to a phone booth, and though her conversation was unheard by the Saint, he felt that he could have written the dialogue.

From that point forward, events moved smoothly and orderly along their predestined path, and the gentleman known as Sam found himself in due course in the apartment of the lady known as Luella— "for a nightcap, Sam, dear."

The nightcap was forthcoming, and Luella was forthright. She sat beside the Saint on a divan, and there was no quibbling about maintaining a space between them in the interests of morality. They touched, shoulder and thigh, and she gave him a long slow glance from long dark eyes.

"It's been such fun, Sam." She put a hand on his and squeezed, ever so lightly.

Somehow the Saint managed a blush.

"It was sure swell of you, Luella. Gosh, do you know this town!"

Luella stood up, after squeezing his hand again.

"Why don't you be comfortable, Sam? Take off that hot old coat." She helped him out of his coat and vest, carried them toward her bedroom. "Excuse me while I get into something cool, Sam."

The Saint leaned back, a little smile flickering on his mouth. He adjusted the black sleeve bands on his pin-striped shirt, loosened his tie, sipped at his drink, and awaited the inevitable.

It came at that moment. Luella's muffled voice called, "Sam, dear, could you help me? My darned zipper is stuck."

The Saint got to his feet, raised Saintly eyes to Heaven, and entered the bedroom.

Luella stood with her dress up over her shoulders, revealing a body of such classic lines that he caught his breath. The body was clad in the scantiest of diaphanous scraps, and the Saint loosened his tie a little more before stepping forward to assist her in getting her head out of the dress. It was in this position, with the dress breaking free from her dark hair, the Saint holding it, obviously having taken it off, that the cameraman caught them.

The blinding flash bulb popped, the shutter clicked from the bedroom doorway, and the Saint whirled, looking as guilty as a little boy caught with his hand in the cooky jar.

Patricia Holm stood there.

"That'll do it, Smith," she said to a young man who carried a Speed Graphic.

She surveyed Simon with magnificent scorn.

The Saint was the picture of a man trying to disclaim any connection with the dress. He held it at arm's length, between thumb and forefinger, and regarded it with astonishment, as if to say, "Now where in the world did that come from?"

Luella was frozen to a tinted statue. She stared at Pat and the photographer with boiled and unbelieving eyes. This sort of thing, her expression said, couldn't happen. It was fully ten seconds before she thought to use her hands in the traditional manner of women caught without clothes.

"Now, dear," Simon began in conciliatory tones, "I can explain—"

"Explain!" Patricia spat the word. "You can explain to the judge, Samuel Taggart. I've been a long time catching you with the goods . . . you, you . . ." Patricia choked, and her voice was awash in a bucketful of tears. "Oh, how could you, Sam? The boys, and—" She turned, covered her face with her hands, and her shoulders began to shake.

The Saint surveyed the grouping of the dramatis personae, through Mr Samuel Taggart's eyeglasses, with an impresario's appreciation, noting that to anyone in the living room only he and the lightly clad Luella would be visible through the open door.

A second flash bulb's blinding glare knifed through his reflections.

"At last!" thundered Matthew Joyson, with the glibness of many past performances. "My lawyer will know how to use—"

Then his voice trailed away, and he stared at the other members of the tableau with the expression of a gaffed fish. Tod Kermein, with the camera, gulped audibly and offered a rather similar impersonation, concentrating most of it on Patricia's lens-bearing companion, and reminding the Saint of a goldfish which had just discovered itself in a mirror.

"And then there were six," Simon murmured. "Busiest bedroom scene I ever saw."

"What the hell—"

Mr Joyson tried again, and again stopped on a note almost of panic.

Luella did her best.

"Honest to God, Matt," she began. "I swear there's nothing—"

Matthew Joyson may have lacked many sterling qualities, but presence of mind was not one of them. As a matter of fact, he had a professional pride in his ability to ad-lib, which had stood him in good stead during his days on the road, when at certain matinees an overindulgence on the night before had dulled his recollection of the script. He realized now that something drastic had gone wrong, that by some incredible coincidence his big scene had been blown up by a rival team who were actually playing it straight, and that the one safe course was to drop the curtain as fast as possible and consider the other angles later.

He turned to Patricia.

"Madam," he said in his most magisterial style, "am I to understand that we are here on the same errand?"

"The brute!" Patricia choked. "The bru-hu-hute! And after all I've done for him. The best years of my life—"

Mr Joyson took command of the situation, so regally that only a captious critic would have noted the undertones of desperation in his behavior.

"Stand back, Kermein," he commanded. "We don't need any more detective work here." He snatched the dress from Simon's unresisting fingers. "By your leave, sir!" He strode over to the still petrified Luella. "May I trouble you to cover yourself?" he grated. "To think that my wife, my own wife . . ." His voice broke for a moment, but he recovered it bravely. He turned to Patricia again, adjusting his mien to something between an undertaker and a floorwalker, if anything can be imagined that would fit into such a narrow gap. "Madam, accept my heartfelt sympathy. I know too well what your feelings must be. I only wish you could have been spared the same betrayal. What a dingy ending to it all!"

"Cedar Rapids Repertory Theatre, 1911," commented the Saint, but he said it to himself, and outwardly maintained a properly hangdog visage.

Patricia regarded Mr Joyson with brimming blue eyes.

"You're so kind . . . But to think that we should have to meet like this!" She dabbed a handkerchief at her tear-stained face. "If only I could have spared you any connection with my tragedy—"

"What had to be, had to be," said Mr Joyson sagely, and edged hastily towards the door. "Don't you bother your pret—er, don't bother about a thing. Just leave all the details to me. I'll see my lawyer in the morning, and we'll discuss what steps to take, and you can get in touch with me at my home at—er—" He dug in his pockets. "I seem to have lost my cardcase. The address is 7522 South Hooper—East Los Angeles. No phone. Now you just contact me, say, tomorrow afternoon. I'll do anything I can to help. Come, Kermein."

He completed his exit with almost indecent haste, but was able to refrain from mopping his brow till he was outside. Tod Kermein fell in step with him on the street, and their steps turned automatically in the direction of the nearest bar.


Kermein, who knew his place, preserved a discreet but sympathetic silence until they had been served, when he permitted himself to say, "Jeez, what a lousy break."

"What a goddam stinking break!" Joyson exploded. "This pigeon was the vice-president of a bank, no less, and carrying a roll you could paper a house with, according to Luella. Whoever'd think his wife'd beat us to it?"

"I guess after all it must happen that way sometimes," Kermein said, awed with a great discovery. "You know, I never thought of that."

Matt Joyson scarcely heard him. The bracing draughts of Kentucky Nectar which he had absorbed were quieting his jangled nerves without impairing his mental processes. And something, something on the instinctive levels of his mind, now that the first blackout curtain of panic began to lift, was irking his consciousness with jagged little edges. He began to wish he had made a less precipitate withdrawal.

"It was too neat," he muttered foggily. "Too pat."

His eyes were murky with unformed suspicion.

Tod Kermein tried to console him.

"You're always seeing somebody under the bed, Matt."

"Once, there was," Joyson reminded him. "Remember that go with the college president in Dallas?"

Kermein grimaced.

From the juke box at one end of the room seeped the voice of a scat singer who longed for some Shoo Fly Pie. At one of the low tables a pretty girl, like the melody, did some mild rhythmic writhing. The bartender, a jovial gent in a toupee, set a fresh drink in front of an aging debutante at the far end of the bar.

"I can't nail it down," Joyson said. "Something smells, and I don't know what it is."

"Because the guy's wife gets there the same time we do? You heard her. She's been followin' the old jerk a long time, she nabs him. at exactly the right minute, which is just our time, too. Bad luck, that's all. One chance in a million."

"One thing's sure." Joyson struck the bar a light blow with a clenched fist. "Somewhere in town right now there's a negative with Luella on it. It's gonna be used by that dame in her divorce action. If one of our old suckers sees it, and we try to go back to him for more—"

He left the sentence unfinished.

"If that blonde really is after a divorce," he enunciated softly. "If she's his wife . . ." He swung off the bar stool. "We're going back to the apartment. I want to talk to Lu about this guy."


They walked along the echoing sidewalk toward the apartment house. Fifty yards from it, Kermein grabbed his companion's arm. With his free hand he pointed.

In the lee of a potted shrub beside the entrance, a man lurked. A camera case was slung over his shoulder, and even in the dark the two men could recognize the photographer who had accompanied Patricia. He was not looking in their direction at the moment, but an elephant could not have lurked more obviously.

Like a sister act, Joyson and Kermein pivoted and walked briskly back to the bar they had just left. There was no more uncertainty in Joyson's mind as they stepped inside.

"But—but what the hell's he doin' there?" mumbled Kermein. "The job was finished when he got his picture. You think the old goat's got another dame in the place?"

"Shut up!" Joyson's tone silenced him. "I don't know and I don't care. It smells. Gimme a nickel."

He went to the phone booth. When Luella's throaty voice answered, he wasted no words.

"Did you get rid of everyone?"

"Yes, Matt. I did the best I could. But I want to know—"

"So do I. But I don't want to wait to find out. Something's screwy. That photographer the dame had with her is still hanging around the front of the building."

"What's the matter? Did—"

"Talk later. All I know is there's going to be some kind of beef. So we're blowing. Put the pictures and the cash in a bag and come down the fire escape. The car's in the alley. We'll meet you there."

"I've got clothes to pack."

"I'm not taking any raps for your wardrobe. I've got a hunch about this. You can get more clothes in San Francisco, but you can't in Tehachapi. We'll give you ten minutes."

Luella Joyson heard the click as he hung up, and wasted some good expletives on an unresponsive microphone.

Then, with a shrug of her comely shoulders, she went to a closet in the bedroom and dragged out a large suitcase and opened it. It contained several bulky envelopes of uniform size, but even after the addition of a dozen thick stacks of medium-denomination currency which she retrieved from various hiding places in the apartment, there was still room for a small armful of her most expensive clothes.

She put on a fur coat, snapped the bag shut, picked it up, and paused for a last regretful look around the inviting room. Then she stepped through the open window onto the fire escape.

She dropped lightly from the bottom of the last ladder to the alley pavement, almost beside a shiny low-slung sedan. Opening the door, she shoved the bag in and looked up and down the gloomy canyon between tall apartment buildings like the one she had left.

Two figures debouched into the alley from the street and came toward her, silhouetted against the opening, and she recognized Joyson and Kermein. She started to climb into the car—and stopped, as the sound of voices reached her.

At the end of the alley, where two shapes had been visible a second ago, there were now four. And then she heard a voice she recognized.

"I want you boys to meet a friend of mine," said the grim tones of Sergeant Bill Harvey, followed on the instant by the sound of knuckles and jaws in violent collision. The group of shadows leaped into frenetic motion and gave off scrambled sound effects of flesh smacking flesh, scuffling feet, smothered grunts, and gasps of pain.

Luella snatched off a high-heeled shoe and hobbled swiftly toward the commotion, but as she ran, it resolved itself into two recumbent shapes, with two more moving swiftly toward the street. They were gone by the time Luella reached the scene.

She had a sickening suspicion of the identity of the fallen two even before she bent over them, but as she stooped, a fresh horrifying sound jerked her bolt upright again. The sound was the starting of a car's engine.

Uttering a small scream, Luella sprang towards the long black sedan.

The taillight seemed to wink mockingly at her as it dwindled toward the far end of the alley and vanished into the street.

The photographer called Smith, whose obviously new civilian clothes would normally have branded him at once to a less rattled Matthew Joyson, leered at the 4x5 print and chuckled.

"Sarge, do you look silly," he remarked.

"Go to hell, Corporal," said Sergeant Harvey genially. He tore the picture and the negative into small pieces and scattered them out of the car window.

"I didn't think they'd ever part with a negative," said the Saint. "You'd have felt fine in a few months when Brother Joyson dropped in and told you how sorry he was he hadn't been able to get any more evidence with your dough, and he was going to have to cite you as correspondent after all—unless, of course, you wanted to finance some more detectives."

"All the pictures have names and address on them," confirmed Patricia, who was going through the suitcase in the back of the car while they drove.

"So a lot of people will have a pleasant surprise when they get 'em back. That's why it had to be played my way, so the gang'd be sure to pack everything up and drop it in our laps. Sometimes I think a great psychologist was lost in me."

Simon Templar eased the sedan around a corner and parked it behind his own convertible.

"A very satisfactory evening," he remarked. "What else have you got in that suitcase besides clothes, Pat?"

She handed him one of the bundles of greenbacks, and the Saint grinned.

"Fourteen hundred bucks, wasn't it, Bill?" He flipped off the bills. "And the rest I suppose we'll have to divvy up and send back to the original donors—less, of course, our fee for collection."

Bill Harvey said, "I can't tell you how swell you've been, sir. If it hadn't been for you—"

"Forget it," said the Saint. "I can't tell you how much fun it was."

Patricia Holm harked back to that, broodingly, some minutes later when they were driving away in their own car.

"I suppose you did have fun," she said thoughtfully. "Maybe it's a good thing you knew I was waiting to break into that bedroom."

Simon chuckled.

"Darling, I'm sure everything would have continued on a high spiritual plane."

"Which reminds me somehow," she said, "did you reserve that Pullman?"

"We aren't going to need it. You don't think for a moment that Luella and Co are going to stop traveling now, do you? We are probably the only people in Los Angeles who know where there's an apartment vacant tonight—and I've still got Luella's keys from their car," said the Saint.

EMILY

Simon Templar propped one well-shod foot on the tarnished brass rail of the Bonanza City Hotel bar, and idly speculated on the assortment of footgear which had probably graced this brazen cylinder in its time—prospectors' alkali-caked boots, miners' hobnails, scouts' buckskins, cowhands' high heels . . . and now his own dully gleaming cordovan, resting there for a long cool one to break the baking monotony of the miles of steaming asphalt which had San Francisco as their goal.

But it was quite certain that none of the boots which in diverse decades had parked themselves on that time-mellowed prop had ever carried a more picturesque outlaw, even though there was no skull and crossbones on his softly battered hat, and no pearl-handled six-shooters clung to his thighs. For Simon Templar had made a new business out of buccaneering, and hardly one of the lawbreakers and law-enforcers who knew him better under his sobriquet of the Saint could have given a valid reason why the source of so much trouble should ever have acquired such a name. The Saint himself would have found that just as hard to answer: in his own estimation he was almost as good as his name, and he would have maintained at the stake that most of the things that happened to him were not of his inviting. The one remarkable thing was how regular they conspired to invite him.

Which was what started to happen again at that precise moment, although as it began he was still far from realizing where it might go.

He was examining the mirrored reflections of sundry characters draped along the mahogany rim (which still boasted the autograph of a Prince of Wales under a screwed-down glass plate) and wondering if any of them inhabited the paintless houses outside, when he felt a touch on his arm.

"Would it be worth a drink t'see the Marvel of the Age, stranger?"

An anticipatory hush seemed to settle gradually on the small dark room. Simon could see in the mirror that each of the characters who decorated the perimeter of the horseshoe stiffened a little as the reedy voice broke the quiet. Brown hands tensed a little around their glasses, and a covert wink was exchanged between the unmistakable cognoscenti.

The Saint turned to look down into a saddle-tanned seamed face studded with mild blue eyes and topped by this gray hair. The blue jeans were faded, so was the khaki shirt, and the red necktie ran through a carven bone clasp. The look in the blue eyes said that their owner expected an order to get the hell from underfoot—or at best the polite brush-off which was already on Simon Templar's lips.

And then, almost as the words were forming, the mind's eye of the Saint visualized a long succession of such brush-offs and he reflected on how small a price was the cost of a drink in return for gratitude in the mild eyes of a lonely old character.

"I don't know the going rate on marvels in these degenerate times," said the Saint gently, "but one drink sounds fair enough."

"Double?" spoke the old-timer hopefully.

The bartender halted the bottle in mid-flight and again the Saint felt a tensing among the habitués along the brass rail.

"Double," Simon agreed, and the bartender relaxed as if a great decision had been reached, and finished pouring the drink.

The little man lifted a battered canvas grip and placed it tenderly on the bar. He reached for the drink and lifted it toward his lips. Then he set the drink back on the bar and drew himself up to a dignified five feet five.

"Beggin' your parding, mister—James Aloysius McDill, an' your servant."

"Simon Templar, and yours, sir," the Saint said gravely.

He lifted his own drink and they clinked glasses in solemn ritual, after which James Aloysius McDill demonstrated just how quickly a double bourbon can slide down a human throat. Then he opened his shabby bag, and took out an oblong box of lovingly polished wood.

It was very much like a small table-model radio. A pair of broad-faced dials on its upper surface sported impressive indicator needles. There was a stirrup handle at either end of the box and a sort of sliding scale on top.

"Nice-lookin' job, ain't she?" the little man appealed to the Saint.

"Mighty pretty," responded the Saint, gazing at it as intelligently as he would have surveyed a cyclotron.

The little man beamed. He spoke diffidently to the bartender.

"Got a silver dollar, Frank?"

The bartender obliged, with the air of one who has done this before, and the other customers duplicated his ennui. Once the Saint succumbed to the pitch for a double rye, the show was pretty well routined.

J. Aloysius McDill tossed the silver dollar across the room. It landed in the sawdust on the floor with a dull thump.

"Watch," he said.

He turned a switch, made some adjustments, and grasped the handles on the varnished box, which thereupon emitted a low hymenopterous humming, and advanced upon the dollar like a hunter stalking skittish game. As he neared the coin, the humming began to keen up the scale. He stood still, and the sound held steady; again toward the dollar and the wail of the box slid up and up until, held directly above the coin, it gave forth the whine of a band saw eating into a pine knot.

The Saint walked over and inspected the setup. He picked up the dollar and tossed it back to the bartender.

"Let's see what it does about this change in my pocket," he said, slapping his trouser leg.

Mr McDill moved the device over the indicated area, but the humming remained at a low murmur. He ceased his efforts and grinned.

"You ain't got any change in your pocket, mister."

Grinning in turn, the Saint pulled out the pocket. It was empty.

"Can't fool the Doodlebug," said McDill complacently. "See"—he held the box for the Saint to look at—"it works the same way for any other kind o' metal."

The Saint duly noted the markings etched along the sliding scale on top. He moved the indicator to "Gold," and the Doodlebug, which had been humming like a happy bee, suddenly whined like an angry mosquito. The Saint jerked back his left wrist with the gold watch on it, and the machine dropped again to a gentle hum. McDill set it on the bar, and it fell completely silent.

"Ain't she a beauty?" the little man demanded.

"Lovely," Simon agreed. "Just what you need any time you drop a silver dollar."

"She's good for more than that," said McDill. "She'll find the stuff they make dollars out of. That's why she's so beautiful. Takes the guesswork out of prospectin'."

"Aw, yes," Simon said. "Have you tested her in the field yet, Mr McDill?"

A rattle of laughter cackled across the barroom. It was as though a whiplash had been laid across the face of the little man; he flinched.

"Ask him," drawled one of the audience, "why his dingus ain't located no claims yet, if it's so good."

McDill faced the speaker, his chin high.

"Jest ain't happened to look in the right places, that's all," he said stoutly, but there was a quaver in his voice. He turned to Simon. "You've seen her, mister. You've seen what she can do. All I need's a grubstake and a little equipment. If you was, maybe, interested in minin', we c'd be pardners."

The Saint saw the general merriment waxing along the bar again, and had one of his ready quixotic impulses.

"Well, Mr McDill," he said in a loud clear voice, "mining's a little out of my own line, but I have a friend I might be able to interest. I'm certainly impressed by your demonstration. Here's my San Francisco address." He scribbled on a card and handed it to James Aloysius McDill, then he dug into another pocket. "And here's fifty dollars for a week's option on your gadget."

He was aware of glasses being set down all along the bar, of incredulous eyes appraising his well-cut gabardines and evaluating, but it was mostly McDill's reaction that he cared about.

The blue eyes in the seamed old face flamed with happiness. They could not resist a single triumphant glance at the hangers-on, then the little man's hand stuck straight out.

"Put 'er there, Mr Templar," he said, with a ring in his voice. "I'll be right here, any time your pardner wants me. Bonanza City Hotel."

Simon shook the thin callused hand, and beckoned the bartender. No longer bored, a sycophant stepped up with alacrity.

"Yes, sir!"

"The same, for Mr McDill and myself," ordered the Saint. "Double," he added.

He drove away from the Bonanza City Hotel through the light bright California sunshine bearing within him a warmth entirely unconnected with alcoholic potations, and pondering on the varied expressions of man's unending search for riches. Perhaps that was what had moved him to dawdle on back roads and in odd corners of the old gold-rush country for a full three days on his way to San Francisco. When the mood was on him, the Saint enjoyed the exploration of seemingly useless, if fascinating, trivia—in this instance, the dreaming gold camps and ghost towns of the forty-niners.

It was a penchant which sometimes paid surprising dividends, so that the Saint had come to have an almost superstitious faith in his infallible destiny, but in this case the connection came even faster and more unexpectedly than usual.

He had been installed in rooms in the Fairmont, high on Nob Hill, for the duration of a sleep and a breakfast, when his telephone asserted itself, for the first time since his arrival.

"I've called every day since I got your card," said Larry Phelan, "and I was pretty sure you'd show up within the year. What trouble did you come here to stir up?"

"None at all," said the Saint virtuously. "I am on a vacation, and I have taken a vow to right no wrong, rescue no young ladies in distress, and acquire no money by fair means or foul, until further notice."

"That's fine," said Phelan. "There's nothing in your vow about rescuing old ladies in distress, is there?"

"Not so fast," said the Saint. "Whose old lady is in distress?"

"My old lady, if you must know."

"Your mother?"

"None other."

"This," said the Saint, "is beginning to sound like a Gilbert and Sullivan duet. You can buy me lunch and tell me all about it."

Larry Phelan was a little shorter than the Coit Tower and much more interesting to know. He had the face of a college sophomore and the mind of the top-drawer mining engineer that he was.

"My mother," he explained gloomily, over *écrevisses au vin blanc*, "is in the situation of any elderly lady with an excess of both time and money. Especially money."

"A rather pleasant situation," commented the Saint, chewing. "Is there such a thing as too much money?"

"Some people seem to think so," said Phelan. "Did you ever hear of a guy called Melville Rochborne?"

Simon shook his head.

"It sounds like the sort of phony name that I wouldn't buy any gold mines from."

"He sold Mother a gold mine," Phelan said.

"Any gold in it?"

"I defy anyone to find any gold in this particular mine," said Phelan sadly. "It's the old Lucky Nugget. Opened up with a big whoop-de-do in 1906, beautiful vein of quartz, eighteen dollars to the ton; closed in 1907—no more quartz. No one's made a nickel on it since—even the tailings are worked out. The stock, which is what Mother bought, wouldn't even serve for wrapping fish."

"There are laws," suggested the Saint, "which take care of folks who misrepresent stocks and bonds to other people."

"That's the trouble," said Phelan. "This Rochborne is an extremely smart operator. There's nothing on record—including Mother's own testimony—to prove he ever claimed there was any gold in the mine."

"Didn't she ask you about it?"

"What would you think? After all," said Phelan bitterly, "I have only two degrees in engineering and one in mining. Why should anyone, even my own dear mother, consult me on such a topic? Obviously, a crystal ball and a turban put my credentials in the shade. I'll admit," he added, in less vehement tones, "I've been up to my ears in some very hush-hush stuff lately—uranium sources, if you must know. Top secret."

"Keep your uranium," said the Saint. "I don't like the things they do with it. What is this stuff about crystal balls?"

"My blessed mother," Phelan said reverently, "has developed an interest in the Occult. In this specific case, a soothsayer from the Mystic East."

"Tea leaves, eh?" said the Saint. "Lucky numbers and cards and so forth?"

"And signs of the zodiac," supplemented Phelan. "A swami, no less. The Swami Yogadevi."

"Sounds like a new cocktail. Where does he come in?"

"The swami," said Phelan sourly, "is the guy who advised Mom to buy the wretched stock. She's sort of gotten into a habit of consulting him, I'm afraid. I suppose he makes a couple of passes at his crystal and evokes a genie, or something. Seems to lay Mother and several dozen other respectable old-ladies-about-town in the aisles, anyway."

Simon cleaned up his plate and lighted a cigarette.

"One gathers, Larry, that Mama has been hornswoggled by a couple of pretty smooth operators. I almost think it's a new combination."

"Combination?"

"Of course. It must be. Don't you see how it works? Your swami spots the suckers who have plenty of moola, and gets their confidence with his mumbo-jumbo. Which isn't illegal if he doesn't claim to predict futures. Your Mr Rochborne peddles stocks and makes no claim for them. You can't prosecute a man for that. Separately, they mightn't get too far. Working together, they're terrific . . . How much," asked the Saint gently, "did your mother pay for the Lucky Nugget mine?"

"Forty-five thousand smackers," Phelan admitted glumly.

The Saint whistled. He proceeded to order coffee and then sank into a lethargy which might or might not have denoted deep thought.

"What are you looking stupid about?" inquired Larry Phelan after five minutes.

"About the vacation I was going to have until you tripped into my life," said Simon wryly. "However," he added thoughtfully, "if Comrade Rochborne has forty-five G's of Mama's, he might have several of someone else's Gs, too. Do you know anything else about him?"

"He has an address—an insurance office—where he picks up his mail. The people there know nothing about him. On a hunch I checked the city business-license records. It seems he was licensed as an assayer from 1930 to 1939. That fits into your picture."

"I'll keep thinking about it," said the Saint.

He did exactly that, although for two days there was nothing to show for his thinking. But to the Saint a hiatus like that meant nothing. He knew better than anyone that those coups of his which seemed most spontaneous and effortless were usually the ones into which the hardest work had gone; that the machinery of his best buccaneering raids was labored and polished as devotedly as any master playwright's plot structure. Even then there had to be an initial spark of inspiration to start the wheels turning, and in this instance the requisite spark eluded him tantalizingly for a full forty-eight hours.

When it came, it was nothing that he had even vaguely expected. It took the form of a chunky oblong package, crudely wrapped, which a bellboy delivered to his room. Simon scanned the label and found a postmark, and had a rather saddening premonition.

There was a note enclosed, printed in sprawling capitals on a sheet of blue-lined note paper.

*Dere Mr. Templar,*

*Ole Jimmy Mc Dill Had One To Meny Double Wiskeys An
Cash In His Chips Las Nite His Last Rekest Was Send You
Ths Here Dingus Account Of You Are A Reel Good Feller
An He Like You A Lot Same Is Inclose.*

*Yrs Truly
The Boys
Bonanza City*

The Saint lifted the glass in his right hand.

"Jimmy McDill," he said softly, "may there be double bourbons and unlimited credit wherever you are."

He was happily playing with the contraption when Larry Phelan arrived to pick him up for dinner that night, and the engineer gazed at him in somewhat condescending puzzlement.

"What the hell are you doing with a Doodlebug, Saint?" he demanded, and Simon was hardly less surprised.

"How the hell did you know what it was?"

"The lunatic fringes of the business were stiff with these things during the Depression. I've seen 'em in all sizes and shapes. Trouble is, none of 'em are worth anything."

"What do you mean, not worth anything?" Simon objected. "I'll bet I can pick up a silver dollar at ten feet with this gadget."

"I'll bet you can too," Phelan said. "I've seen it done, and by queerer-looking numbers than this one. I've seen 'em with loop aerials, knee action, and floating power."

Simon produced a silver cartwheel and threw it on the carpet. Grasping the stirrup handles, he lifted the box, and the same humming sound he had heard in the Bonanza City bar filled the room.

"Listen to the hum," he said.

"They all hum," said Larry Phelan.

Simon made sure the scale pointer indicated "Silver," and advanced upon the dollar. Just as it had done for James Aloysius McDill, the humming keened up the scale until, as the Saint stood over the dollar, a malignant whining came from between his hands. He turned to Phelan triumphantly.

"This one works," he said.

"Sure," rejoined Phelan. "Now let's see how well it works."

He picked up a San Francisco telephone directory and the classified directory and piled them on top of the dollar, and the humming stopped abruptly.

"They're all the same," Phelan said sympathetically. "It seems to be possible to bounce some kind of oscillation off different metals, and make it selective according to their atomic structure, but the beam hardly has any penetration. Your lode would have to be practically on the surface, where you could see it anyhow, before a thing like this would detect it at all. I hope you didn't pay much for it."

"Only fifty bucks and a couple of drinks, and it was worth that," said the Saint, and the thought deepened in his blue eyes. "In fact, I think this is just what we needed to square accounts with Brother Rochborne and your swami."

The Swami Yogadevi had never seen a Doodlebug, but he had his own effective methods of ascertaining the presence of precious metals. His techniques depended for their success upon certain paraphernalia unknown to electronics, such as a large spherical chunk of genuine optical glass; celestial charts populated by crabs, bulls, goats, virgins, and other mythological creatures; and many yards of expensive drapery embroidered with esoteric symbols, the whole enshrined in a gloomy and expensive apartment on Russian Hill.

There was nothing about the place to suggest that the Swami Yogadevi had once been Reuben Innowitz, known to the carnival circuit as Ah Pasha, the Mighty Mentalist. Mr Innowitz's wants had been simple in those days, expressed mainly in terms of tall bottles and tall blondes, and they were much the same now, under his plush exterior. There were times, the Swami Yogadevi told himself, when he wished he hadn't met Melville Rochborne, profitable though the partnership had turned out to be. For instance, there was this Professor Tattersall business.

"How should I know who's Professor Simeon Tattersall?" he asked with asperity.

Mr Rochborne eyed the mystic with some distaste.

"I don't expect you to know anything," he said coldly. "All I want you to do is read it—if you can."

The seer pushed his turban back on his forehead and picked up the newspaper clipping again. It was from the front page of the final afternoon edition of a San Francisco daily.

*CLEMENTINE VALLEY, CALIF, [by a staff correspondent]—*

*There's a lot of gold still lying around the long-abandoned Lucky Nugget mine near here if someone will just come along with the right kind of divining rod, water witch, or a sensitive nose.*

*Professor Simeon Tattersall not only says that the gold is there, but asserts freely that he has the gadget that will find it. Said gadget, his own invention, he modestly styles the Tattersall Magnetic Prospector, and he plans to demonstrate its worth at the Lucky Nugget Thursday morning at 10:30 P.S.T.—*

"Say!" bleated the soothsayer. "Ain't this Lucky Nugget mine the same one you sold that old Phelan dame?"

"It is," said Mr Rochborne concisely. "What I want to know now, Rube, is who this Tattersall is and why he picks the Lucky Nugget to demonstrate his screwball gadget, just three weeks after we made a deal with it."

"It says here he thinks there's gold in it," said the swami brightly.

"Baloney!" said Mr Rochborne. "There isn't a nickel's worth of gold in that mine and hasn't been since 1907. There's something about this Tattersall that smells."

"He sounds mighty suspicious to me," agreed the oracle sagely.

Mr Rochborne favored him with a look of contempt and got to his feet. He was a large man with hulking shoulders and a tanned kindly face, of the type which inspires instant trust in dogs, children, and old ladies.

"One thing I'd bet on—there's no such person as Professor Simeon Tattersall. There never was a name like that. There couldn't be."

"What're you going to do about it, Mel?" asked the sage.

"I don't know," said Mr Rochborne darkly. "Maybe nothing. Maybe something. But one thing I do know, I'm going to be there when this 'Professor'"—he put quotation marks around the title—"holds his 'demonstration' tomorrow morning. It's probably a lot of horseshoes, but we can't afford to take any chances."


Simon Templar might have hoped for a more impressive turnout in response to his carefully planted publicity, but he could also have been guilty of discounting Larry Phelan's estimate of the skepticism of local wiseacres in the matter of Doodlebugs. The Lucky Nugget mine site on Thursday morning was fairly uncrowded by seven male and two female citizens of the nearby town of Clementine Valley, all more or less the worse for wear; four small boys; three cynical reporters, two dogs, and a passing hobo attracted by the crowd. But to Simon Templar the most important spectator was a large well-built man, conspicuous in city clothes, with a kindly face, to whom the dogs and small boys aforesaid were immediately attracted, and whose eyes missed no detail of the proceedings in the intervals of ministering to posterity and its pets.

The Saint had arrayed himself for the occasion in what seemed a likely professorial costume of Norfolk jacket, pith helmet, and riding boots, with the addition of a gray goatee which sat rather strangely on his youthful brown face.

He eyed the gathering individually and collectively with an equal interest as he stepped from Clementine Valley's only taxicab, tenderly bearing the wooden box, replete with knobs and dials, which was obviously the one and only Tattersall Magnetic Prospector.

"Good morning, gentlemen," he said.

"Hey, Prof," queried a high thin voice from the group, "will she bring in London?"

This sally elicited a wave of home-town laughter, to which Simon professorially paid no heed. He reconnoitred situation and terrain with the bold eye and flaring nostril of an intrepid conquistador.

When one spoke of the Lucky Nugget mine, one meant nine hundred and twenty-eight feet of partially caved-in tunnel sunk into the bowels of a red-dirt pine-freckled hill. The tunnel entrance was half blocked by fallen dirt and broken timbers. From it emerged two streaks of rust which had once been rails for ore cars to run on, and which descended a gentle slope to the remains of a stamp mill.

Professor Simeon Tattersall sapiently eyed the tunnel mouth, grasped his device, and took a step toward the opening. "Mind if I look at your gadget, Professor?" said a genial voice.

Simon looked around, and found the man in the city clothes standing at his elbow.

"And who are you, sir?" he inquired frostily.

"Just an interested observer, Professor," was the response, accompanied by a smile that crinkled the corners of the speaker's eyes.

"Well, sir," said the Saint, in his most precise pedantic voice, "in the first place, this is not a 'gadget'; it is a highly involved and intricate extrapository reactodyne, operating according to an entirely new principle of electronics. Later, perhaps, after the demonstration is concluded, you may—"

"Not afraid I might find something phony, are you?" The big man stepped very close. "And haven't I seen your picture somewhere before?"

Professor Simeon Tattersall lowered his eyes for a single fleeting instant, then raised their candid blue gaze to the stranger's.

"You may have read about my work in mineral detection—"

"That's what it said in the paper," assented the large man jovially. "I must have been thinking about someone else. The name's on the tip of my tongue—but you wouldn't know about that." He beamed. "Anyway, Prof—I've been in the mining game a long time. Know all the dodges. Thought some of them up myself. I'll be watching your demonstration with great interest."

He chuckled tranquilly and rejoined the motley gallery.

There followed what radio commentators call an "expectant hush."

Simon picked up his instrument, with barely visible nervousness, and started up the slope from the mill to the small mountain of "muck" fanning out below the old mine entrance. He skirted around its base, his audience following, and approached the steep hillside itself.

Suddenly he grasped the handles on the box again and, to the obbligato of the resultant humming, began moving along the base of the hill, moving the device to and fro as he went. The humming continued in the same even key. The trailing onlookers listened breathlessly—or perhaps their concentrated breathing merely gave that impression.

Ahead of the exploration lay a large slide of loose dirt brought down by recent rains. He neared it, and all at once the box's tone slid up an octave. The Saint stopped; he moved the box to the right, away from the hill, and the tone dropped; he swung it toward the slide, and it climbed infinitesimally; he moved toward the slide, and the tone mounted until at the base of the fresh clods it was a banshee wail.

Simon Templar put down the box. In the ensuing sinusoidal silence, he jointed a small collapsible spade and poked tentatively in the dirt.

Suddenly he dived down with one hand, and came up with it held high, and between his thumb and forefinger glittered a tiny pea-sized grain of yellow.

"The Tattersall Prospector never makes a mistake," he began in his best classroom manner. "I hold in my hand a small nugget of gold. Obviously, somewhere on the hillside above, we will find the source of this nugget. I predict—"

His words were lost in a yell as the small crowd, like one man, started up the steep bank toward the source of the slide. As Simon turned to stare at them, he found the big city observer at his elbow.

"Not good." The large man shook his head. "If I were you, Professor, I'd get the hell out of here before those boys up there find out that you salted this slide." He shook his head again. "I just remembered where I saw your face—and I expected something better from the Saint," he said. "Listen—you may have been a hot shot in your own league, but you didn't really expect to take Melville Rochborne into camp, did you?"

"It was always worth trying," said the Saint sheepishly. He poked his spade into the slide and turned over the loose earth.

"All right, Mel," he said. "You win this time. Have yourself a shoeshine on the house."

And with a rather childish gesture he spilled a shovelful of dirt deliberately over Mr Rochborne's shining pointed toes before he threw down the spade and turned away.

Mr Rochborne's geniality blacked out for a moment, and then he bent to dust off his shoes.

Suddenly he seemed to stiffen. He bent down and picked up a fragment of powdery pale yellow stuff, and crumbled it in his fingers.

A strange look came into his face, and he straightened up quickly, but the Saint was already surrounded by the bored but dutiful news hawks. Mr Rochborne recklessly scuffed his beautifully polished shoes more extensively into the loose earth, bent down to probe it deeper with his manicured fingers . . .

A mere few hours later, which seemed to him like a few years, he was clutching his hat to his bosom and trying to hold his temperature down to an engaging glow while Mrs Lawrence Phelan, Sr, gushed, "Why, Mr Rochborne! What a pleasant surprise!"

He still felt a little out of breath, but he tried to conceal it.

"As a matter of fact, Mrs Phelan," he admitted, with the air of a schoolboy caught in the jam closet, "I'm here on business. I hate to impose on you, but . . ."

"Go on, Mr Rochborne," she fluted. "Do go on. Business is business, isn't it?"

"I might as well come right out with it," Rochborne said wearily. "It's about that Lucky Nugget stock you bought, Mrs Phelan. I—well, it turns out it was misrepresented to me. I'm not at all sure it's a good investment."

"Oh, dear!" Mrs Phelan sat down suddenly. "Oh, dear! But . . . my . . . my forty-five thou—"

"Now, Mrs Phelan, don't excite yourself. If I weren't prepared to—"

"Telephone, Mrs Phelan." A maid stood in the doorway.

"Excuse me," said Mrs Phelan. "Oh, dear!"

"Mrs Phelan," said a deep mellifluous voice on the wire, "this is Swami Yogadevi."

"Oh . . . oh, Swami!" The old lady sighed with relief. "Oh, I am so glad to hear from you!"

"Dear Mrs Phelan, you are in trouble. I know. I could feel the disturbance in your aura. That was why I called."

"Oh, Swami! If you only knew . . . I—it's my mining stock, Swami. The stock you said I should buy, remember? And now—"

"He wants to buy it back from you. Yes."

"He . . . does . . .? Oh, then it's all right . . ."

"Sell, Mrs Phelan. But for a profit, of course."

"But how much should I—"

"Not a penny less than seventy thousand, Mrs Phelan. No, not a penny less. Peace be with you. Your star is in the ascendant. You will not say that I have talked to you, naturally. Good-bye."

When Mr Melville Rochborne heard the price, he barely escaped being the first recorded case of human spontaneous combustion.

"But, Mrs Phelan . . . I've just told you. The stock is no—well, it's been misrepresented. It's not really worth the price you paid me. I thought if I gave you your money back . . ."

"The stars," said Mrs Phelan raptly, "control my business dealings. I am asking seventy thousand for the stock."

"Oh, sure, the stars." Mr Rochborne thought rapidly. "May I use your telephone?"

He dialed a certain unlisted number for nearly five minutes, with the same negative results that had rewarded him even before he called at Mrs Phelan's house. At the end of that time he returned, slightly frantic and flushed of face.

"Mrs Phelan," he said, "we can discuss this, I know. Suppose we say fifty-five thousand."

"Seventy, Mr Rochborne," said Mrs Phelan.

"Sixty-two fifty," cozened Rochborne, in pleading tones.

"Seventy," repeated the implacable old lady.

Mr Rochborne thought fleetingly of the mayhem he was going to perform upon the luckless frame of Reuben Innowitz when he caught him.

"Very well," he groaned. "I'll write you a check."

"My swami told me all deals should be in cash," said Mrs Phelan brightly. "I'll get the stock and go with you to the bank."

An hour later, minus practically his entire bank roll but grimly triumphant, with the stock of the Lucky Nugget mine in his pocket, Mr Melville Rochborne met Mr Reuben Innowitz on the doorstep of the apartment house on Russian Hill, and finally achieved a much-needed self-expression.

"You stupid worthless jerk!" he exploded. "What's the idea of being out all day—and on a day like this? You just cost us twenty-five grand!"

"Listen," shrilled the prophet, "who's calling who a jerk! What did you do about that mine?"

"I got it back, of course," Rochborne told him short-windedly. "Even though the old bag took me for twenty-five G's more than she put into it—just because you weren't around to cool her down. But I didn't dare take a chance on waiting. There were some old-time prospectors around, and if any of them recognized the carnotite—"

"The what?" Innowitz said.

"Carnotite—that's what uranium comes from. The Lucky Nugget is full of it. You know what that's worth today. If any of those miners spotted it and the story was in the papers tomorrow morning, you couldn't buy that stock for a million dollars . . . It was the Saint, of course," Mr Rochborne explained, becoming even more incoherent, "and he was trying to put over the most amateurish job of mine-salting I ever saw, but when he reads about this—"

The swami was staring at him in a most unspiritual way.

"Just a minute, Mel," he said. "Are you drunk, or what? First you send me a wire and tell me to meet you at the airport. I watch all the planes come in until my ears are buzzing. Then you send me another wire there about some new buyer for the Lucky Nugget, and tell me to phone the Phelan dame and tell her to hold out for seventy grand—"

A horrible presentiment crawled over Mr Rochborne.

"What are you talking about?" he asked weakly. "I never sent you—"

"I've got 'em right here in my pocket." His colleague's voice was harsh, edged with suspicion.

"Ohmigod," breathed Mr Melville Rochborne. "He couldn't have salted it twice . . . he couldn't have . . ."

It was Simon Templar's perpetual regret that he was seldom able to overhear these conversations. But perhaps that would have made his life too perfect to be borne.

# DAWN

# INTRODUCTION

I suppose no feat of cerebration exercises an imaginative person so much as the deathbed speech that he or she would make if he or she (and this ghastly grammar has got to stop somewhere) knew for sure that it was their (oh, goody!) positively final utterance, the crystallization of a life by which posterity would remember it, whatever else it might have lived.

"It is a far, far better thing . . ."

"Kiss me, Hardy . . ."

Oh, great!

You know what you'll probably say?

"Why the hell didn't that fool dim his lights?"

Or, "The Government should have done something about it!"

A writer who was been writing for a long time may legitimately begin to feel even more apprehension about what might be his last story. And a lot more may well be expected of him. After all, his life has been built on nothing but words. His last ones should give a good account of him. They should summarize, somehow, everything he has thought and learned, every technique he had acquired.

His last story, dramatically, should be his best.

But who knows which will be his last story?

Thus we come to the story in this book, at any rate. And it is certainly one of the latest written. And it is not the best.

But it is placed here because there is an element in it which you will have to read to discover, which in a collection of this kind is almost impossible to top. Anyhow, I am not yet ready to try.

*—Leslie Charteris (1951)*

Simon Templar looked up from the frying pan in which six mountain trout were developing a crisp golden tan. Above the gentle sputter of grease, the sound of feet on dry pine needles crackled through the cabin window.

It didn't cross his mind that the sound carried menace, for it was twilight in the Sierras, and the dusky calm stirred only with the rustlings of nature at peace.

The Saint also was at peace. In spite of everything his enemies would have said, there actually were times when peace was the main preoccupation of that fantastic freebooter; when hills and blue sky were high enough adventure, and baiting a hook was respite enough from baiting policemen or promoters. In such a mood he had jumped at the invitation to join a friend in a week of hunting and fishing in the High Sierras—a friend who had been recalled to town on urgent business almost as soon as they arrived, leaving the Saint in by no means melancholy solitude, for Simon Templar could always put up with his own company.

The footsteps came nearer with a kind of desperate urgency. Simon moved the frying pan off the flames and flowed, rather than walked, to where he could see through windows in two directions.

A man came out of the pines. He was traveling on the short side of a dead run, but straining with every gasping breath to step up his speed. He came, hatless and coatless, across the pine-carpeted clearing toward the cabin door.

He burst through it, and in spite of his relaxation the Saint felt a kind of simmer of anticipating approval. If his solitude had to be intruded on, this was the way it should happen. Unannounced. At a dead run.

The visitor slammed the door, shot the bolt, whirled around, and seemed about to fold in the middle. He saw the Saint. His jaw sagged, swung adrift on its hinges for a moment, then imitated a steel trap.

After the sharp click of his teeth, he said, "How did you get in here? Where's Dawn?"

"Dawn?" Simon echoed lazily. "If you're referring to the rosy-fingered goddess who peels away the darkness each morning, she's on the twelve-hour shift, chum. She'll be around at the regular time."

"I never dreamed you here," the man said. "Who are you?"

"You dropped a word," the Saint said. "'I never dreamed you *were* here' makes more sense."

"Nuts, brother. You're part of my dream, and I never saw you before. You don't even have a name. All the others have, complete with backgrounds. But I can't place you. Funny . . . Look here, you're not real, are you?"

"The last time I pinched myself, I yelped."

"This is crazy," the man muttered.

He walked across the pine floor to within a couple of feet of the Saint. He was breathing easier now, and the Saint examined him impassively.

He was big, only a shade under the Saint's six feet two, with sandy hair, a square jaw, and hard brown eyes.

"May I?" he said, and pinched the Saint. He sighed. "I was afraid this was happening. When I put my arms around Dawn Winter in my dreams, she—"

"Please," the Saint broke in. "Gentlemen don't go into lurid detail after the lady has a name."

"Oh, she's only part of my dream." The stranger stared into space, and an almost tangible aura of desire formed about him. "God!" he whispered. "I really dreamed up something in her."

"We must swap reminiscences someday," the Saint said. "But at the moment the pine-scented breeze is laden with threshings in the underbrush."

"I've got to hide. Quick! Where can I get out of sight?"

The Saint waved expressively at the single room. In its four hundred square feet, one might hide a large bird if it were camouflaged as an atlas or something, but that would be about the limit.

The two bunk beds were made with hospital precision, and even a marble would have bulged under their tight covers. The deck chairs wouldn't offer sanctuary for even an undernourished mouse, the table was high and wide open beneath the rough top, and the small bookcase was made to display its contents. "If we had time," the Saint mused, "I could candy-stripe you—if I had some red paint—and put on a barber's smock. Or . . . er . . . you say you're dreaming all this?"

"That's right."

"Then why don't you wake up—and vanish?"

The Saint's visitor unhappily gnawed his full underlip.

"I always have before, when the going got tough, but—Oh, hell, I don't know what's going on, but I don't want to die—even in my dream. Death is so . . . so . . ."

"Permanent?"

"Mmm, I guess. Listen, would you be a pal and try to steer these guys away? They're after me."

"Why should I?"

"Yeah," the man said. "You don't owe me a damn thing, but I'm trying to help Dawn. She—"

He broke off to fish an object out of his watch pocket. This was a small chamois bag, and out of it he took something that pulsed with incredible fires. He handed it to the Saint.

"That's Dawn."

The circular fire opal blazed with living beauty—blue, green, gold, cerise, chartreuse—and the Saint gasped with reverent wonder as he looked at the cameo head carved on the unbelievable gem.

There is beauty to which one can put a name. There is beauty that inspires awe, bravery, fear, lust, greed, passion. There is beauty that softens the savage blows of fate. There is beauty that drives to high adventure, to violence.

That stone, and above all the face cut eternally on its incandescent surface, was beauty beyond belief. No man could look on that face and ever know complete peace again.

She was the lily maid of Astolat, the lost loveliness that all men seek and never find, the nameless desire that haunts the ragged edge of sleep, that curls a lonely smile and sends vacant eyes searching far spaces.

Her face was made for—and of? the Saint asked himself—dreaming.

"Count me in, old boy."

He went outside. Through the dusky stillness the far-off unseen feet pounded nearer.

The feet were four. The men, with mathematical logic, two. One might be a jockey, the other a weight lifter. They tore out of the forest and confronted the Saint.

"Did you see a kind of big dopey-lookin' lug?" the jockey asked.

The Saint pointed to the other side of the clearing where the hill pitched down.

"He went that way—in a hell of a rush."

"Thanks, pal."

They were off, hot on the imaginary trail, and the sounds of their passage soon faded. The Saint went inside.

"They'll be back," he said. "But meanwhile we can clear up a few points. Could you down a brace of trout? They've probably cooled enough to eat."

"What do you mean, they'll be back?"

"It's inevitable," Simon pointed out as he put coffee on, set the table, and gathered cutlery. "They won't find you. They want to find you. So they'll be back with questions. Since those questions will be directed at me, I'd like to know what not to answer."

"Who are you?"

"Who are you?" the Saint countered.

"I'm—oh, blast it to hell and goddam. The guy you're looking at is Big Bill Holbrook. But he's only something I dreamed up. I'm really Andrew Faulks, and I'm asleep in Glendale, California."

"And I am the queen of Rumania."

"Sure, I know. You don't believe it. Who would? But since you've got me out of a tight spot for the time being, I'd like to tell you what I've never told anybody. But who am I telling?"

"I'm Simon Templar," said the Saint, and waited for a reaction.

"No!" Holbrook-Faulks breathed. "The Saint! What beautiful, wonderful luck. And isn't it just like a bank clerk to work the Saint into his dream?" He paused for breath. "The Robin Hood of Modern Crime, the twentieth century's brightest buccaneer, the devil with dames, the headache of cops and crooks alike. What a sixteen-cylinder dream this is."

"Your alliterative encomia," the Saint murmured, "leave me as awed as your inference. Don't you think you'd better give out with this—er—bedtime story? Before that unholy pair return with gun-lined question marks?"

The strange man rubbed his eyes in a dazed helpless way.

"I don't know where to begin," he said conventionally.

But after a while, haltingly, he tried.

Andrew Faulks, in the normal course of events, weathered the slingshots and arrows of outrageous playmates and grew up to be a man.

As men will, he fixed his heart and eyes on a girl and eventually married her. As woman will, she gave birth in due course to a boy, Andy Jr, and later a girl, Alexandria.

He became a bank clerk, and went to and from home on an immutable schedule. He got an occasional raise; he was bawled out at times by the head teller; he became a company man, a white-collar worker, and developed all the political ills that white-collared flesh is heir to. And he dreamed. Literally.

This was what Big Bill Holbrook told the Saint in the mountain cabin to which Simon had retired to await the blowing over of a rather embarrassing situation which involved items duly registered on police records.

"In the first dream, I was coming out of this hotel, see. And *whammo!* Bumping into her woke me—Oh, the hell with it. Whoever was dreaming woke up, but it was me bumped into her. And I was sorry as hell, because, brother, she was something."

Some two weeks later, Big Bill said, he bumped into her again. The dream started exactly as its predecessor, progressed exactly to the point of collision.

"But I didn't awaken this time. We each apologized all over the place and somehow we were walking along together. Just as I was about to ask her to have dinner, I woke up again."

"Or Andy did," the Saint supplied.

"Yeah. Whoever. Now this is what happened. Every ten days or two weeks, I'd be back in this dream, starting out of the hotel, crashing into her, walking along, having dinner, getting to know her better each dream. Each one started exactly the same, but each one went a little further into her life. It was like reading the same book over and over, always starting back at the beginning, but getting one chapter further every time. I got so used to it that I'd say to myself, 'This is where I woke up last time,' and then after the dream had gone on a bit further I'd begin to think, 'Well, I guess this must be getting near the end of another installment,' and sure enough, about that time I'd wake up again."

The accidental encounter began to develop sinister ramifications, picked up unsavory characters, and put Big Bill Holbrook in the role of a Robin Hood.

"Or a Saint," he amended, "rescuing a beautiful dame from a bunch of lugs."

And there was, of course, the jewel.

It had a history. The fire opal, which seemed to be eternal yet living beauty, had carved upon it the likeness of Dawn's great-great-grandmother, of whom the girl was the living image.

The talented Oriental craftsman who had chiseled those features which were the essence of beauty—that wily fellow had breathed upon the cameo gem a curse.

The curse: It must not get out of the possession of the family—or else.

Death, deprivation, and a myriad other unpleasantries were predicted if the stone fell into alien hands.

The name of Selden Appopoulis sort of slithered into the tale. This was a fat man, a lecherous fat man, a greedy fat man, who wanted—not loved—Dawn, and who wanted—and loved—the cameo opal. In some fashion that was not exactly clear to the Saint, the fat man was in a position to put a financial squeeze on her. In each succeeding dream of Andrew Faulks, Glendale bank clerk, Dawn's position became more and more untenable. In desperation she finally agreed to turn the jewel over to Appopoulis. The fat man sent for the jewel by the two henchmen whom the Saint had directed off into the Holbrook-bare woods.

"Now in this dream—this here now dream," Holbrook said, "I took it away from him, see? Andy Faulks went to sleep in Glendale Saturday night and—say, what day is it now?"

"Tuesday."

"Yeah, that's the way it seems to me too. And that's funny. If you're really part of this dream you'd naturally think it was Tuesday, because your time and my time would be the same. But you don't seem like part of a dream. I pinched you and—oh, nuts, I'm all mixed up."

"Let's try and be clear about this," said the Saint patiently. "You know that it's Tuesday here, but you think you're dreaming all this in Glendale on Saturday night."

"I don't know," said the other wearily. "You see, I never dreamed more than one day at a stretch before. But tonight it's been going on and on. It's gone way past the time when I ought to have woken up. But I don't seem to be able to wake up. I've tried . . . My God, suppose I don't wake up! Suppose I never can wake up? Suppose I never can get back, and I have to go on and on with this, being Big Bill Holbrook—"

"You could take a trip to Glendale," Simon suggested gravely, "and try waking Faulks up."

Holbrook-Faulks stared at him with oddly unfocused eyes.

"I can't," he said huskily. "I thought of that—once. But I couldn't make myself do it. I . . . I'm scared . . . of what I might find . . . Suppose—"

He broke off, his pupils dilated with the formless horror of a glimpse of something that no mind could conceive.

Simon roused him again, gently: "So you took the jewel—"

Holbrook snapped out of his reverie.

"Yeah, and I lammed out for this cabin. Dawn was supposed to meet me here. But I guess I can't control all these characters. Say," he asked suddenly, "who do you suppose I am? Faulks or Holbrook?"

"I suggest you ask your mother, old boy."

"This ain't funny. I mean, who do you really suppose I am? Andy Faulks is asleep and dreaming me but I've got all his memories, so am I a projection of Andy or am I me and him both? None of these other characters have any more memories than they need."

Simon wondered if the two men chasing Holbrook were his keepers; he could use a few. In fact, Simon reflected, keepers would fit into the life of Holbrook-Faulks like thread in a needle. But he sipped his brandy and urged the man to continue.

"Well, something's happened," Holbrook-Faulks said. "It never was like this before. I never could smell things before. I never could really feel them. You know how it is in a dream. But now it seems like as if you stuck a knife in me I'd bleed real blood. You don't suppose a . . . a reiterated dream could become reality?"

"I," said the Saint, "am a rank amateur in that department."

"Well, I was too—or Andy was, whichever of us is me—but I read everything I could get my hands on about dreams—or Andy did—and it didn't help a bit."

Most men wouldn't have heard the faint far-off stirring in the forest. But the Saint's ears, attuned by long practice to detect sound that differed from what should be there, picked up evidence of movement toward the cabin.

"Some one," he said suddenly, "and I mean one, is coming. Not your pursuers—it's from the opposite direction."

Holbrook-Faulks listened.

"I don't hear anything."

"I didn't expect you to—yet. Now that it's dark, perhaps you'd better slip outside, brother, and wait. I don't pretend to believe your yarn, but that some game is afoot is so obvious that even Sherlock Holmes could detect it. I suggest that we prepare for eventualities."

The eventuality that presently manifested itself was a girl. And it was a girl who could have been no one but Dawn Winter.

She came wearily into the cabin, disheveled, her dress torn provocatively so that sun-browned flesh showed through, her cloud of golden hair swirled in fairy patterns, her dark eyes brooding, her mouth a parted dream.

The Saint caught his breath and began to wonder whether he could really make Big Bill Holbrook wake up and vanish.

"Do you belong to the coffee and/or brandy school of thought?" he asked.

"Please." She fell carelessly into a chair, and the Saint coined a word.

She was glamorous beyond belief.

"Miss Winter, pull down your dress or I'll never get this drink poured. You've turned me into an aspen. You're the most beautiful hunk of flesh I've ever seen. Have your drink and go, please."

She looked at him then, and took in the steel-cable leanness of him, the height of him, the crisp black hair, the debonair blue eyes. She smiled, and a brazen gong tolled in the Saint's head.

"Must I?" she said.

Her voice caught at the core of desire and tangled itself forever there.

"Set me some task," the Saint said uncertainly. "Name me a mountain to build, a continent to sink, a star to fetch you in the morning."

The cabin door crashed open. The spell splintered into shining shards. Holbrook-Faulks stood stony-faced against the door.

"Hello, Bill," the girl said, her eyes still on the Saint. "I came, you see."

Bill's gaze was an unwavering lance, with the Saint pinioned on its blazing tip.

"Am I gonna have trouble with you too, Saint?"

The Saint opened his mouth to answer, and stiffened as another sound reached his ears. Jockey and weight lifter were returning.

"We'll postpone any jousting over the fair lady for the moment," Simon said. "We're about to have more company."

Holbrook stared wildly around.

"Come on, Dawn. Out the window. They'll kill us."

Many times before in his checkered career the Saint had had to make decisions in a fragment of time—when a gun was leveled and a finger whitening on the trigger, when a traffic accident roared toward consummation, when a ship was sinking, when a knife flashed through candlelight. His decision now was compounded of several factors, none of which was the desire for self-preservation. The Saint rarely gave thought room to self-preservation—never when there was something more important to preserve.

He did not want this creature of tattered loveliness, this epitome of what men live for, to get out of his sight. He must therefore keep her inside the cabin. And there was no place to hide . . .

His eyes narrowed as he looked at the two bunks. He was tearing out the mattresses before his thought was fully formed. He tossed the mattresses in a corner where shadows had retreated from the candle on the table. Then he motioned to Holbrook.

"Climb up. Make like a mattress."

He boosted the big man into the top bunk, and his hands were like striking brown snakes as he packed blankets around him and remade the bed so that it only looked untidily put together.

"Now you," he said to the girl.

She got into the lower bunk and lay flat on her back, her disturbing head in the far corner. The Saint deposited a swift kiss upon her full red lips. They were cool and soft, and the Saint was adrift for a second.

Then he covered her. He emptied a box of pine cones on the mattresses and arranged the whole to appear as a corner heap of cones.

He was busy cleaning the dishes when the pounding came on the door.

As he examined the pair, Simon Templar was struck by the fact that these men were types, such types as B pictures had imprinted upon the consciousness of the world.

The small one could be a jockey, but one with whom you could make a deal. For a consideration, he would pull a horse in the stretch or slip a Mickey into a rival rider's sarsaparilla. In the dim light that fanned out from the door, his eyes were small and rat-like, his mouth a slit of cynicism, his nose a quivering button of greed.

His heavier companion was a different but equally familiar type. This man was Butch to a T. He was large, placid, oafish, and an order taker. His not to reason why; his but to do——or cry. He'd be terribly hurt if he failed to do what he was ordered; he'd apologize, he'd curse himself.

It crossed the Saint's mind that a bank clerk such as Andrew Faulks had been described would dream such characters. "So you lied to us," the little man snarled. The Saint arched an eyebrow. At the same time he reached out and twisted the little man's nose, as if he were trying to unscrew it.

"When you address me, Oswald, say 'sir.'" The little man sprang back in outraged fury. He clapped one hand to his injured proboscis, now turned a deeper purple than the night. The other hand slid under his coat.

Simon waited until he had the gun out of the holster, then leaped the intervening six feet and twisted it from the little man's hand. The Saint let the gun swing from his finger by its trigger guard.

"Take him, Mac!" grated the disarmed man. Mac vented a kind of low growl, but did nothing but fidget as the Saint turned curious blue eyes on him. The tableau hung frozen for a long moment before the little man shattered the silence.

"Well? Ya afraid of 'im?"

"Yup," Mac said unhappily. "Criminy, Jimmy, 'f he c'n get the best uh you, well, criminy, Jimmy."

Jimmy moaned, "You mean you're gonna stand there and let just one guy take my gun away from me? Gripes, he ain't a army."

"No," Mac agreed, growing more unhappy by the second, "but he kind of seems like one, Jimmy. Didja see that jump? Criminy, Jimmy."

The Saint decided to break it up.

"Now, Oswald—"

"Didn'ja hear, Mac? Name's Jimmy."

"Oswald," the Saint said firmly, "is how I hold you in my heart. Now, Oswald, perhaps you'll pour oil on these troubled waters, before I take you limb from muscle and throw you away."

"We don't want no trouble," Jimmy said. "We want Big Bill. You got him, but we got to take him back with us."

"And who is Big Bill, and why do you want him, and why do you think I have him?"

"We know you got him," Jimmy said. "This here's Trailer Mac."

The Saint nodded at Mac.

"Hey, Jimmy," Mac broke in, "this guy's a phony."

"Charmed, I'm sure." Jimmy blinked.

"Owls," Mac explained, "can't swim."

"What the damblasted hell has owls to do with it?" Jimmy demanded.

"He said pour owls on the something waters. So that," Mac said in triumph, "proves it."

This, the Saint thought, wanders. He restrained Jimmy from assaulting Mac, and returned to the subject.

"Why should the revelation of this gent's identity be regarded as even an intimation that I have—what was the name?—Big Bill?"

"Holbrook," Jimmy said. "Why, this is Trailer Mac. Ain't you never heard of him? He follered Loopie Louie for eighteen years and finally caught 'im in the middle of Lake Erie."

"I never heard of him," Simon said, and smiled at Mac's hurt look. "But then there are lots of people I've never heard of."

This, he thought as he said it, was hardly true. He had filed away in the indexes of his amazing memory the dossiers of almost every crook in history. He was certain that he'd have heard of such a chase if it had ever occurred.

"Anyway," Jimmy went on, "we didn't go more'n a couple miles till Mac he says Big Bill ain't here, 'n he ain't been here, neither. Well, he come this far, 'n he didn't go no farther. So you got him. He's inside."

"The cumulative logic in that series of statements is devastating," the Saint said. "But logicians veer. History will bear me out. Aristotle was a shining example. Likewise all the boys who gave verisimilitude to idiocy by substituting syllogisms for thought processes, who evaded reality by using unsemantic verbalisms for fact-facing and, God save the mark, fact-finding."

Mac appealed to the superior intellect in his crowd.

"Whut'n hell's he talkin' about, Jimmy?"

"I mean," the Saint said, "Big Bill ain't here. Come in and case the joint."

"Whyn't cha say so?" Mac snarled, and pushed inside.

They searched nook and cranny, and Mac fingered a knothole hopefully once. They gave the bunk beds a passing glance, and were incurious about the seeming pile of pine cones in the corner. Mac boosted Jimmy up on the big central beam to peer into ceiling shadows, and they scanned the fireplace chimney.

Then they stood and looked at the Saint with resentment.

"Sump'n's fishy," Jimmy pronounced. "He's got to be here. This here"—he pointed—"is Trailer Mac."

"Maybe we better go get the boss, huh, Jimmy?"

"Yeah," Jimmy agreed. "He'll find Big Bill."

"Who," the Saint inquired, "is the boss?"

"You'll see," Jimmy promised. "He won't be scared of you. He's just down the hill in the town. Stopped off to play a game of billiards. So we'll be seein' ya, bub."

They went off into the night, and the Saint stood quite still for a moment in a little cloud of perplexity.

Never before had he been faced with a situation that was so full of holes.

He added up known data: a man who had a fabulous jewel, who claimed to be the projected dream of his alter ego; a girl of incredible beauty said to be another creation of that dream; and two characters who were after two men and/or the jewel and/or—perhaps—the girl.

Mac and Jimmy had searched the cabin. They professed to have overlooked an object the size of Big Bill Holbrook. Their proof that they had overlooked him: "This here's Trailer Mac." They assumed he would remain here while they walked four miles to the settlement and back with their boss who was said to have stopped off to shoot a game of billiards.

But would a man on the trail of that fire opal stop off to play billiards? Would two pseudo-tough guys go away and leave their quarry unguarded?

No, the Saint decided. These were the observable facts, but they were unimportant. They masked a larger, more sinister pattern. Great forces must be underlying the surface trivia. Undeniably, the jewel was a thing to drive men to madness. It could motivate historic bloodshed. The girl, too, possessing the carven features of the gem, could drive men to—anything. But for the life of him, the Saint could not get beneath the surface pattern to what must be the real issues. He could only cling to the conviction that they had to exist, and that they must be deadly.

He turned back to the bunk beds.

"Come on out, kids," he said. "The big bad wolves have temporarily woofed away."

Fear lingered in the dark depths of Dawn Winter's eyes, making her even more hauntingly beautiful. The Saint found strange words forming on his lips, as if some other being possessed them.

He seemed to be saying, "Dawn . . . I've seen the likeness of every beauty in history or imagination. Every one of them would be a drab shadow beside you. You are so beautiful that the world would bow down and worship you—if the world knew of your existence. Yet it's impossible that the world doesn't know. If one single person looked at you, the word would go out. Cameramen would beat a path to your door, artists would dust off their palettes, agents would clamor with contracts. But somehow this hasn't happened. Why? Where, to be trite, have you been all my life?"

He couldn't define the expression which now entered her eyes. It might have been bewilderment, or worry, or fear, or an admixture.

"I . . . I . . ." She put a hand as graceful as a calla lily against her forehead. "I . . . don't know."

"Oh, don't let's carry this too far." It sounded more like himself again. "Where were you born, where did you go to school, who are your parents?"

She worried at him with wide, dark eyes.

"That's just the trouble. I . . . don't remember any childhood. I remember only my great-great-grandmother. I never saw her, of course, but she's the only family I know about."

Big Bill's facial contortions finally caught the Saint's eye. They were something to watch. His mouth worked like a corkscrew, his eyebrows did a can-can.

"I gather," said the Saint mildly, "that you are giving me the hush-hush. I'm sorry, comrade, but I'm curious. Suppose you put in your two cents."

"I told you once," Big Bill said, "I told you the truth."

"Pish," Simon said. "Also, tush."

"It's true," Big Bill insisted. "I wouldn't lie to the Saint."

The girl echoed this in a voice of awe.

"The Saint? The Robin Hood of Modern Crime, the twentieth century's brightest buccaneer, the"—she blushed—"the devil with dames."

It occurred to Simon, with a shock of remembrance, that her phrases were exactly those of Big Bill's when he learned his host's identity. And even they had been far from new. The Saint thought of this for a moment, and rejected what it suggested. He shook his head.

"Let's consider that fire opal then, children. It's slightly fabulous, you know. Now, I don't think anybody knows more than I do about famous jools. Besides such well-known items as the Cullinan and the Hope diamonds, I am familiar with the history of almost every noteworthy bauble that was ever dug up. There's the Waters diamond, for example. No more than a half dozen persons know of its existence, its perfect golden flawless color. And the Chiang emerald, that great and beautiful stone that has been seen by only three living people, myself included. But this cameo opal is the damn warp of history. It couldn't be hidden for three generations without word of it getting out. In the course of time, I couldn't have helped hearing about it. But I didn't . . . So it doesn't exist. But it does. I know it exists; I've held it in my hand—"

"And put it in your pocket," Big Bill said.

The Saint felt in his jacket.

"So I did." He pulled out the chamois bag with its precious contents and made as if to toss it. "Here."

Big Bill stopped him with flared hands.

"Please keep it for me, Mr Templar. Things will get rather bad around here soon. I don't want Appopoulis to get his fat hands on it."

"Soon? Surely not for a couple of hours."

Big Bill frowned.

"Things happen so quickly in dreams. This may seem real, but it'll still hold the screwy pattern you'd expect."

The Saint made a gesture of annoyance.

"Still sticking to your story? Well, maybe you're screwy or maybe you just think I am. But I'd rather face facts. As a matter of fact, I insist on it." He turned back to the girl. "For instance, darling, I know that you exist. I've kissed you."

Big Bill growled, glared, but did nothing as the Saint waited calmly.

Simon continued, "I have the evidence of my hands, lips, and eyes that you have all the common things in common with other women. In addition you have this incredible, unbelievable loveliness. When I look at you, I find it hard to believe that you're real. But that's only a figure of speech. My senses convince me. Yet you say you don't remember certain things that all people remember. Why?"

She repeated her gesture of confusion.

"I . . . don't know. I can't remember any past."

"It would be a great privilege and a rare pleasure," the Saint said gently, "to provide you with a past to remember."

Another low growl rumbled in Big Bill's chest, and the Saint waited again for developments. None came, and it struck the Saint that all the characters in this muddled melodrama had one characteristic in common—a certain cowardice in the clutch. Even Dawn Winter showed signs of fear, and nobody had yet made a move to harm her. It was only another of the preposterous paradoxes that blended into the indefinable unreality of the whole.

Simon gave it up. If he couldn't get what he thought was truth from either of these two, he could watch and wait and divine the truth. Conflict hung on the wind, and conflict drags truth out of her hiding place and casts her naked before watching eyes.

"Well, souls," he said, "what now? The unholy three will be back sometime. You could go now. There is the wide black night to wander in."

"No," Big Bill said. "Now that you're in this, give us your help, Saint. We need you."

"Just what, then," Simon asked, "are we trying to prevent, or accomplish?"

"Selden Appopoulis must not get his hands on the opal or Dawn. He wants both. He'll stop at nothing to get them."

"I believe you mentioned a curse breathed on this gewgaw by some Oriental character."

Dawn Winter's voice once more tangled itself in Simon's heart. As long as he could remember that quality—of far-off bells at dusk, of cellos on a midnight hill—time would never again pass slowly enough.

"Death shall swoop on him," she chanted, "who holds this ancient gem from its true possessor, but all manner of things shall plague him before that dark dread angel shall come to rest at his shoulder. His nights shall be sleepless with terror, and hurts shall dog his accursed steps by day. Beauty shall bring an end to the vandal."

The mood of her strange incantation, far more than the actual words, seemed to linger on the air after she had finished, so that in spite of all rationality the Saint felt spectral fingers on his spine. He shook off the spell with conscious resolution.

"It sounds very impressive," he murmured, "in a gruesome sort of way. Reminds me of one of those zombie pictures. But where, may I ask, does this place me in the scheme of dire events? I have the jewel."

"You," Big Bill Holbrook said, "will die, as I must, and as Trailer Mac and Jimmy must. They stole it from Dawn; I stole it from them."

The Saint smiled.

"Well, if that's settled, let's pass on to more entertaining subjects bordering on the carnal. Miss Winter, my car is just down the hill. If Bill is resigned to his fate, suppose we leave him and his playmates to their own fantastic devices and drift off into the night."

Her face haloed with pleasure.

"I'd like it," she said. "But I . . . I just can't."

"Why not? You're over three years old. Nobody is sitting on your chest."

"I can't do what I like, somehow," she said. "I can only do what I must. It's always that way."

"This," the Saint said to nobody in particular, "sounds like one of those stories that fellow Charteris might write. And what's the matter with you?" he demanded of Holbrook. "A little earlier you were eager to get rough with me because I admired the lady. Now you sit listening with disgusting indifference to my indecent proposal. I assure you it was indecent, from your viewpoint."

Big Bill grinned.

"It just occurred to me. She can't go with you. She must do what she must. She can't get out of my sight. Good old Andy," he added.

The Saint turned his eyes away and stared into space, wondering. His wandering gaze focused on a small wall mirror that reflected Dawn Winter. Her features were blurred, run together, an amorphous mass. Simon wondered what could have happened to that mirror.

He swung back to face Bill Holbrook.

"I'm afraid," he said softly, but with the iron will showing through his velvet tones, "that we must have some truth in our little séance. Like the walrus, I feel the time has come to speak of many things. From this moment, you are my prisoners. The length of your durance vile depends on you. Who are you, Miss Winter?"

The look she turned on him made his hands tingle. Hers was a face for cupping between tender palms. Dark and troubled, her eyes pleaded for understanding, for sympathy.

"I told you all I know," she pleaded. "I've tried and tried, ever since I could remember anything, to think of—well, all those things you think of at times."

Again she passed a hand across her face, as if wiping away veils.

"I don't ever remember snagging a stocking on the way to an important appointment," she said. "And I know that girls do. I never had to fight for my"—she colored—"my honor, whatever that is. And I know that girls like me have fought for this something I don't understand, by the time they've reached my age. Whatever that is," she added pensively. "I don't even know how old I am, or where I've been."

A pattern suddenly clicked into place in the Saint's brain, a pattern so monstrous, so inhuman as to arouse his destructive instincts to the point of homicidal mania. The look he turned on Big Bill Holbrook was ice and flame.

His voice was pitched at conversational level, but each word fell from his lips like a shining sword.

"Do you know," he said, "I'm beginning to get some new ideas. Not very nice ideas, chum. And if I'm guessing right about what you and your fellow scum have done to this innocent girl, you are liable to cost your insurance company money."

He moved toward Holbrook with a liquid grace that had all the co-ordination of a panther's movement—and the menace. Big Bill Holbrook leaned back from it.

"Stop acting the knight in armor," he protested. "What in hell you talking about?"

"It should have been obvious before," Simon Templar said. "Up on your feet, Holbrook."

Holbrook remained at ease.

"If you've got an explanation for all this that doesn't agree with mine, I want to know it."

The Saint paused. There was honest curiosity in the man's voice—and no fear. That cowardice which had characterized him before was replaced with what seemed an honest desire to hear the Saint's idea.

"This girl," the Saint said, "whoever she is, has breeding, grace, and beauty out of this world. She has been brought up under expensive and sheltered surroundings. You can see that in her every gesture, every expression. She was bred to great wealth, perhaps nobility, or even royalty."

Big Bill leaned forward in almost an agony of concentration. Every word of Simon Templar's might have been a twenty-dollar gold piece, the way he reached for it with every sense.

The Saint patted his jacket pocket.

"This jewel is the symbol of her position—heiress, princess, queen, or what have you. You and your unsavory companions kidnapped her, and are holding her for ransom. That would be wicked enough, but you've done worse. Somewhere in the course of your nasty little scheme, it seemed like a good idea to destroy a part of her beauty that could be dangerous to you and your precious pals. So you destroyed her mind. With drugs, I have no doubt—drugs that have dulled her mind until she has no memory. Your reasons are clear enough—it was just a sound form of insurance. And now your gang has split up, fighting over the spoils. I don't know who would have come out on top, if you hadn't happened to run into me. But I know what the end is going to be now—and you aren't going to like it. Get on your feet!"

The command was like a pistol shot, and Big Bill Holbrook jumped. Then he leaned back again and chuckled in admiration.

"Everything that's been said about you is true. There's nobody like you. That's so much better than Andy Faulks did there's no comparison. Say, that really would have been something, and look, it'd have explained why she couldn't remember who she was. Saint, I got to hand it to you. Too bad you're not in bed in Glendale."

For once of a very few times in his life, the Saint was taken aback. The words were spoken with such ease, such sincerity, that Simon's deadly purpose cooled to a feeling of confusion. While it is true that a man who is accustomed to danger, to gambling for high stakes with death as a forfeit, could simulate feelings he did not actually feel, it is seldom that a man of Big Bill Holbrook's obvious IQ can look annihilation in the face with an admiring grin.

Something was still wrong, but wrong in the same way that everything in the whole episode was wrong—wrong with that same unearthly off-key distortion that defeated logical diagnosis.

The Saint took out a cigarette and lighted it slowly, and over the hiss of the match he heard other sounds which resolved themselves into a blur of footsteps.

Simon glanced at his watch. Jimmy and Mac had been gone less than half an hour. It was impossible for them to be returning from the village four miles away.

What had Holbrook said? Something about everything happening faster in dreams? But that was in the same vein of nonsense. Maybe they'd met the boss at the foot of the hill.

Holbrook said, "What is it? Did you hear something?"

"Only your friends again."

Fear came once more to Holbrook and Dawn Winter. Their eyes were wide and dark with it, turning instantly toward the bunk beds.

"No," Simon said. "Not this time. We'll have this out in the open."

"But he'll kill us!" Holbrook began to babble. "It's awful, the things he'll do. You don't know him, Saint. You can't imagine, you couldn't—"

"I can imagine anything," said the Saint coldly. "I've been doing that for some time, and I'm tired of it. Now I'd prefer to know."

He crossed the room as the footsteps outside turned into knuckles at the door.

"Welcome to our study club," the Saint said.

Trailer Mac and Jimmy preceded an enormous hulk through the door and, when they saw Holbrook and Dawn, charged like lions leaping on paralyzed gazelles.

The Saint moved in a lightning blur. Two sharp cracks of fist on flesh piled Mac in one corner, Jimmy in another. They lay still.

A buttery chuckle caused the Saint to turn. He was looking into a small circular hole. A .38, he computed. He raised his eyes to twins of the barrel, but these were eyes. They lay deep in flesh that swelled in yellowish-brown rolls, flowing fatly downward to describe one of the fattest men the Saint had ever seen. They could only have belonged to a man called Selden Appopoulis.

"Mr Sydney Greenstreet, I presume?" Simon drawled.

The buttery chuckle set a sea of flesh ebbing and flowing.

"A quick action, sir, and an efficient direction of action. I compliment you, and am saddened that you must die."

The Saint shrugged. He knew that this fat man, though butter-voiced, had a heart of iridium. His eyes were the pale expressionless orbs of a killer. His mouth was thin with determination, his hand steady with purpose. But Simon had faced all those indications before.

"I hate to disappoint you, comrade," he said lightly, "but that line has a familiar ring. And yet I'm still alive."

Appopoulis appraised and dismissed the Saint, though his eyes never wavered. He spoke to Holbrook.

"The opal. Quickly!"

The butter of his voice had frozen into oleaginous icicles, and Holbrook quailed under the bite of their sharp edges.

"I haven't got it, Appopoulis. The Saint has it."

Simon was astonished at the change in the fat man. It was subtle, admittedly, but it was there nonetheless. Fear came into the pale gray eyes which had been calmly contemplating murder as a climax to unspeakable inquisitions. Fear and respect. The voice melted butter again.

"So," he said warmly. "Simon Templar, the Robin Hood of Modern Crime, the twentieth century's brightest buccaneer, the . . . ah . . . devil with dames. I had not anticipated this."

Once more it struck the Saint that the descriptive phrases were an exact repetition of Holbrook's. And once more it struck him that the quality of fear in this weird quintet was not strained. And once more he wondered about Holbrook's fantastic tale . . .

"You are expecting maybe Little Lord Feigenbaum?" Simon asked. "Or what do you want?"

"The cameo opal, for one thing," Appopoulis said easily. "For the other, the girl."

"And what do you intend to do with them?"

"Cherish them, sir. Both of them."

His voice had encyclopedic lust and greed, and the Saint felt as if small things crawled on him.

Before he could make an answer, stirrings in their respective corners announced the return of Mac and Jimmy to another common plane of existence. Without a word they got groggily to their feet, shook their heads clear of trip hammers, and moved toward the Saint.

"Now, Mr Templar," said Appopoulis, "you have a choice. Live, and my desires are granted without violence, or die, and they are spiced with emotions at fever heat."

Mac and Jimmy had halted: one small and thunderstruck, one large and paralyzed.

"Boss," quavered Jimmy, "did youse say Templar? Da Saint?"

"The same." Simon bowed.

"Chee!" Mac breathed. "Da Saint. Da Robin Hood of Modern Crime, da—"

"Please," Simon groaned. "Another record, if you don't mind."

"Boss, we ain't got a chance," Jimmy said.

Appopoulis turned his eyes on the little man.

"He," the boss said, "has the opal."

This news stiffened their gelatinous spines long enough to set them at the Saint in a two-directional charge.

The Saint swerved to meet it. He held Jimmy between himself and the unwavering gun of Appopoulis with one hand. With the other he wrought havoc on the features of Mac.

It was like dancing, like feathers on the breeze, the way the Saint moved. Even to himself it had the kind of exhilaration that a fight may only experience once in a lifetime. He had a sense of power, of supernatural co-ordination, of invincibility beyond anything he had ever known. He cared nothing for the knowledge that Appopoulis was skipping around on the outskirts of the fray, trying to find an angle from which he could terminate it with a well-placed shot. Simon knew that it was no fear of killing Jimmy that stayed the fat man's finger on the trigger—it was simply the knowledge that it would have wasted a shot, that the Saint could have gone on using Jimmy as a shield, alive or dead. The Saint knew this coolly and detachedly, as if with a mind separate from his own, while he battered Mac's face into a vari-colored pulp.

Then Mac's eyes glazed and he went down, and the Saint's right hand snaked hipwards for his own gun while his left flung Jimmy bodily at the paunch of Appopoulis.

And that was when the amazing, the incredible, and impossible thing went wrong. For Jimmy didn't fly away from the Saint's thrust, as he should have, like a marble from a slingshot. Somehow he remained entangled with the Saint's arm, clinging to it as if bogged in some indissoluble bird-lime, with a writhing tenacity that was as inescapable as a nightmare. And Simon looked down the barrel of Appopoulis's gun and saw the fat man's piggy eyes brighten with something that might have been lust . . .

The Saint tried to throw a shot at him, but he was off balance, and the frenzied squirming of his erstwhile shield made it like trying to shoot from the back of a bucking horse. The bullet missed by a fraction of an inch, and buried itself in the wall beside the mirror. Then Appopoulis fired back.

The Saint felt a jar, and a flame roared inside his chest. Somehow, he couldn't pull the trigger any more. The gun fell from his limp fingers. His incredulous eyes looked full in the mirror and saw a neat black hole over his heart, saw it begin to spread as his life's blood gushed out.

It was strange to realize that this was it, and it had happened to him at last, as it had always been destined to happen someday, and in an instant he was going to cheat to the back of the book for the answer to the greatest mystery of all. Yet his last conscious thought was that his image was sharp and clear in the mirror. When he had seen Dawn's reflection, it had been like one seen in an agitated pool . . .

When he opened his eyes again it was broad daylight, and the intensity of the light told him that it must have been more than twelve hours since he had been shot.

He was lying on the floor of the cabin. He felt for his heart. It was beating strongly. His hand did not come away sticky with blood.

His eyes turned hesitantly down to his shirt. There was no hole in it. He jumped to his feet, felt himself all over, examined himself in the mirror. He was as whole as he'd ever been, and he felt fine.

He looked around the cabin. The mattresses were piled in the corner under the pine cones, the bunks unmade. Otherwise there were no signs of the brawl the night before. No trace of Jimmy and Mac, or Appopoulis. No Big Bill Holbrook. No Dawn . . .

And no hole in the wall beside the mirror where his hopeless shot at Appopoulis had buried itself.

The Saint shook his head. If it had all been a dream, he might have to seriously consider consulting a psychiatrist. Dreams reach only a certain point of vividness. What he remembered was too sharp of definition, too coherent, too consecutive. Yet if it wasn't a dream, where were the evidences of reality, the bullet hole in his chest, in the wall?

He went to the door. There should be footprints. His cabin had rated with Grand Central Station for traffic last night.

There were no footprints, other than his own.

Simon reached for a cigarette, and suddenly sniffed it suspiciously before he put it in his mouth. If some joker, either in fun or malice, had adulterated his tobacco with some more exotic herb . . . But that, too, was absurd. A jag of those dimensions would surely bequeath a hangover to match, but his head was as clear as the mountain air.

He fumbled in his pockets for a match. Instead, his questing fingers touched something solid, a shape that was oddly familiar— yet impossibly alien. The tactile sensation lasted only for an instant, before his hand recoiled as if the thing had been red hot. He was afraid, actually afraid, to take it out.


The address of Andrew Faulks was in the Glendale directory. The house was a modest two-bedroom affair on a side street near Forest

Lawn Memorial Park. A wreath hung on the door. A solemn gentleman who looked like, and undoubtedly was, an undertaker opened the door. He looked like Death rubbing white hands together.

"Mr Faulks passed on last night," he said in answer to the Saint's query. Unctuous sorrow overlaid the immediate landscape.

"Wasn't it rather sudden?"

"Ah, not exactly, sir. He went to sleep last Saturday, passed into a coma, and never awakened."

"At what time," Simon asked, "did he die?"

"At ten-forty," the man replied. "It was a sad death. He was in a delirium. He kept shouting about shooting someone, and talked about a saint."

Simon had moved into the house while listening to the tale of death and found himself looking off the hallway into a well-lighted den. His keen eyes noted that while most of the shelves were gay with the lurid jackets of adventure fiction, one section was devoted to works on psychology and psychiatry.

Here were the tomes of Freud, Adler, Jung, Brill, Bergson, Krafft-Ebing, and lesser lights. A book lay open on a small reading table.

The Saint stepped inside the room to look at it. It was titled *In Darkest Schizophrenia* by William J Holbrook, Ph.D.

Simon wondered what the psychic-phenomena boys would do with this one. This, he thought, would certainly give them a shot in the aura.

"Mrs Faulks is upstairs, sir," the professional mourner was saying. "Are you a friend of the family? I'll be glad to ask whether she can see you."

"I wish you'd just show her this." Simon forced one hand into a pocket. "And ask her—"

He never finished the question. Never.

There was nothing in the pocket for his hand to find. Nothing to meet his fingertips but a memory that was even then darkening and dying out along his nerves.

# PUBLICATION

# HISTORY

The eight stories in this book were all written, initially, for magazine publication: "Judith" first appeared in the January 1934 edition of *The American Magazine* with a subsequent first British appearance being in the April 1934 edition of *The Strand Magazine*. "Iris" was based on a radio script entitled "The Man Who Murdered Shakespeare," an original script written by Irvin Ashkenazy for the very first series of *The Saint* on the radio, which aired on 22 March 1945. The prose version of the story then appeared in the Winter 1948 edition of *Mystery Book Magazine* before being collected in this volume. "Lida" first appeared in the August 1947 edition of *Ellery Queen's Mystery Magazine* whilst "Jeannine" made it in to the February 1948 edition of *Argosy* prior to this book. "Lucia" is one of the older stories, having first made print in the November 1937 edition of *Double Detective* magazine; "Teresa," meanwhile, is almost as old, as it first appeared in the 5 November 1938 edition of *The Winnipeg Tribune* under the title of "Masquerouge" and was subsequently syndicated to a number of newspapers around that date. "Luella" appeared in the October 1946 edition of *Rex Stout's Mystery Quarterly* whilst "Emily" debuted in the November 1948 edition of *Ellery Queen's Mystery Magazine*. "Dawn," which is an unusual story for Leslie Charteris and the Saint anyway, first appeared under the title of "The Darker Drink" in the October 1947 edition of *Thrilling Wonder Stories*. It was then retitled to fit in with the ethos of this book, but subsequent magazine and book publications have reverted back to its original title.

The book was first published in late 1948 by the Doubleday Crime Club with a British edition following in August 1949. A French translation appeared in 1949 under the not terribly complicated title of *Le Saint at les femmes* whilst a Spanish edition, with the even less complicated title of *El Santo errante*, appeared in 1958.

All but two of the stories in this book were adapted for *The Saint* with Roger Moore: "Judith" appeared as part of the first season, initially airing on Thursday, 3 October 1963 and starring Julie Christie as the eponymous lady. "Teresa" followed the week after, whilst "Iris" had to wait until 7 November. "Luella" first aired on 23 January 1964 whilst "Lucia," for reasons lost in the mists of time, was retitled "Sophia" and in an episode directed by Roger Moore first appeared on 27 February 1964. "Lida" and "Jeannine" had to wait until the third season and were first broadcast on 4 October 1964 and 11 October 1964 respectively.

# ABOUT THE AUTHOR

*I'm mad enough to believe in romance. And I'm sick and tired of this age—tired of the miserable little mildewed things that people racked their brains about, and wrote books about, and called life. I wanted something more elementary and honest—battle, murder, sudden death, with plenty of good beer and damsels in distress, and a complete callousness about blipping the ungodly over the beezer. It mayn't be life as we know it, but it ought to be.*

—*Leslie Charteris in a 1935 BBC radio interview*

Leslie Charteris was born Leslie Charles Bowyer-Yin in Singapore on 12 May 1907.

He was the son of a Chinese doctor and his English wife, who'd met in London a few years earlier. Young Leslie found friends hard to come by in colonial Singapore. The English children had been told not to play with Eurasians, and the Chinese children had been told not to play with Europeans. Leslie was caught in between and took refuge in reading.

"I read a great many good books and enjoyed them because nobody had told me that they were classics. I also read a great many bad books which nobody told me not to read . . . I read a great many popular scientific articles and acquired from them an astonishing amount of general knowledge before I discovered that this acquisition was supposed to be a chore."[1]

One of his favourite things to read was a magazine called *Chums*. "The Best and Brightest Paper for Boys" (if you believe the adverts) was a monthly paper full of swashbuckling adventure stories aimed at boys, encouraging them to be honourable and moral and perhaps even "upright citizens with furled umbrellas."[2] Undoubtedly these types of stories would influence his later work.

When his parents split up shortly after the end of World War I, Charteris accompanied his mother and brother back to England, where he was sent to Rossall School in Fleetwood, Lancashire. Rossall was then a very stereotypical English public school, and it struggled to cope with this multilingual mixed-race boy just into his teens who'd already seen more of the world than many of his peers would see in their lifetimes. He was an outsider.

He left Rossall in 1924. Keen to pursue a creative career, he decided to study art in Paris—after all, that was where the great artists went—but soon found that the life of a literally starving artist didn't appeal. He continued writing, firing off speculative stories to magazines, and it was the sale of a short story to *Windsor Magazine* that saved him from penury.

He returned to London in 1925, as his parents—particularly his father—wanted him to become a lawyer, and he was sent to study law at Cambridge University. In the mid-1920s, Cambridge was full of Bright Young Things—aristocrats and bohemians somewhat typified in the Evelyn Waugh novel *Vile Bodies*—and again the mixed-race Bowyer-Yin found that he didn't fit in. He was an outsider who preferred to make his own way in the world and wasn't one of the privileged upper class. It didn't help that he found his studies boring and decided it was more fun contemplating ways to circumvent the law. This inspired him to write a novel, and when publishers Ward Lock & Co. offered him a three-book deal on the strength of it, he abandoned his studies to pursue a writing career.

When his father learnt of this, he was not impressed, as he considered writers to be "rogues and vagabonds." Charteris would later recall that "I wanted to be a writer, he wanted me to become a lawyer. I was stubborn, he said I would end up in the gutter. So I left home. Later on, when I had a little success, we were reconciled by letter, but I never saw him again."[3]

*X Esquire*, his first novel, appeared in April 1927. The lead character, X Esquire, is a mysterious hero, hunting down and killing the businessmen trying to wipe out Britain by distributing quantities of free poisoned cigarettes. His second novel, *The White Rider*, was published the following spring, and in one memorable scene shows the hero chasing after his damsel in distress, only for him to overtake the villains, leap into their car . . . and promptly faint.

These two plot highlights may go some way to explaining Charteris's comment on *Meet—the Tiger!*, published in September 1928, that "it was only the third book I'd written, and the best, I would say, for it was that the first two were even worse."[4]

Twenty-one-year-old authors are naturally self-critical. Despite reasonably good reviews, the Saint didn't set the world on fire, and Charteris moved on to a new hero for his next book. This was *The Bandit*, an adventure story featuring Ramon Francisco De Castilla y Espronceda Manrique, published in the summer of 1929 after its serialisation in the *Empire News*, a now long-forgotten Sunday newspaper. But sales of *The Bandit* were less than impressive, and Charteris began to question his choice of career. It was all very well writing—but if nobody wants to read what you write, what's the point?

"I had to succeed, because before me loomed the only alternative, the dreadful penalty of failure . . . the routine office hours, the five-day week . . . the lethal assimilation into the ranks of honest, hard-working, conformist, God-fearing pillars of the community."⁵

However his fortunes—and the Saint's—were about to change. In late 1928, Leslie had met Monty Haydon, a London-based editor who was looking for writers to pen stories for his new paper, *The Thriller*— "The Paper with a Thousand Thrills." Charteris later recalled that "he said he was starting a new magazine, had read one of my books and would like some stories from me. I couldn't have been more grateful, both from the point of view of vanity and finance!"⁶

The paper launched in early 1929, and Leslie's first work, "The Story of a Dead Man," featuring Jimmy Traill, appeared in issue 4 (published on 2 March 1929). That was followed just over a month later with "The Secret of Beacon Inn," starring Rameses "Pip" Smith. At the same time, Leslie finished writing another non-Saint novel, *Daredevil*, which would be published in late 1929. Storm Arden was the hero; more notably, the book saw the first introduction of a Scotland Yard inspector by the name of Claud Eustace Teal.

The Saint returned in the thirteenth issue of *The Thriller*. The byline proclaimed that the tale was "A Thrilling Complete Story of the Underworld"; the title was "The Five Kings," and it actually featured Four Kings and a Joker. Simon Templar, of course, was the Joker.

Charteris spent the rest of 1929 telling the adventures of the Five Kings in five subsequent *The Thriller* stories. "It was very hard work, for the pay was lousy, but Monty Haydon was a brilliant and stimulating editor, full of ideas. While he didn't actually help shape the Saint as a character, he did suggest story lines. He would take me out to lunch and say, 'What are you going to write about next?' I'd often say I was damned if I knew. And Monty would say, 'Well, I was reading something the other day . . .' He had a fund of ideas and we would talk them over, and then I would go away and write a story. He was a great creative editor."⁷

Charteris would have one more attempt at writing about a hero other than Simon Templar, in three novelettes published in *The Thriller* in early 1930, but he swiftly returned to the Saint. This was partly due to his self-confessed laziness—he wanted to write more stories for *The Thriller* and other magazines, and creating a new hero for every story was hard work—but mainly due to feedback from Monty Haydon. It seemed people wanted to read more adventures of the Saint . . .

Charteris would contribute over forty stories to *The Thriller* throughout the 1930s. Shortly after their debut, he persuaded publisher Hodder & Stoughton that if he collected some of these stories and rewrote them a little, they could publish them as a Saint book. *Enter the Saint* was first published in August 1930, and the reaction was good enough for the publishers to bring out another collection. And another . . .

Of the twenty Saint books published in the 1930s, almost all have their origins in those magazine stories.

Why was the Saint so popular throughout the decade? Aside from the charm and ability of Charteris's storytelling, the stories, particularly those published in the first half of the '30s, are full of energy and joie de vivre. With economic depression rampant throughout the period, the public at large seemed to want some escapism.

And Simon Templar's appeal was wide-ranging: he wasn't an upper-class hero like so many of the period. With no obvious background and no attachment to the Old School Tie, no friends in high places who could provide a get-out-of-jail-free card, the Saint was uniquely classless. Not unlike his creator.

Throughout Leslie's formative years, his heritage had been an issue. In his early days in Singapore, during his time at school, at Cambridge University or even just in everyday life, he couldn't avoid the fact that for many people his mixed parentage was a problem. He would later tell a story of how he was chased up the road by a stick-waving typical

English gent who took offence to his daughter being escorted around town by a foreigner.

Like the Saint, he was an outsider. And although he had spent a significant portion of his formative years in England, he couldn't settle.

As a young boy he had read of an America "peopled largely by Indians, and characters in fringed buckskin jackets who fought nobly against them. I spent a great deal of time day-dreaming about a visit to this prodigious and exciting country."[8]

It was time to realise this wish. Charteris and his first wife, Pauline, whom he'd met in London when they were both teenagers and married in 1931, set sail for the States in late 1932; the Saint had already made his debut in America courtesy of the publisher Doubleday. Charteris and his wife found a New York still experiencing the tail end of Prohibition, and times were tough at first. Despite sales to *The American Magazine* and others, it wasn't until a chance meeting with writer turned Hollywood executive Bartlett McCormack in their favourite speakeasy that Charteris's career stepped up a gear.

Soon Charteris was in Hollywood, working on what would become the 1933 movie *Midnight Club*. However, Hollywood's treatment of writers wasn't to Charteris's taste, and he began to yearn for home. Within a few months, he returned to the UK and began writing more Saint stories for Monty Haydon and Bill McElroy.

He also rewrote a story he'd sketched out whilst in the States, a version of which had been published in *The American Magazine* in September 1934. This new novel, *The Saint in New York*, published in 1935, was a significant advance for the Saint and Leslie Charteris. Gone were the high jinks and the badinage. The youthful exuberance evident in the Saint's early adventures had evolved into something a little darker, a little more hard-boiled. It was the next stage in development for the author and his creation, and readers loved it. It became a bestseller on both sides of the Atlantic.

Having spent his formative years in places as far apart as Singapore and England, with substantial travel in between, it should be no surprise that Leslie had a serious case of wanderlust. With a bestseller under his belt, he now had the means to see more of the world.

Nineteen thirty-six found him in Tenerife, researching another Saint adventure alongside translating the biography of Juan Belmonte, a well-known Spanish matador. Estranged for several months, Leslie and Pauline divorced in 1937. The following year, Leslie married an American, Barbara Meyer, who'd accompanied him to Tenerife. In early 1938, Charteris and his new bride set off in a trailer of his own design and spent eighteen months travelling round America and Canada.

*The Saint in New York* had reminded Hollywood of Charteris's talents, and film rights to the novel were sold prior to publication in 1935. Although the proposed 1935 film production was rejected by the Hays Office for its violent content, RKO's eventual 1938 production persuaded Charteris to try his luck once more in Hollywood.

New opportunities had opened up, and throughout the 1940s the Saint appeared not only in books and movies but in a newspaper strip, a comic-book series, and on radio.

Anyone wishing to adapt the character in any medium found a stern taskmaster in Charteris. He was never completely satisfied, nor was he shy of showing his displeasure. He did, however, ensure that copyright in any Saint adventure belonged to him, even if scripted by another writer—a contractual obligation that he was to insist on throughout his career.

Charteris was soon spread thin, overseeing movies, comics, newspapers, and radio versions of his creation, and this, along with his self-proclaimed laziness, meant that Saint books were becoming fewer and further between. However, he still enjoyed his creation: in 1941 he indulged himself in a spot of fun by playing the Saint—complete with monocle and moustache—in a photo story in *Life* magazine.

In July 1944, he started collaborating under a pseudonym on Sherlock Holmes radio scripts, subsequently writing more adventures for Holmes than Conan Doyle. Not all his ventures were successful—a screenplay he was hired to write for Deanna Durbin, "Lady on a Train," took him a year and ultimately bore little resemblance to the finished film. In the mid-1940s, Charteris successfully sued RKO Pictures for unfair competition after they launched a new series of films starring George Sanders as a debonair crime fighter known as the Falcon. But he kept faith with his original character, and the Saint novels continued to adapt to the times. The transatlantic Saint evolved into something of a private operator, working for the mysterious Hamilton and becoming, not unlike his creator, a world traveller, finding that adventure would seek him out.

"I have never been able to see why a fictional character should not grow up, mature, and develop, the same as anyone else. The same, if you like, as his biographer. The only adequate reason is that—so far as I know—no other fictional character in modern times has survived a sufficient number of years for these changes to be clearly observable. I must confess that a lot of my own selfish pleasure in the Saint has been in watching him grow up."[9]

Charteris maintained his love of travel and was soon to be found sailing round the West Indies with his good friend Gregory Peck. His forays abroad gave him even more material, and he began to write true-crime articles, as well as an occasional column in *Gourmet* magazine.

By the early '50s, Charteris himself was feeling strained. He'd divorced his second wife in 1943 and got together with a New York radio and nightclub singer called Betty Bryant Borst, whom he married in late 1943. That relationship had fallen apart acrimoniously towards the end of the decade, and he roamed the globe restlessly, rarely in one place for longer than a couple of months. He continued to maintain a firm grip on the exploitation of the Saint in various media but was writing little himself. The Saint had become an industry, and Charteris couldn't keep up. He began thinking seriously about an early retirement.

Then in 1951 he met a young actress called Audrey Long when they became next-door neighbours in Hollywood. Within a year they had married, a union that was to last the rest of Leslie's life.

He attacked life with a new vitality. They travelled—Nassau was a favoured escape spot—and he wrote. He struck an agreement with *The New York Herald Tribune* for a Saint comic strip, which would appear daily and be written by Charteris himself. The strip ran for thirteen years, with Charteris sending in his handwritten story lines from wherever he happened to be, relying on mail services around the world to continue the Saint's adventures. New Saint books began to appear, and Charteris reached a height of productivity not seen since his days as a struggling author trying to establish himself. As Leslie and Audrey travelled, so did the Saint, visiting locations just after his creator had been there.

By 1953 the Saint had already enjoyed twenty-five years of success, and *The Saint Detective Magazine* was launched. Charteris had become adept at exploiting his creation to the full, mixing new stories with repackaged older stories, sometimes rewritten, sometimes mixed up in "new" anthologies, sometimes adapted from radio scripts previously written by other writers.

Charteris had been approached several times over the years for television rights in the Saint and had expended much time and effort during the 1950s trying to get the Saint on TV, even going so far as to write sample scripts himself, but it wasn't to be. He finally agreed a deal in autumn 1961 with English film producers Robert S. Baker and Monty Berman. The first episode of *The Saint* television series, starring Roger Moore, went into production in June 1962. The series was an immediate success, though Charteris himself had his reservations. It reached second place in the ratings, but he commented that "in that distinction it was topped by wrestling, which only suggested to me that the competition may not have been so hot; but producers are generally cast in a less modest mould." He resented the implication that the TV series had finally made a success of the Saint after twenty-five years of literary obscurity.

As long as the series lasted, Charteris was not shy about voicing his criticisms both in public and in a constant stream of memos to the producers. "Regular followers of the Saint saga . . . must have noticed that I am almost incapable of simply writing a story and shutting up."[10] Nor was he shy about exploiting this new market by agreeing to a series of tie-in novelisations ghosted by other writers, which he would then rewrite before publication.

Charteris mellowed as the series developed and found elements to praise too. He developed a close friendship with producer Robert S. Baker, which would last until Charteris's death.

In the early '60s, on one of their frequent trips to England, Leslie and Audrey bought a house in Surrey, which became their permanent base. He explored the possibility of a Saint musical and began writing some of it himself.

Charteris no longer needed to work. Now in his sixties, he supervised the Saint from a distance whilst continuing to travel and indulge himself. He and Audrey made seasonal excursions to Ireland and the south of France, where they had residences. He began to write poetry and devised a new universal sign language, Paleneo, based on notes and symbols he used in his diaries. Once Paleneo was released, he decided enough was enough and announced, again, his retirement. This time he meant it.

The Saint continued regardless—there was a long-running Swedish comic strip, and new novels with other writers doing the bulk of the work were complemented in the 1970s with Bob Baker's revival of the TV series, *Return of the Saint*.

Ill-health began to take its toll. By the early 1980s, although he continued a healthy correspondence with the outside world, Charteris felt unable to keep up with the collaborative Saint books and pulled the plug on them.

To entertain himself, Leslie took to "trying to beat the bookies in predicting the relative speed of horses," a hobby which resulted in several of his local betting shops refusing to take "predictions" from him, as he was too successful for their liking.

He still received requests to publish his work abroad but had become completely cynical about further attempts to revive the Saint. A new Saint magazine only lasted three issues, and two TV productions—*The Saint in Manhattan*, with Tom Selleck look-alike Andrew Clarke, and *The Saint*, with Simon Dutton—left him bitterly disappointed. "I fully expect this series to lay eggs everywhere . . . the only satisfaction I have is in looking at my bank balance."[11]

In the early 1990s, Hollywood producers Robert Evans and William J. Macdonald approached him and made a deal for the Saint to return to cinema screens. Charteris still took great care of the Saint's reputation and wrote an outline entitled *The Return of the Saint* in which an older Saint would meet the son he didn't know he had.

Much of his time in his last few years was taken up with the movie. Several scripts were submitted to him—each moving further and further away from his original concept—but the screenwriter from 1940s Hollywood was thoroughly disheartened by the Hollywood of the '90s: "There is still no plot, no real story, no characterisations, no personal interaction, nothing but endless frantic violence . . ." Besides, with producer Bill Macdonald hitting the headlines for the most un-Saintly reasons, he was to add, "How can Bill Macdonald concentrate on my Saint movie when he has Sharon Stone in his bed?"

The Crime Writers' Association of Great Britain presented Leslie with a Lifetime Achievement award in 1992 in a special ceremony at the

House of Lords. Never one for associations and awards, and although visibly unwell, Leslie accepted the award with grace and humour ("I am now only waiting to be carbon-dated," he joked). He suffered a slight stroke in his final weeks, which did not prevent him from dining out locally with family and friends, before he finally passed away at the age of eighty-five on 15 April 1993.

His death severed one of the final links with the classic thriller genre of the 1930s and 1940s, but he left behind a legacy of nearly one hundred books, countless short stories, and TV, film, radio, and comic-strip adaptations of his work which will endure for generations to come.

> *I was always sure that there was a solid place in escape literature for a rambunctious adventurer such as I dreamed up in my youth, who really believed in the old-fashioned romantic ideals and was prepared to lay everything on the line to bring them to life. A joyous exuberance that could not find its fulfilment in pinball machines and pot. I had what may now seem a mad desire to spread the belief that there were worse, and wickeder, nut cases than Don Quixote.*
>
> *Even now, half a century later, when I should be old enough to know better, I still cling to that belief. That there will always be a public for the old-style hero, who had a clear idea of justice, and a more than technical approach to love, and the ability to have some fun with his crusades.* [12]

---

1 *A Letter from the Saint*, 30 August 1946
2 "The Last Word," *The First Saint Omnibus*, Doubleday Crime Club, 1939
3 *The Straits Times*, 29 June 1958, page 9

4 Introduction by Charteris to the September 1980 paperback reprint of *Meet—the Tiger!* (Charter), the last ever print edition.

5 *The Saint: A Complete History*, by Burl Barer (McFarland, 1993)

6 PR material from the 1970s series *Return of the Saint*

7 From "Return of the Saint: Comprehensive Information" issued to help publicise the 1970s TV show

8 *A Letter from the Saint*, 26 July 1946

9 Introduction to "The Million Pound Day," in *The First Saint Omnibus*

10 *A Letter from the Saint*, 12 April 1946

11 Letter from LC to sometime Saint collaborator Peter Bloxsom, 2 August 1989

12 Introduction by Charteris to the September 1980 paperback reprint of *Meet—the Tiger!* (Charter).

# WATCH FOR THE SIGN

# OF THE SAINT!

# THE SAINT CLUB

*And so, my friends, dear bookworms, most noble fellow
drinkers, frustrated burglars, affronted policemen, upright
citizens with furled umbrellas and secret buccaneering
dreams that seems to be very nearly all for now. It has been
nice having you with us, and we hope you will come again,
not once, but many times.*

*Only because of our great love for you, we would like
to take this parting opportunity of mentioning one small
matter which we have very much at heart . . .*

—*Leslie Charteris,* The First Saint Omnibus *(1939)*

Leslie Charteris founded The Saint Club in 1936 with the aim of
providing a constructive fanbase for Saint devotees. Before the War, it
donated profits to a London hospital where, for several years, a Saint
ward was maintained. With the nationalisation of hospitals, profits
were, for many years, donated to the Arbour Youth Centre in Stepney,
London.

In the twenty-first century, we've carried on this tradition but have
also donated to the Red Cross and a number of different children's
charities.

The club acts as a focal point for anyone interested in the adventures of Leslie Charteris and the work of Simon Templar, and offers merchandise that includes DVDs of the old TV series and various Saint-related publications, through to its own exclusive range of notepaper, pin badges, and polo shirts. All profits are donated to charity. The club also maintains two popular websites and supports many more Saint-related sites.

After Leslie Charteris's death, the club recruited three new vice-presidents—Roger Moore, Ian Ogilvy, and Simon Dutton have all pledged their support, whilst Audrey and Patricia Charteris have been retained as Saints-in-Chief. But some things do not change, for the back of the membership card still mischievously proclaims that . . .

> *The bearer of this card is probably a person of hideous antecedents and low moral character, and upon apprehension for any cause should be immediately released in order to save other prisoners from contamination.*

## To join . . .

Membership costs £3.50 (or US$7) per year, or £30 (US$60) for life. Find us online at www.lesliecharteris.com for full details.